THE TIGER'S TALE

THE TIGER'S TALE

Undercover Cat Series, Book 3

KELLE Z. RILEY

Published by
Curtis Brown Unlimited.
Ten Astor Place
New York, NY 10003

Cover Artist: Jaycee DeLorenzo, Sweet 'N Spicy Designs

Dedication

To Kandy Zeiher Petrovic

Because sisters make everything better

ACKNOWLEDGEMENTS

This work would not be possible without the help of many. Thanks go to:

- My agent, Laura Blake Peterson, of Curtis Brown Ltd., for her unfailing support; you've been a faithful partner during this journey.
- The dedicated staff at CBLtd., for their tireless work.
- Author Denise Swanson, for continued support and inspiration in this crazy business.
- My writer community—CARA; Windy CityRWA, GRW, TGN, CWG. If you can figure out the alphabet soup, you know who you are! Your encouragement, advice, critiques and support keep me motivated, sane and humble.
- My science colleagues—you know who you are. My work with you helped bring these characters to life.

Most of all to my beloved husband, Tom Riley. You are an unfailing cheerleader, unpaid assistant, and baker extraordinaire. You light up my life, and make everything worthwhile—and much more fun! I love you.

CHAPTER 1

Six months ago, Bree had been a confirmed dog person—until she'd inherited a cat from her murdered boss. Now, she held a tiger by the tail. Or rather, by a leash. But when it came to tigers, the difference was just splitting hairs.

"This way," shouted the tour guide, his thick Australian accent a sharp contrast to the murmurings of the local Thai tiger trainers. "And stay with your tigers."

Bree was fairly certain he didn't mean for her to follow the energetic tiger cub over the dusty, rock-strewn flatlands to her right. But it tugged on the leash, intent on exploring, so she followed.

Sweat trickled down her back as she scrambled over the barren, baked earth of the Thailand Tiger Sanctuary. Her foot caught on a rock and she stumbled when the wayward cub pulled her forward.

A strong male hand grabbed the leash and jerked the tiger back onto the path. Bree suppressed a shiver of awareness and turned to Matthew Tugood, both grateful for—and irritated by—his presence.

"I can't believe we're doing this," he grumbled. "Why are we here again?"

"Are you seriously asking me that?" Bree resisted the temptation to roll her eyes. Barely. "You know my sorority is donating a rescued tiger cub to the Terrance U animal clinic."

He scowled at her. Or maybe the sun was in his eyes. "If you recall, *I'm* the one who cut through the red tape for the donation. Not your sorority. Not Terrance University. Not the exotic animal clinic. *Me.*"

Enough already. How many times did she have to thank him? He might be as handsome as the devil, but she didn't owe him eternal gratitude for a simple favor. And she wasn't about to feed his overblown ego by gushing over his efforts. She ignored him and focused on her tiger cub.

Tugood slowed his pace, widening the gap between them and the rest of the tour group. "Let me rephrase. Why are we spending the day in a tourist trap?"

"I wanted to meet the cub's trainer and get firsthand experience."

Matthew answered with a dissatisfied grunt. His mouth firmed into a tight line as he scanned the horizon, squinting against the bright sunlight. "You're wasting time you could spend preparing for your assignment." His voice dropped low and he kept his eyes trained on the distance. After a slow pivot, he leaned close, his breath warm on her ear despite his harsh tone. "Or have you forgotten about your mission?"

Bree disentangled the leash from his hands. "I liked you better before I knew you were a spy."

"No, you liked my cover story." His voice softened, and he glanced her way. "That's not the same thing. And you *do* like me now. I happen to like you too." Despite the ninety-degree heat, a shiver raced down Bree's spine as if he'd touched her rather than just looked at her.

"What I don't like is that you never stop thinking about your mission. Not for a minute. Look around you, Matthew." She gestured to landscape, the tourists, and the tigers. "We're exploring a new culture. Bottle-feeding tiger cubs. Having adventures. Living. And you're missing it."

"Lower your voice. We don't want to be overheard."

Bree eyed the terrain, wondering if the clumps of scrub grass and rocks were cleverly disguised surveillance devices. She dismissed the idea with a snort. "Can't you think about something besides the mission?"

"May I remind you that my single-minded focus on the mission saved your life on more than one occasion?"

Bree dropped the argument. For one thing, his interference *had* saved her life when a murderer—make that two murderers—had wanted her out of the picture. On the other hand, she hadn't found a single dead body before she met Matthew. So, in her mind, it was a toss-up.

"I helped you with your project." He glowered at the tiger cub.

"Thank—"

"You can repay me by focusing on our mission. I don't need thanks, I need you to complete your *assignment*."

"Fine. You've made yourself very clear." Bree shrugged. "Next topic." Beside her, Matthew bristled. Bree hid her smile, taking secret delight in being able to needle him the same way he constantly needled her.

"The Thai Energy Summit starts at 7:00 p.m. tomorrow. Zed is always early. So you need to be there early, too."

"I'm ready," she insisted. "I'm using the same cover as last time."

"Of course." Matthew shrugged. "Zed is convinced you're a brilliant researcher with access to cutting edge technology."

Bree stopped in her tracks so fast the tiger cub did a backflip at the end of his leash. She whirled on Matthew. "In case you've forgotten, I *am* a real researcher, complete with a PhD in science. Just because my cover story involves a fictional company doesn't negate my *real* experience." Behind her, the tiger cub let out a noise—something between a growl and a whine—as if to support Bree's statement.

"Your science degree isn't the only reason you're an asset to the Sci-Spy organization."

Another yowl accompanied by a tug on the leash made Bree turn back to her tiger cub. The rest of the tour group was no longer in sight. Ning, the tiger trainer she'd come to meet, hurried to them, chattering in Thai and gesturing. "Hurry," she said, pointing in the direction where the others had disappeared.

Bree followed Ning and her tiger, moving quickly to catch up with the group. Tugood kept pace, his voice low and insistent in her ear. "Like it or not, your days as a simple researcher ended when you signed on with Sci-Spy. Your fictional energy research could be the key to thwarting a terrorist."

"The meeting isn't until tomorrow."

"You need to prep for it today."

"We've prepped for weeks. In the office. After hours at home. On the flights here." Bree stopped again at the edge of the tour group and turned to Matthew. "Please. I need a day to do something fun. Something … normal."

As if anything about her days could be normal. Across the clearing, a large tiger roared, shaking the ground under her feet. The tour guide explained the procedure for approaching—and being photographed with—the massive, 500-pound animal.

Bree surrendered her leash to Ning without releasing Matthew's gaze. When he nodded in reluctant agreement, she turned to the tour group, but all thoughts of fun—and normal—had fled at Matthew's mention of the man they'd code-named Zed. Tomorrow, she'd have to confront him while trying to find information to link him to his network of associates.

Compared to that, even the quarter-ton tiger seemed docile.

❧   ❧   ❧

Dread lodged in Bree's gut as she shimmied into the black, knee-length cocktail dress. The sheer material clung to her curves and proved—once again—that Spanx alone wouldn't mold her curvy shape into svelte lines. Guilt settled next to the dread. She should have listened to Matthew and prepped more intensively for tonight's meeting with Zed.

They had discovered the meeting rooms for the Summit had technology that shielded communications, preventing Matthew from coaching her via hidden camera and in-ear audio. She couldn't count on his help in person, either, since he might be recognized from his former undercover work in one of Zed's research facilities.

"You can do this." She looked at her reflection, trying to summon confidence, but a blonde, green-eyed, more-than-a-little-terrified stranger stared back at her. She longed to rip off the wig, throw away the contacts and hide behind her boring brown hair and brown eyes where she'd be safe.

She paced her hotel room, reviewing the situation. Zed believed she had a technique to safely store and transport large quantities of natural gas. She could navigate any technical conversations regarding her fictional product. The trick was to get him to fund her research so Matthew would have a money trail to follow while she worked to uncover Zed's technical organization.

Bree returned to the mirror and fastened an ornate necklace and matching earrings into place. They sparkled against the understated black dress, lending her costume a layer of elegance. A quick sound and video check assured her the cameras and microphones hidden within the necklace worked as expected. Matthew couldn't monitor her conversations in real time, but they would scour the recordings later that night, searching for information.

Time to get into character. She closed her eyes and focused on breathing as she'd learned in her high school acting classes. From the moment she walked out the door, Dr. Gabriella Catherine Mayfield-Watson—chemist turned corporate spy—would no longer exist. Instead she'd be Dr. Catherine Holmes, researcher at *Energy Unlimited.*

Unease twisted in her gut as she envisioned dozens of ways the mission could fail. Her eyes popped open and she grabbed her cell phone to activate a program to hide all information except that which was appropriate for Cat Holmes.

Her fingers hovered over the button, but instead of tapping it, she opened her message screen. A few keystrokes later, she'd drafted a message to her family and scheduled it for delivery tomorrow. If all went well, she'd erase it before the program sent it. If not...

She refused to ponder that alternative.

Hours later, the burn in Bree's feet rivaled enemy torture, thanks to the heels she wore. She ignored the pain and juggled her glass of Merlot, a plate of cheese, and conversation with three men. Two of them tried to pry technical information out of her. The third, an elderly investment banker, seemed more interested in her cleavage than her conversation.

She angled her body away from him and sent a covert glance toward Zed—whose real name was Dr. Lei Chan. After keeping him at arm's length throughout the cocktail hour, his exaggerated body language told Bree he was desperate to talk to her. So far, so good. The PA system crackled to life, asking everyone to be seated for dinner. Dr. Chan waved her toward his table.

Bree smiled and headed in his direction, only to be stopped when the banker tugged on her elbow. "A word, Dr. Holmes?"

She cringed as he leaned close. His minty breath did little to ease her trepidation when a hairy finger brushed her neck.

"Be still, Bree," he whispered. "You have a wire showing in your necklace."

"Matt—"

"Shh. Even deep cover is risky around Zed." He tucked the wire away and leaned back, cackling as if they'd shared a joke.

Bree clamped her jaw shut and tightened her lips into a smile. How had rugged Matthew Tugood transformed himself into a stooped, graying, lecherous old man?

He took her arm and escorted her to Zed's table where, to her surprise, he took a seat beside her. As she sat between Matthew and Zed, a tiny part of her felt relief. Despite Matthew's obnoxious disguise, she took comfort in his presence.

If tonight's mission failed, at least they'd fail together.

"You did a good job." Matthew twisted in the front seat of the car and addressed Bree. Beside him, a woman—who he'd introduced as Sasha Markovich—sped through the early morning streets of Bangkok.

"The information Zed gave you at dinner, plus his follow-up emails yesterday are already giving us solid financial leads."

Warmth at his praise spread through her. She leaned forward from the back seat and cast a sidelong glance in Sasha's direction. Bree lowered her voice, unable to believe she could trust the woman despite Tugood's assurances. "How were you able to follow the money trail so quickly?"

"I have resources," Sasha answered, her thick eastern European accent making the words sound like a villain of a cold-war era spy thriller. She eyed Bree in the rearview mirror. "You played the role of a chemist well, but it is time for those with experience to take over."

"Dr. Mayfield-Watson has plenty of experience," Matthew interjected before Bree could give the irritating blonde a piece of her mind.

"Of course, *Matthew*. That is what you're calling yourself these days, isn't it?" Sasha's voice took on a syrupy quality that set Bree's teeth on edge. "But perhaps our target would be more responsive to *Mr. Steven Hibbs*. We should bring him back." Sasha put her hand on Matthew's knee.

"Steven Hibbs is dead." He removed her hand and faced forward, his profile sinking into granite-hard lines. "I burned that alias years ago."

Unease slipped beneath Bree's irritation. The man she knew as Matthew Tugood had once been Steven Hibbs? She pulled her purse from her phone and clicked on the record function while pretending to scan texts. In the front seat, Sasha said something in Russian to Matthew. He replied in clipped tones.

"English, Sasha," he said after another minute of conversation.

"Of course, darling." Sasha eyed Bree again in the mirror and winked. "*Matthew*," she said emphasizing the name as if it was an inside joke, "has always been protective of his assets. You did a credible job at the summit. I intended no disrespect." She pulled the car into the departure lane at the Bangkok International Airport.

Bree stashed her phone and exited the car, glad to be away from the tension. The sooner she and Matthew were away from Sasha, the happier she'd be.

Matthew exited the car, but Sasha called him back, continuing her conversation in Russian. Unfortunately, Bree was too far away to hear—or record—their conversation.

The trunk of the vehicle popped open and Matthew rounded the car to haul Bree's suitcase out before she could reach for it. His brow furrowed, and his eyes darkened to storm cloud gray, unreadable. Shutting her out. Bree felt a chill as he swung her suitcase and laptop bag onto the curb.

"This is where we part ways, Watson."

"You're not returning to Chicago?" Her mouth hung agape and Bree struggled to understand. They'd booked first class tickets for the flight home. "I thought—"

"Plans change." His mouth tightened, and he trained his gaze toward model-beautiful driver of the car. Before Bree could pull away, he cupped the back of her neck and leaned in close. He brushed a lingering kiss across her cheek. "Trust me on this. I'll be home as soon as I can," he whispered, his breath warm in her ear.

He backed away. "Safe travels, Watson," he called, all traces of warmth gone as he sprinted to the car. Before she could reply, Sasha and Matthew disappeared into the morning traffic, leaving Bree alone.

CHAPTER 2

Exhaustion weighed on Bree like a fifty-pound backpack as she escorted Ning through the maze that was the international terminal at O'Hare airport. Determination, double espresso, and a sense of duty kept her on her feet.

"Chicago is cold," Ning whispered, wrapping a scarf tighter around her neck as if the short blast of air from the jetway had chilled her to the bone.

The tiger trainer from Thailand had become Bree's responsibility—at least as far as getting her to the university, along with the tiger. Along the way, Bree had formed a friendship of sorts with the young woman. Bree knew what it was like to be left alone, and she didn't wish it on the young Thai woman.

"It's only September. It will get much colder. But you'll adjust." Bree tried to put herself in the girl's shoes, alone in an unfamiliar country risking everything for a chance at a better life. "Are you excited about starting school?"

A smile lit Ning's face. "I will work hard and make my family proud."

"Have fun too. Life isn't only about work." Bree spotted a sign with the Terrance University logo and steered Ning toward the group of students clustered around a trim, brown-haired woman several inches shorter than Bree's five and a half feet. "It looks like some of your new classmates have already arrived."

A woman broke away from the group and headed to Bree and Ning, clipboard in hand. "I'm Professor Miriam Cook, exchange student liaison and International Studies teacher at TU." Her gaze flitted to Bree before settling on Ning. "Welcome. You are?"

When Ning hesitated, Bree stepped in. "I'm Dr. Mayfield-Watson, and this is Ning." Bree pointed to Ning's Thai name—Phailin Sintawichai—on the clipboard.

Professor Cook gave Ning a wide, encouraging smile. "Welcome to Terrance University. We'll have you settled in no time. You'll be rooming with a peer mentor from the U.S. who will help you with anything you need. Meanwhile, let me introduce you to the other freshmen."

In moments, Professor Cook eased Ning into a conversation with several new students and then assured Bree she'd handle everything from that point on.

One weight lifted from her shoulders, Bree headed to retrieve her own luggage. The hypnotic clicks of the empty baggage carrousel and the over-warm press of bodies lulled her into a state where the whirlwind of the mission, the nineteen-hour flights between Chicago and Bangkok, and the multiple time zone changes blurred into a hazy jumble.

She was home. She should relax. And sleep. But whenever she closed her eyes, images of Mathew—*damn him*—Tugood intruded on her peace. He should have been here with her. Not gallivanting across the Pacific with a former colleague.

Sasha.

The memory of the lithe blonde with her exotic accent and deep connections to Tugood pecked away at the confidence Bree had built the past months. A flick of Sasha's little finger and Tugood abandoned Bree at the Bangkok airport with barely a good-bye.

Hardly the behavior of a real boyfriend.

Your love relationship with Tugood is just a cover story. A cover story she'd thought held a grain of truth based on the way

Tugood looked at her. The way he kissed her. The things he said at the tiger sanctuary.

Sasha put an end to that delusion. Especially when Bree had used a language app to translate Sasha's Russian conversation with Matthew. A conversation about their former cover as *a married couple.*

Even Matthew's brusque dismissal of the incident left Bree feeling cold. Bree's searing kisses while posing as Matthew's girlfriend probably didn't compare to whatever he'd shared with Sasha while undercover. Or under the covers, as the case may be. And if he could dismiss Sasha, how much easier could he dismiss Bree?

Damn Matthew for making her think there was more. That she was special.

When people jostled Bree to grab at their luggage, she shoved thoughts of Matthew *No*-good and Sasha aside. She hefted her suitcase from the conveyor and headed to the exit, ready to catch a taxi for home. She could do this part in her sleep.

"Hey, beautiful. Welcome home." A familiar voice interrupted her trek to the exit. James O'Neil stood by the doors, his thousand-watt grin almost hidden behind the bouquet of flowers he held. She must have smiled in return, because he moved in and wrapped her in a bear hug, crushing a few sprigs of baby's breath between them. "I've missed you."

"Thanks for taking care of my cat while I was traveling. It means a lot to me. Is everything okay at home?" She wiggled out of his embrace and searched his face for clues.

"Your menace of a cat is still alive and well, if that's what you're asking. He's been moping and crying for you."

"Somehow I doubt that. Sherlock's always had a soft spot for you." Bree smiled at the memory of James delivering the cat to her door last spring.

"Maybe in the beginning, but he's definitely your cat now. I spent time with him, like you asked. I even stopped by *The Barkery* to buy some of his favorite Tiny Tuna Treats, but he wasn't interested."

"Is he sick?"

"No. He just missed you." The dimple in James's cheek popped out as he grinned. "So have I." He stepped close and this time Bree accepted his embrace.

James wasn't pretending when he offered her affection. And after months of keeping the handsome detective at arm's length while believing her relationship with her spy handler went beyond pretend, maybe it was time to rethink her decisions. Having something—someone—in her life that wasn't complicated tempted her more than she cared to admit.

"I can offer a ride home, American comfort food, and anything else you desire. But for starters—" James bent close and his lips captured hers.

Bree didn't pull away. For years, she'd fought to be smarter, tougher, and more driven than her male colleagues just to be taken seriously. Not giving up when the going got tough was ingrained in her DNA. Even so, the process severely limited moments where she could let her guard down. Being a spy was even worse, because it kept her constantly—

Damn. James stiffened and drew away, as if sensing her wandering thoughts. The look on his face sent a prickle of unease down Bree's spine.

"What's wrong?"

"We seem to have gathered an entourage."

Bree followed his gaze to Ning. The girl stood, flanked by a knot of exchange students, studying the stitching on her duffle bag as if its pattern held cryptic secrets. Until she sensed Bree's eyes on her.

Smiling, she dropped the bag and stepped forward. *"Khun Dr. Bree,"* she said, using the traditional Thai title of honor, "Professor Cook does not know about Lucky."

Miriam Cook pushed through the crowd, her earlier composure gone. A hank of frizzed brown hair escaped from the clip at her nape, as wild and uncertain as the look in her eyes.

"Ning insists that she traveled with another student, Bun-Ma "Lucky" Benjakalyani. The students are my responsibility and I don't have Ms. Benjakalyani on my list." She thrust the clipboard at Bree. "Do you know what she's talking about?"

"I can clear that up," Bree said. "Ning is the trainer accompanying a tiger cub that Terrance University adopted."

Understanding smoothed the furrow between Professor Cook's brows. She swiped a hand through her hair, freeing an errant strand caught on her diamond stud earring and restoring order with a practiced adjustment of her hair clip. "So, she's the one with the special arrangements. Where is the tiger?" Miriam's eyes darted around the baggage claim area as if expecting the tiger to materialize with the other luggage.

"Lucky—Benjakalyani—is the tiger. She was sent directly from quarantine to the vet school. I'll come by in the morning to handle any necessary details."

"Isn't there a restriction on import of exotic animals? Or did Tugood *handle* things for you?" James frowned, all traces of good humor and the tantalizing dimple disappearing at the mention of Matthew Tugood.

"Actually, a Kappa Zeta Rho sorority sister from the Brookfield Zoo handled the paperwork. I just went to Thailand to meet Ning and facilitate her introduction to the university."

"Well, then," Professor Cook scribbled a note on her papers, "I'll get the students settled on campus for the night and I'll see you," she hesitated, her hands fluttering, "later." She rounded up her students and headed off.

"Is that all you did in Thailand? Escort Ning and her tiger home to the university?" Curiosity and a hint of professional distance replaced the earlier warmth in James's eyes.

"Of course." The lie tasted sour in Bree's mouth and she swallowed the urge to say more. *Never explain.* Tugood's admonition on the art and science of lying played in her mind like the refrain of a song she couldn't get out of her head. No matter how much she wanted to.

By the time they reached her condo, Bree still had not managed to recapture the earlier warmth with James. Friendly, yet aloof, he made her wonder if she'd jumped to conclusions earlier. Or if her ruminations on Matthew had made her finally ruin the chance for a real relationship.

As she swung the front door open, a thud shook the floorboards and Sherlock, her twenty-pound orange fur-baby, raced to her, mewing at the top of his kitty lungs.

Exactly three and three-quarters strokes later, he slapped her hand away with his paw, turned to present her with a ramrod straight tail, and sauntered away.

"Typical," James said behind her, a hint of laughter in his voice. "I know how he feels." Before she could respond to the barb, he lifted her suitcase. "Where do you want me to put this?"

While he stashed the suitcase at the foot of her bed, Bree headed to the kitchen to put her flowers in water. When James joined her, his eyes held questions. "So, has my bad temper turned you off to the idea of sharing dinner? Or are you up for it? It's still early."

She gave him a smile. "I'd say I'm the one with a bit of a temper tonight. It's been a busy trip. But I should try to stay awake a while before I crash. Would you mind if we had a quick dinner and an early evening?"

"No problem. And I'm glad you agreed, because I stocked your fridge with burgers and other goodies before I came to the airport to surprise you. All I need now is a grill." He started to gather his grilling supplies.

"Calling my hibachi a grill is a little grandiose, but I'd love a burger." Her stomach rumbled. This was so much better than the airline's idea of breakfast——green tea-flavored porridge—or lunch——a mystery meat dubbed kimchi fusion deluxe.

"Done. Why don't you freshen up and relax while I cook?"

While James took the meat out to the grill on her balcony, Bree headed to the bedroom. As she wrestled her suitcase onto the chest at the foot of the bed, Sherlock slid out from under it. How the tubby tabby managed to get underneath the bed was a mystery.

"Still mad at me?" He blinked, then licked his paws and rubbed them across his face, not responding to Bree. "Guess so."

She opened the suitcase and tossed her laundry in a heap near the hamper, ready for the wash later that night after James had gone. Sherlock stopped his bathing and stalked to the pile as if expecting to find a mouse underneath.

A foot away, he arched his back and hissed. His tawny orange hair stood straight up on his back, making him appear twice his size—no small feat. He took a cautious step forward, sniffed and hissed again.

"What's the matter, baby? It's just my laundry. Dirty clothes from my day at—" *The Tiger Sanctuary.* Bree lowered herself to the floor and put a hand out for Sherlock to sniff. "Do you smell tigers? Are you jealous? They aren't as pretty as my boy. No. Never."

The sound of her voice appeared to calm him, and he sniffed her hand. A tentative lick later, he allowed her to pet him. Five full strokes this time before he turned and stalked off to wiggle his bulk under her bed again.

Fickle, she thought. *Just like all the other men in her life.* She turned from the cat to see if she could salvage the remainder of the evening with James.

The next morning, fortified with extra strong coffee and a layer of jet-lag-concealing makeup, Bree greeted a receptionist at Terrance University and was given directions to the office of the Vice President of Student Affairs housed in the original historic section of the administration building.

A long, empty hallway connected the newer building entrance to a suite of elegant, if aging, offices on the upper floor. A handful of cubicles designed to house student employees sat empty in the anteroom outside the office. Bree crossed the expanse and knocked on the frame of the partially closed door.

"Dr. Mayfield-Watson, it's a pleasure to meet you." The VP rose, one hand smoothing his already perfect tie. He rounded the desk and crossed the room toward her, hand extended. "I'm Quentin Christianson. My colleagues call me Quint." Sharp eyes, the watery pale blue of skim milk, raked over her.

Despite his smile, Bree shivered as her instincts snapped to attention. Automatically she committed his description to memory. Just under six feet tall, tending to the heavy side. Light hair—once blond now gray—immaculately cut and styled. Smooth, pale skin. Blunt fingers, buffed nails, the indent of a wedding ring on his bare left hand.

"On behalf of the athletic department, the veterinary college, and the alumni association, I want to thank you for your help in bringing our tiger cub to us."

Bree gripped Quint's hand and pasted on a smile. "The alums from the Kappa Zeta Rho sorority did the hard work. I simply took advantage of a business trip to escort Ning and the cub stateside. Speaking of which, how is Ning settling in?"

Quint's brow creased, echoing the frown on his lips. Bree catalogued his micro expressions, assessing and weighing them as if she were still on a Sci-Spy mission.

"Ning?" Quint's face relaxed even as his eyes narrowed. "You must mean the student who came with the cub. There have been some," his eyes darted to a cabinet at the far end of his massive office "irregularities with the new student."

Bree strolled to the desk, took a seat and pulled a notebook out of her purse, not looking to see if Quint followed. "I'm sure I can clear up any questions you might have."

"Yes. Well," Quint's voice sounded behind her and out of the corner of her eye she saw him return to the desk with long, firm strides. "I would appreciate any help you can offer." He pinned her with a look, his brow still slightly creased as he sat.

"Was there a problem with her admission packet? Her visa? Her passport?" Bree raised her brows, forcing herself not to smile.

"You are a feisty one, aren't you, Dr. Watson?" Quint's eyes searched her face then slipped lower, resting on her cleavage. "I could get used to having someone like you on staff."

"What are the issues with Ning?"

Quint's gaze snapped to her face, darted to the cabinet, then fell to a folder on his desk. He opened it and flipped through the pages. "The legal paperwork appears to be in order. Ms. Cook, our International Studies teacher, is in charge of getting the students settled."

Bree waited.

Quint's jaw shifted, firmed, before he lifted his eyes to hers. "I am generally kept in the loop."

"And this time?"

"I like to get to know the students before they are admitted. It smooths the process. That didn't happen with the Thai girl."

"She's a vibrant young woman with a bright, curious mind. You'll have ample chances to meet with her, especially since she'll accompany the cub on her athletic club appearances."

Quint smiled and pushed the folder aside. "I'm sure you're correct. Now, if you don't mind, tell me more about yourself. I understand your company has undergone major changes within the last year."

"We went from being a research-based company to a scientific staffing company." Bree handed him a business card.

"Sci-PHi. Science Professionals for Hire." He glanced up. "Not the most prestigious place for someone with your resume."

"I've found the work both challenging and interesting. Nothing is ever routine at Sci-PHi."

"And your clients?"

"We handle everything from forensic lab analyses to contract research for start-up companies."

"Any clients in education?"

Bree tensed. The memory of being undercover at another local college while solving a murder knotted her muscles. She inhaled slowly, trying to quell the reflexive action. "We have had a few academic clients."

Quint nodded. "Good to know. Now, if you can spare a few minutes, may I show you around?" He rose and rounded the desk to pull her chair out for her.

Bree tucked her notebook away and followed Quint across the office to the wall of display cases. Artifacts of various sizes clustered beneath display lights. The hilt of a Celtic sword rested in a place of honor next to a pile of old Roman coins.

Geodes and polished gem stones winked at her from another shelf. Elsewhere what appeared to be medieval instruments of torture, including a pair of lethal looking tongs, a claw-shaped backscratcher, and wrought iron handcuffs pitted with rust. Bree shifted her gaze to a collection of bottles and jars with foreign inscriptions on the labels.

"You have a fascinating collection."

Quint unlocked the case with a small key which he stashed in his pocket. "Many international students have given me gifts over the years. Cultural items from their homes reminds me of the value that can be gleaned from diversity."

He plucked something from the outstretched hands of a many-armed elephant god draped in Indian style robes. "This," he said with pride as he placed it in Bree's palm, "is a lotus flower. The leaves are made from emerald set in rhodium. The petals are diamond, sapphire, and ruby. Very rare. Very valuable."

"It's exquisite." Bree's hand shook slightly as she returned the thousands of dollars' worth of gems to him.

"There are other gems too. Less valuable, but equally fascinating. Opals from Australia. Diamonds from Africa. Amethyst from Brazil. I also collect local remedies from around the world. And ancient artifacts such as the Roman coins and medieval weapons." He reached for another item but stopped when the phone rang.

As he took the call, Bree scanned the office, noting the door through which she'd entered, a small door in the back of the room, and an expanse of windows overlooking an oval of grass covered in early autumn leaves where students gathered.

No apparent security cameras. No assistant at a desk in the anteroom. No students working in the cluster of cubicles outside, either. And a case containing gems whose worth rivaled the GDP of a small nation state protected by a thin sheet of glass and a small, easily-picked lock. A security nightmare.

But not her business.

Behind her, Quint cut off the call.

"My apologies, Dr. Mayfield-Watson. I must take another meeting." He locked the cabinet, saw her to the door, and made his farewells.

As Bree crossed the empty outer office, she shivered. Her thoughts shifted from the cold office behind her and its harsh, calculating occupant to Ning. Alone in an unfamiliar world, the girl might have trouble adjusting. She would need all the help she could get.

CHAPTER 3

Outside the oppressive, artifact-filled room, the brightness of the day and the crisp September air energized Bree, a welcome reprieve from the hot, muggy days in Thailand. When she returned to her Sci-PHi office, she booted up her computer and grabbed coffee before heading to her friend Norah's desk.

"You're back!" Norah jumped from her chair in the cubicle outside the boss's office and gave Bree a quick hug. "How was the trip?"

"I brought you something." Bree handed Norah a small package wrapped in tissue.

Despite Norah's black and purple attire and preference for skull and bones jewelry, Bree had picked out a soft pink silk scarf for the girl. Because underneath the admin's devil-may-care attitude lurked a shy young woman.

Norah's quick intake of breath told Bree she'd made the right choice. "It's beautiful. Pink, just like my aura."

Bree held her tongue, declining to comment on Norah's supposed aura. Working with scientists hadn't dampened Norah's enthusiasm for her alternative, bordering-on-whacky, beliefs.

"So, tell me about the trip."

"It was the adventure of a lifetime."

Too late, the thud of footsteps alerted Bree to her boss's presence seconds before he spoke. "And here I thought it was a business trip on behalf of our client." Troy lifted his lips in a sneer. "Since you missed this morning's department meeting, why don't you come in and tell me all about your adventures."

A muscle spasm in her neck sent a shaft of pain through Bree's head as she settled across the desk from Troy. She massaged the corded muscles.

"Are you all right?" Troy's normally grating voice held a hint of real concern and, for once, he wasn't scowling at her.

"Too many hotels. Too much sleeping on the plane."

"Too many jobs for the Special Projects Division?" A calculating gleam sparked in his eyes. "I know you think I don't like sharing you with Matthew Tugood's department because I'm a control freak—"

"You are."

Troy leaned back in his chair with a sigh. "Maybe. A little. But I don't want to end up in a lifeless pile under the desk like our last boss."

"Technically, *I* was your last boss." The words slipped out before Bree could censor them.

"Right. And I don't know why the new owners put me in this office instead of you. But they did. And if they see I can't keep track of my primary researcher, what will they think about my ability to run the department?"

They'll think you're too self-involved to notice that Sci-PHi is a front for our real business. Spying. At least that was the argument Bree had given Tugood when they'd discussed who to promote to the department head position. So far, the ruse had worked, keeping the company and its many employees afloat with contract business while hiding the handful of people who worked on the spy side.

"Has anyone complained about your job performance?" she asked.

"No, but—"

"Have they complained about my job performance?"

"No, they—"

"Then my advice, Troy, is to focus on the department's consulting work and not create trouble where it doesn't exist."

Troy raked a hand through his gelled blond hair, then buried his face in his palms. "Easy for you to say. But now that your other boss is out of town, I'm getting Special Projects requests too."

Bree straightened, the pains in her neck and head forgotten. She glanced at her watch. Nearly ten o'clock local time. Which meant it was ten at night in Thailand. If Tugood wanted her, why hadn't he called her directly? *Because barely thirty-six hours after we parted in Bangkok, he's too involved with Sasha to bother.*

"This came through an hour ago." Troy pushed a contract across the desk.

Bree scanned the document. "Terrance University wants to hire me to teach introductory chemistry for the fall semester?" Quint hadn't been joking when he asked if she did contract work in education.

"Actually, they want to contract Sci-PHi, but they did request you. Since you're back from the Thai Energy Summit," he spread his hands wide, "I can't spare anyone from the forensics project. And Tugood won't be breathing down your neck until he returns from the Pacific. You're the perfect candidate." He paused. "Unless you think you're overqualified?"

"I think," Bree said slowly, tightening her lips into a slight frown, "that teaching a college course and continuing my *Energy Unlimited* contract research adds up to a full plate." In reality, it gave her a chance to watch over Ning while recovering from the recent spate of activities involving Zed.

And while Tugood was busy in the Pacific playing spy games with Sasha, Bree would prove she couldn't be brushed aside. She might not have the resources to do financial forensics, but with her research skills, she could dig into the geo-politics of energy terrorism and learn more about Zed's potential targets. Let Matthew try to push that aside.

Bree listened with one ear to Troy's instructions while she laid out her plans for the next weeks. At least this time when she entered the university, she'd be using her own name and credentials.

The tension in her muscles ebbed. A few weeks of teaching and private research. No undercover spying. No dead bodies. No deceiving Troy, her best friend Kiki, or even Norah while Bree worked outside of the office.

Bree arrived at Quint's office half an hour before her first job as a Terrance University contractor—an evening faculty mixer. He waved her in.

"I'm delighted that Sci-PHi agreed to lend me your expertise. Our chemistry professor left us in the lurch when he quit this morning."

"It's a clear violation of his contract." A woman stood near Quint's desk, her dark eyes cool and assessing as she tapped a file folder against her hand.

"Bree, let me introduce you to Ms. Fiona Fancier." He gave her name a stylish, French pronunciation. "Ms. Fancier is our legal counsel." Bree took in the statuesque woman's tight, low-cut cocktail dress and immediately regretted choosing a business suit for the event.

Everything from Fiona's upswept hair to the sapphire and diamond drop earrings and necklace that matched her dress, to her stiletto heels exuded a commanding presence and indicated the mixer was a more formal event than Bree had expected.

She shook hands with Fiona. The woman slid easily into Quint's chair. "Thank you for coming early." Fiona flashed her a smile. "Quint and I were just discussing how to deal with Professor Shore's violation of his employment contract."

"He won the lottery, bought a small plane, and decided to give flying lessons." Quint shrugged. "He's pursuing his dream."

"And we're pursuing a settlement," Fiona said sharply. "He owes us at least two weeks' notice." She looked at Bree. "I'm sure you can appreciate that, having been burned, we want to ensure our contract with you is iron clad, Dr. Watson."

"It's Mayfield-Watson."

Fiona glanced at the paperwork in front of her. "Of course. The contract specifies …"

Bree listened to the legalese of the contract with one ear, more interested in the way Fiona's breasts threatened to spill out of her dress with each inhale. And the way Quint's eyes tracked the sight. Fiona toyed with the necklace at her cleavage, never once breaking the flow of the mundane, legal wording in the contract while the air around her thickened with tension.

"… if you agree with the specification outlined in the contract," Fiona angled her body away from Quint, focusing entirely on Bree as she pointed to the printouts, "then sign and initial here, here, and here."

After Bree slid the signed forms back, Fiona opened another file. "I understand you've also agreed to act as the sponsor for …" She frowned at the paperwork.

"Ning? The Thai tiger trainer?"

"Yes, that is correct."

"It's a good thing she has a short version of her name for the English-speaking students to use. In any case, please read over this agreement and sign."

Although Bree hadn't planned on sponsoring Ning, she had committed herself to helping the girl acclimate to university life. After a careful read, Bree signed as Ning's sponsor.

"Wonderful. By the end of tomorrow, I'll have a mailbox set up for you in the office and an employee manual waiting for you. Welcome aboard." Fiona flashed her a brilliant smile and slid the folders into the top drawer of Quint's desk. "I'll make sure to stop by in the morning to file these with HR. If that's all right with you." She tilted her head in Quint's direction.

"Of course." Quint's eyes roamed the expanse of Fiona's pale, exposed décolletage. "Now we should introduce Bree to the rest of the staff. She'll want to know who she's working with."

They left the office, pausing while Quint locked the doors. As they headed to the elevator, Fiona clutched Quint's arm—maybe for balance in the stilettos although she didn't appear to need help—making Bree suppress a squirm. She was either a third wheel or a witness to a tangled web of sexual harassment, depending on how reciprocal the relationship was.

Bree breathed a sigh of relief when they reached the faculty lounge and she was no longer alone with Fiona and Quint. The warm, wood-paneled expanse gave off a 1950's Ivy-league vibe. The waitstaff consisted of students formally garbed in black and white. Everyone else had opted for more casual wear. She accepted a canape—salmon mousse topped with caviar—from a passing server.

Fiona headed to the bar while Quint steered Bree toward a small group. "Coach Fleek," he called, waving a heavily muscled man over. "I want you to meet our newest staff member. This is Dr. Mayfield-Watson."

"You can call me Bree. It's easier." *Barrel-chested. A few inches shorter than Quint. Dark hair enhanced with cheap dye. Frown lines bracketing his mouth.* Bree filed the information away in the seconds it took to flash through her mind.

"Pleasure to meet you, Bree. I'm Rich. Rich Fleek. Most people just call me Coach." Coach Fleek engulfed her hand in his and pumped it a couple times before offering a grin. She winced as his thick, gold-banded ring dug into her flesh. "What brings you to Terrance University?"

"Good luck," Quint answered before Bree could reply. "Dr. Mayfield-Watson, Bree, agreed to fill in for our missing introductory chemistry professor."

"Huh. Science was never my strong point."

"Good thing we hired you to coach football." Quint laughed and slapped the coach on the arm. "You just keep the team winning."

"Will do." Coach Fleek held up his hand and pointed to the thick, square shaped front of his ring, which reminded Bree of the ones given to Super Bowl winners. Gold and diamonds glinted in the light. "A record season like last year and I can add another one of these babies to my collection." He winked at Bree. "The fans love these displays of Tiger Power."

"Speaking of things the fans will love, Bree was instrumental in getting that new mascot of yours."

"You brought us the tiger cub?" Coach's eyes widened as he looked at Bree. "I can't tell you how much Terry—that's what we're calling him—is going to help the athletic booster club. The private boxes are almost sold out with donors who want to get up close and personal with Terry the Tiger."

He turned to Quint. "Donations are up thirty percent over last year—and that's before Terry makes his debut." He grinned widely at Bree. "Tiger Power—it's more than just the team motto now."

"I understood that the cub was primarily here as part of the exotic animal veterinarian program," Bree said. "*She* has a genetic feature the vet teams want to study."

Coach Fleek waved a dismissive hand. "As long as he shows up for the games, I don't care what the vet school does. I'm happy to share him with the vets as long it doesn't impact the football schedule."

"Or publicity events," Quint added.

"Right." Coach nodded, his smile slipping. "Say, I met that that little Chinese girl that came with the cub. What do you know about her?"

"That's Ning." Bree dug deep for patience. "She's actually from Thailand, where she worked at an animal sanctuary. Ning has been with Lucky—the cub—since *she* was born." Bree stressed the name and gender of the cub.

"Thailand. Got it." Coach smiled again, nodding thoughtfully. "Hope you can forgive my ignorance. I've never traveled further than Texas. Anyway, the Thai girl is a mite shy. Doesn't look big enough to handle a house cat, let alone a tiger cub. I better lay down the law to my players to make sure they watch their manners around her."

"I'm sure you'll do fine, Coach." Quint steered Bree away from him. "He's a good coach and a reasonable man when he isn't crossed. Keeps the players in line. He won't give you any trouble."

A shiver of awareness, one she'd come to think of as her spy-sense, whispered across Bree's nerve endings. Why should Quint assume the coach would give her trouble? Other than being a little culturally out-of-touch, he hadn't seemed like a bad person.

"Ah, here's Ms. Cook. How are you doing, my dear?" Quint brushed a kiss on the teacher's cheek. "Miriam is our International Studies teacher at the university. I believe you and Bree met at the airport, didn't you?"

Miriam blushed, the deep rose a pretty contrast to the soft brown curls that framed her face. A dusky blue knit dress skimmed her body, the hem stopping just above the knee. Gone was the frazzled professional from the airport, reminding Bree of the power of a makeup brush and a change of clothing.

"A pleasure to meet you again, Dr. Watson. I must apologize if I was short with you the other day. We have more new international students this year than we've had in quite some time."

"It's all due to your extraordinary efforts, Miriam. I believe in giving credit where it's due." Quint winked at her. "Diversity is one of our prime initiatives, after all."

"Does that mean I'm up for that promotion? Tenure?" Miriam brought a hand to her ear, fiddling flirtatiously with her diamond studs.

"That's a discussion for another day." A server passed Quint a note and he scanned the page. "Miriam, I hate to impose, but could you introduce Dr. Mayfield-Watson to some of the other staff? Something's come up that I need to deal with."

Miriam watched Quint move through the crowd, stopping to shake hands here and there. She nodded to the door where a stunning older woman in a sparkling white mini dress and sporting platinum hair gave Quint a cool kiss. "Looks more like *someone* than *something*. That's Pamela Christianson. You'd think after all these years, Quint would learn to escort his wife to official university events."

She tucked a strand of hair behind her ear, her gaze thoughtful. "She's a tolerant woman, but not one who likes to be ignored. At least in public."

"Quint never mentioned a wife." An image of the indent on his naked ring finger flashed through Bree's mind.

"He likes a good work-wife balance." Miriam giggled, waving away the issue as if shooing a troublesome gnat. "I'll fill you in over coffee if you're interested. Speaking of which, I'd like you to meet my friend Heather." She pointed to a high-top table where a petite redhead with a closely cropped pixie-style cut sipped coffee beside several other younger teachers.

Giant, dangling dream catcher earrings fluttered beneath a second ear piercing sporting a tiny diamond stud, an odd contrast of the flamboyant with the traditional. Elsewhere, flamboyant carried the day. Heather's brightly colored, flowing tunic, black leggings, and ballet flats reminded Bree, rather uncomfortably, of the disguise she wore while undercover at her last university assignment.

The other teachers scattered as Miriam and Bree approached.

"Heather Beauchamp is our English teacher. Heather, this is Dr. Mayfield-Watson—Bree—our new chemistry professor."

"So good to meet you." Heather abandoned her coffee and gave Bree a critical, searching look before smiling and embracing her in a patchouli-scented hug. "I'm excited to have a woman with her chemistry PhD on staff. Another glass ceiling shattered. And a chance for us to influence young women everywhere. Don't you agree?"

"I hadn't really thought about it that way," Bree began. "Of course, I've barely had time to think about it at all. This morning I was just the woman who'd facilitated bringing the university's tiger cub from Thailand."

Heather pursed her lips as if she'd tasted something sour. "Enslaving animals for the sake of athletic department theatrics is cruel. The money Coach convinced the university to invest in that misguided venture could have been much better spent. Anti-bullying training for his players comes to mind." She sighed, her whole body deflating. "Not that anyone with power would listen to the likes of me."

"If it helps," Bree signaled to a server circling the room with a coffee pot, "the cub is actually here at the behest of the vet school. She has a rare genetic disorder that wouldn't allow her to live in the wild."

Heather returned to her perch on the stool. "In that case, I won't hold it against you. Or call out SWAP."

Bree groaned, hoping Heather's joking tone didn't hold a dark side. SWAP—the Suburban West Animal Protection group—had picketed her former company over an issue regarding the

Canadian Goose population. Even though the group's antics helped Bree uncover a murderer, she had no love for them.

"Don't worry." Heather sent her an impish grin. "I was just kidding about SWAP. Even I think they take things too far. But back to the situation with Dick Fleek. Don't let him push you, the cub, or the trainer around."

"Ning is tougher than she looks." Bree accepted a cup of coffee and inhaled the caffeinated goodness. She sipped, hoping to force her jet-lagged brain to function for a few more hours.

"I doubt she's a hundred pounds, soaking wet. But then," Heather spread her arms wide, "neither am I, and I guarantee I could hold my own against any man."

"Ning handled tigers more than twice her size without flinching. And she was brave enough to leave everything she knew behind to chase her dreams of a better education. I'm sure she can handle herself."

"Good for her." Heather clapped her hands, setting her multiple bangles jingling. "Maybe she'll join one of our women's self-defense classes. She might teach me a thing or two about handling wild beasts of the two-legged variety."

Across the room someone started playing the piano. The sounds of chatter lowered to a dull hum as the music worked its magic. Bree scanned the crowd, her gaze drawn to Quint and his wife as they strolled the perimeter of the room, the royal couple of the university holding court.

They stopped near Fiona and Coach. The women embraced, Fiona bending toward the smaller woman, both throwing air kisses and smiles, their bodies angled toward one another, shutting the men out, creating a sense of intimacy between the women. Just like best friends, except for the exaggerated personal space between them.

Rivals for Quint's affection.

"More coffee?" The cultured British accent of the server was at odds with his young face. Bree accepted a refill. The server puttered around the table, setting out small silver cream and sugar sets. Without being asked, he refilled Heather's cup.

"If you like coffee, you should visit the coffee house I sponsor near campus." Heather smiled at the server. "Nigel is a regular there. A good barista and a better poet."

"I thought the coffee house closed down," he murmured.

"That was temporary." Heather lowered her voice. "We're opening again this semester. With a few changes."

Miriam drew Bree away from the table where Nigel and Heather spoke in low tones. "The coffee shop is one of the few places my international students feel free to express themselves. Heather's done a wonderful job with making it a safe haven for free thinking. Students who don't quite fit in elsewhere tend to gather there." She cocked her head, clearly expecting a reply.

"I take it people like Coach—who don't know the difference between China and Thailand—are less comfortable there?"

Miriam nodded. "Exactly. You should visit to see for yourself what a wonderful place it is. But I warn you—it's an independent, off-campus venture."

"Meaning Quint and the university haven't approved of its existence? Or do they not know it exists?"

"Exactly."

Before Bree could ask for clarification, Miriam returned her to Quint and his wife. "Lovely to see you, Mrs. Christianson," Miriam said, lightly embracing the woman.

"And you." Mrs. Christianson broke from the embrace, then turned her back on Miriam while extending a hand to Bree. "Dr. Watson, I presume? My husband has told me little about you, except that you have impressive science credentials. Why don't you and I have a cozy little chat and get to know one another?"

She scooped two glasses of Champagne from a nearby tray and steered Bree away from the others.

Then, with the skill of a seasoned interrogator, Pamela Christianson questioned Bree about topics ranging from her grad school GPA to her love life, prying into every corner.

And Bree, PhD chemist and spy-in-training, told Pamela everything. And nothing at all. Just the way Matthew taught her.

CHAPTER 4

L ife as a university professor suited her more than she'd ever imagined. Bree buttoned her lab coat as twenty students filed into the university chem lab. "Starting today," she said once everyone was in their assigned workspace, "you must wear your safety glasses before entering the lab."

"But we keep our glasses in the lab drawer," said a student from the back of the room.

"From now on you can take them with you and bring them back each day, or you can leave them here." Bree pointed to a dispenser by the lab door containing safety glasses. "Either way, once you cross this line," she indicated a line of yellow safety tape affixed to the floor two feet inside the door, "your glasses need to be on."

Bree ignored the chorus of groans. "You get one warning. After that, if you are without your glasses, you won't be allowed to complete or get credit for the day's assigned experiment."

"That's not fair."

"Everything we work with is safe."

Variations on the theme erupted from around the room until Bree silenced the students. "Who hates to open their eyes underwater at the swimming pool?"

Bree pointed to a student who had raised her hand. "Why?"

"The chlorine in the water stings."

"And yet," Bree said, "it is considered safe. Now, let's see what happens when eyes are exposed to laboratory chemicals." Bree cued up a video, knowing images of cow eyes exposed to chemicals would drive her point home. When Bree stepped to the side to dim the lights, an admin motioned to her from outside the lab. Bree slipped out, keeping one eye on the students.

"What's wrong?"

The admin smiled apologetically as she passed a note to Bree. "It's appears Miss Ning needs your help."

Again. Bree scanned the note. "Tell Vice President Christianson and Coach Fleek that I'll speak with her."

"Ning, we've talked about this." Bree slipped inside the door and leaned back against the bars of the large, white-tiled holding area where the tiger cub was housed. She cast a wary eye on the sleeping animal. "You have a dorm, a suitemate, and a bed of your own. You can't stay here at the vet school."

Across the enclosure, Ning sat on a low cot, Lucky curled on her lap like an overlarge housecat. The girl's fingers stroked the sleeping tiger. "The pet school doctors gave me *this* bed," she insisted stubbornly. "Lucky cries when I am not here."

Lucky's contented rumble sounded more like a chainsaw than a purr, but Bree couldn't argue that the tiger seemed calm with Ning. "Even though Lucky couldn't survive in the wild, she's still a predator at heart. It isn't safe for you to sleep here. Her teeth—"

"Lucky *cries.*"

Bree switched topics. "Do you want to tell me what happened with Coach Fleek today?"

"Lucky likes the football grass. We play on it, but Coach made me put her back in the cage. Lucky hates the cage."

Bree's lips twitched at the image of Lucky playing on the football field when the players came to practice. She pressed her lips together to hold back the smile. "Lucky has to be transported in the cage. And stay there during football practice. For everyone's safety. Even Lucky's."

"Yes. Mrs. Fancy—"

"*Fan-cee-eh*," Bree corrected.

"Mrs. *Fan-cee-er* made me sign papers that said so." Ning's fingers stilled. "But ... the football team is mean. Especially the quarter—" she closed her eyes in thought, "quarter-boy. He try to scare Lucky by banging on her cage and throwing things. Mr. Coach did not see him."

"The quarterback antagonized Lucky?"

Ning nodded. "He said she should be fierce, like the team. Mr. Coach only listens to his boys. He tells me I am lying. So, I took Lucky away."

"On a leash. By yourself."

"Lucky is a good girl. Walking made her calm. We did not hurt anybody. We came back here." Ning shrugged as if nothing had happened. "I don't like Mr. Coach."

Bree sat on the cot, wordlessly offering support while inwardly planning to confront Coach Fleek about the behavior of his players. Lucky shifted, leaning her warm, heavy weight against Bree's thigh. Without thinking, she stroked the cat's fur. This time she didn't hold back the smile.

After a few minutes, she disentangled her fingers from Lucky's rough fur. "Vice President Christianson would like to see you in the morning. To discuss Lucky's—" she chose her words carefully "—public appearances. Reporters from the *Terrance Tattler* and the *Plainville Herald* will probably be there."

Ning frowned and sent Bree a questioning look.

"They're newspapers—from the school and the city. Everyone is interested in meeting Lucky and taking photos with her. You'll need to be there to make sure everyone knows how to treat Lucky during the photo shoot. And to keep her calm."

"Lucky is a good girl," Ning repeated, "a pretty girl." She cuddled the cub close and dropped a kiss behind Lucky's ear. "She will take good pictures."

After a few more minutes, Bree made Ning promise to sleep in her dorm tonight, then left the vet school. She checked her watch and picked up her pace. Office hours started in five minutes. Her conversation with Coach Fleek would have to wait until tomorrow.

The odor of day-old sweat permeated the suite of offices assigned to Coach Fleek and his staff, even though the locker rooms were on another floor of the athletic complex. Bree unscrewed the cap on her commuter mug hoping the scent of vanilla-infused dark roast would mask the less pleasant smells.

As she strode through the outer office, motivational posters filled her peripheral vision. She neared the coach's massive desk. A slam of a desk drawer put her on alert. But when a slender young man popped up from behind the desk, she relaxed.

Slight and rather small for a football player, he looked unimpressive against the backdrop of massive trophies lining shelves behind him. "Sorry, dropped something," he mumbled, straightening. "You looking for Coach?"

"Yes. I wanted to—"

"Hey! You're the new chemistry teacher. I'm in your Chemistry Concepts class this semester. Josh Gibbons." He hurried out from behind the desk then froze, a foot or two from her, hands stuck in his pockets, weight resting on one leg, looking at her expectantly.

Bree sipped the scalding coffee, using the moment to envision the auditorium style classroom filled with students in the basic science class. All two hundred of them. A cluster of athletes, some sporting the Terrance Tigers logo on their clothing, had occupied the upper left corner of the room, nearest the doors.

"Of course," she said taking a guess. "You and several of your friends from the team like to sit in the back."

The young man's face lit up. "Yeah. That's us." He wrinkled his nose as if smelling sweaty socks. "I don't think I'm going to sit with them anymore. I'd rather hear what you have to say. The class is kind of interesting."

"My office door is always open if you need help with the material," Bree offered. If she was making science "kind of" interesting to the athletes, she must be doing something right. "Is Coach in?"

"Nah," Josh hurried into the outer office, leaving Bree no choice but to follow. "He went to meet old man Christianson. Something about Tanner and yesterday's practice. Told me to clean the office, then run laps till he got back." Josh's gaze narrowed, and he pivoted the toe of one sneaker as if grinding out a cigarette butt. "He wasn't too happy with me this morning."

I shouldn't get involved. I shouldn't. "Anything you want to talk about?" *So much for not getting involved.*

Josh looked up, lips parted. Then he shrugged. "Nothing worth mentioning. You wanna leave a note for Coach or something?"

Bree waved the idea aside. "I'll stop back later." As she left the office, Josh resumed his cleaning with a vigor that left Bree wondering if he was trying to impress the coach with thoroughness, or delay running laps.

Outside the athletic building, a track wound around the football field. A memory hit her, hard and fast.

"You can do this, Watson." Matthew winked at her before she could remind him it was Mayfield-Watson. "We'll start out easy."

Bree eyed the Sci-PHi parking lot while trudging toward the path encircling the complex. It was nearly empty. Good thing. She didn't need her colleagues gawking at the extra pounds she tried to hide beneath her baggy shorts and tee shirt.

Matthew reached the track first and started jogging in place, his clothing revealing, rather than hiding, his physique. Who was she kidding? No one would give her a second glance with that kind of eye-candy on display.

"Hurry up, slowpoke." His teasing voice drifted to her on a summer breeze. "Let's tackle this challenge."

The minute her feet hit the hard asphalt, he started off at a brisk walk. Her blood thumped, first slow, then faster as she kept pace with him. She pulled in air, her lungs expanding with the effort, then puffed it out only to drag in more. "I walk this track every day. Just not at warp speed."

Tugood looked down at her and the evening air heated. "It's easier to run than walk this fast, Watson."

"I don't," she gasped for more air, "run."

"Come on. Try it." He switched from a walk to a slow run, loping along beside her.

She tried. Bouncing off the ball of one foot and landing on the heel of the other, step by step. Amazed to discover it did take less effort than the fast walk.

"See?" Matthew moved in front of her, turned and jogged backward while encouraging her efforts. "Not so bad, is it?"

"It's okay," she managed, keeping her eyes on the terrain in front of her.

"Don't look down. Look at me. Look at the scenery. Don't think about it."

Don't think about the way her legs burned? The way her breasts and hips bounced with each stride? Impossible. Especially when Matthew's gaze slipped from her eyes to her chest. Damn sports bra. Wasn't it supposed to keep everything still and tucked away?

"Bree. Focus. Look at me."

She stared at his face. His eyes. "I'm fine." The words came out in a labored huff.

"You look distressed."

"I'm fine." She kept her focus fixed on his face. Hopefully he'd think her flushed cheeks were only from the run. "Why are we doing this?"

"Training."

"Ha. You think I need to amp up my workouts."

"You do."

Disappointment pounded through her, more powerful than the thud of the hard track against her feet. She'd thought he was different. Not one to judge a woman by her weight.

"Watson? Bree?"

"Sorry to disappoint you by being too fat to be a spy." She slowed her pace, hoping to put distance between them.

"That's what you think this is about?"

"Isn't it?"

He moved back to her side, matching her pace even as she slowed to a walk. "Bree, I didn't hire you for your body. I hired you for your sharp mind. And as lovely *as I find your curvy, sweet self, I'm not going to let you skip training." He slipped an arm around her waist and pulled her closer. "I'll learn to live with a smaller version of you if I have to."*

She moved away from his embrace. "Don't kid yourself. Or me. Everyone wants a smaller version of women."

"No." Matthew curled his fingers around her arm. Not tightly, but insistent. He turned her to face him. "I want a stronger version of you. A safer version. Because one day, if you keep going into the field, you will be running. Not for training. For your life. And I'll be damned if I let you die because I was too soft to push you during training."

A door slammed nearby, sending the memory fleeing. Josh Gibbons brushed past her. "Still waiting for Coach?"

Bree shook her head. "Have a good run, Josh." She turned away as he hit the track. Later tonight, she'd run herself. In case her Sci-Spy work ever involved more than creating fake chemical products and lying to a would-be terrorist.

⚜   ⚜   ⚜

Halfway between the athletic complex and her office, Bree's cell phone vibrated in her pocket. She picked up the call. *"Khun Dr. Bree, come quickly."* Ning's panicked voice snapped Bree's senses to high alert.

"What's wrong?"

"Dr. Christianson." Ning spat out a string of Thai words that Bree couldn't follow.

"Ning, where are you?"

"His office. Come." Words dissolved into sniffles punctuated with Lucky's feral growls before the call cut off.

Bree headed to the administration building, barely conscious that she'd shifted from a walk to a run at the sound of Ning's panicked voice. She slowed her pace as she entered the back door.

Years ago, this had been the front entrance. The historic entrance retained a wide marble vestibule with old world grandeur that was far different from the modern new entrance on the other side of the building. Lucky's cage sat near the elevator, door open.

Bree slid into the old-style elevator, pulling wrought iron and heavy steel doors closed before punching in the button for the third floor. The motor whirred and kicked into a jerky, noisy ride.

The assistant desk and cubicles outside Quint's office were quiet, empty, as usual. Quint's door stood open. Broken glass littered the floor and the strong scent of alcohol permeated the air. Inside, Ning and Lucky huddled together beside the massive curio cabinet staring wide-eyed.

Bree followed her gaze. Past the floor littered with papers and knickknacks from the desk. To Quint.

Motionless. Sprawled beside his desk on the crimson stained carpet. Congealed blood caked his once white hair and painted red streaks stood out on the waxy white skin of his torso. Not streaks, Bree realized when she saw his ripped shirt. Bloody claw marks. The glassy white of his eyes told her she didn't need to check for a pulse.

Quentin Christianson was dead.

Chapter 5

After calling the police, Bree turned her attention to Ning and Lucky. "It's all right," she told the girl, "but I need to know what happened."

"I take Lucky to her cage first."

The cub's growl made Bree wish that were possible. "No. We have to stay here and do our best not to touch or disturb anything." Although, given that Ning had walked in on a crime scene, tiger in tow, before summoning Bree, that seemed unrealistic.

She moved slightly to block Ning's view of the body, but there was no need. The girl had her face buried in the cub's fur. Bree knelt by the pair. "Start at the beginning," she encouraged. "What happened this morning?"

"I came to see Dr. Christianson. With Lucky for the newspaper pictures."

Oh no. When had the photographers been scheduled to come? Bree checked her watch, a sinking feeling weighing her gut. They were due at Quint's office any minute now.

"Go on," she said hoping the reporters were delayed.

"I take Lucky in her cage, like you said. But the lift is too small to carry the cage." She raised eyes glazed with tears to Bree. "Mrs. *Fan-cee-eh* yelled and shut the door when I walk past her. Then I came here."

"And you found Dr. Christianson?"

Ning nodded. "Yes. With Coach. They make me lock Lucky in the bathroom before I talk to them. I let her play in water to keep calm." She pointed to the small door at the rear of Quint's office.

Water? Either Quint's private bathroom had a tub in it or Lucky had been playing in the toilet. The thought almost made Bree smile until a glance at the dead man doused her humor.

"So, he was alive when you visited?"

"Alive. With Coach. Arguing. They stop when I come in. But start again to argue about me and Lucky. And the quarterboy's performance."

"Anything else?" Bree struggled to follow Ning. The girl's accent thickened even as her grasp on English grammar thinned while relaying the events of the morning.

"We left." Her words dropped to a whisper. "I am sorry, *Kuhn* Dr. Bree. I took the new lift and forgot Lucky's cage. We walked to the pet school."

No doubt cutting across the main campus oval in sight of students and teachers. Unlike the tourists and staff at Thai tiger sanctuary where Lucky and Ning had roamed in freedom, the people of Terrance University were unaccustomed to seeing wild animals walking on a leash.

A ghost of a smile lit Ning's wan face. "Lucky played in the fountain. She have so much fun, even in the cold Plainville water. And students take her picture."

Pictures. Crap. "Unfortunately, the pictures might cause some parents and teachers to worry. Lucky should only go on walks when she's on the vet school grounds."

Ning made a face. "No fountain at the pet school. And too many dogs barking at Lucky. Not nice."

That was a discussion for later. Bree's phone vibrated and she pulled it out. A text from James let her know the police detectives were on their way. "Why did you come back here?"

Bree asked, trying to get the rest of Ning's story before the detectives arrived.

"Dr. Christianson text me. Ask me to come back and bring Lucky. We find him like this when we come in. So, I call you." A quiver was back in her voice and her small body trembled. Bree squeezed Ning's shivering shoulder.

Footsteps sounded outside in the hallway. James appeared in the door, taking in everything, his eyes cool and professional. "Ladies, if you'll just wait a minute, I'll be able to get you out of here."

"What the hell?" a young officer gasped. "He's been clawed to death." His gaze flitted between the victim, O'Neil, and Lucky, whose growls had drawn his attention. "That animal—"

"—is under control at the moment." James's crisp manner quelled the younger man's panic and reassured Bree, but increased Ning's tremors. "Don't make assumptions about the crime scene. Just view the evidence."

With James taking charge, the crime scene techs had soon photographed, recorded, and sampled a path to allow Bree, Ning, and Lucky to pass. But just outside the door, an officer stopped them. Bree recognized her as Shana Westerman, who'd worked with James when Bree's boss had been found murdered the past spring.

"We'd like a word with each of you. Individually," Officer Westerman said after introducing herself to Ning. "If you and your dog could follow me ..." She cast a wary eye at Lucky.

"No need to separate them, Westerman." James strode onto the scene. "Dr. Mayfield-Watson is still under contract as a consultant to the PD. Plus, she is Ning's sponsor. And," he swallowed, "apparently she's also in charge of the tiger."

The blood rushed from Officer Westerman's face and she took two giant steps away from Ning and Lucky. "Tiger? I thought it was some kind of weird dog."

"Either way, we'll need to quarantine the animal." He turned to Ning and Bree. "I'm sorry, but it's procedure."

Ning pushed past Bree, her fears momentarily forgotten. "Lucky no hurt anyone. He dead when we arrive!" She faced O'Neil and Westerman with bravado, but her tight knuckled grip on the leash told another story.

"—it's protocol—"

"—nothing to worry about—"

"—you can trust the detectives—"

O'Neil, Westerman, and Bree all tried to calm the situation at once, speaking over one another is a cacophony punctuated by Lucky's cries.

"Just what is going on here?" A strident voice broke through the noise, silencing them. The sharp click of high heels sounded on the tile floor as Fiona Fancier walked toward them.

Behind her a cluster of reporters—some with the campus newspaper some with the local publication—took in the scene and started snapping photographs as fast as their cell phones would let them. A lone police officer tried to remove them from the scene without much success.

"I came to show the reporters to Quint's office. What are the police doing here?"

Seeing Officer Westerman talking to Ning, Fiona hurried over. Without hesitation she edged past the detectives and put an arm around Ning's shoulder. "I'm this young woman's attorney." She turned to the girl. "Don't say a word to anyone but me," she instructed as she began to walk Ning away from the crowd, cutting through the reporters.

Ning planted her feet and stood her ground. "Lucky no hurt anyone," she repeated. "Mrs. *Fan-cee-eh* Lucky's attorney too."

Fiona started, as if just noticing Lucky. "Ning, not another word. I'll sort this out. Let Dr. Mayfield-Watson handle the cub." She disentangled the leash from Ning's hand and thrust it at Bree.

"Come to my office later." With that she shepherded Ning away, against the girl's muffled protests.

"How—" James paused and rubbed his forehead, wincing as his fingers dug into the inflamed sinus area. Across his desk, Bree sat, notebook in hand, looking at him with an expectant gaze. "How on earth do you get involved in these things? You're like the angel of death, finding murder wherever you go." He mentally kicked himself for the accusatory tone in his voice.

"I thought you weren't supposed to assume it was murder until after a thorough examination of the evidence." Bree lightened the mood with a wink and a smile.

James grunted. "A man is found dead in his office with claw marks on his chest and a dented skull. I'm pretty sure that wasn't an accident."

"You do know Lucky isn't responsible, don't you?"

"The tiger?" *That's what she was worried about?* She and a student were found with the body and her first thought was for *the tiger*? "I doubt *malice aforethought* is part of a tiger's attack plan, if that's what you mean. Even so, we'll probably have to put the cub down." He reached across the desk and covered Bree's hand with his own. "I'm sorry. For both you and Ning."

Bree gripped his hand with her free one, tightening her fingers in a demand for his attention. "No, you won't have to put her down. Lucky is incapable of producing those claw marks."

"I know you think the girl had her under control, but the scratches are consistent with—"

"With something else. James, the cub has a rare genetic disorder. One of the manifestations is that she has no claws. Just calloused lumps of flesh. My fingernails are more capable of scratching than Lucky's clawless toes. And her teeth aren't much stronger. That's why the vet school wants to study her. And why she couldn't survive in the wild."

Shit. His hopes for a quick resolution to the case disappeared faster than witnesses at a mugging. James pulled his hand from Bree's grip and opened a steno pad. "Things are not always what they appear to be," he murmured as he scribbled.

"You can say that again."

"I have," he looked up from his notes. "Many times. We drill it into the heads of every new recruit. But even an experienced investigator needs reminding sometimes. The claw marks on the victim's body ..." He shrugged. "I've seen a lot in my day, but this ... Let's just say it makes the tiger look guilty."

"I've already told you that Ning said Christianson was dead by the time she and Lucky arrived on the scene. So, we have enough to construct a timeline."

"*You* said. Not Ning." James shoved his chair back and headed toward the coffee pot. Bree followed. "We don't have an official statement from Ning. And the university attorney seems unlikely to allow her to talk with us." He handed Bree a cup of coffee, then sipped his own cup thoughtfully.

"She's just doing her job."

"Really?" His brows raised. "When exactly did Ning hire an attorney?"

Bree rolled her eyes and let out an exaggerated sigh. "Ning didn't hire her. She's the university liaison for all the international students. And her office is on the same floor as Quint's. She probably heard the officers come in and hurried to see what was happening. I'm sure she's only doing what she thinks is best for her charges."

"Sounds more like the university version of ambulance chasing to me." God knew he'd dealt with enough of *those* people in his day.

"Maybe—but without the chance for financial gain. None of the international students strike me as spoiled rich kids."

"Things are not always what they appear to be." He grinned at Bree. "Take you, for instance. Who would have thought an ivory tower chemistry teacher would turn into a crime-solving super sleuth?"

"You. I hope."

"Touché. Now let's get back to work. Tell me everything you know about today's events."

Bree scribbled in her notebook while James grilled her on the events of the day. Every time he was tempted to soften his questions, he reminded himself that they both knew the stakes. Sure, he was attracted as hell to her, but that didn't mean he'd compromise the investigation. Nor would she want him to.

"James?" Bree's puzzled frown indicated he'd missed something. Like a rookie cop.

"Sorry." He drained his lukewarm coffee and ambled back to the pot to refill the cup. "It's been a long day." He lifted the pot and nodded toward Bree.

"No thanks," she said with a shake of her head. "It's too late for me to indulge if I want to sleep tonight."

When he returned to the desk, she pinned him with her gaze. "So?"

"So, what?"

"Did your crime techs search the contents of the curio cabinet?"

Ah. That's what he'd missed. He shook his head. "The cabinet was unlocked, but no glass was broken. As far as we could tell, robbery wasn't the motive."

Bree flipped through the pages of her notebook. "I wish I'd been able to take notes at the crime scene, like before," she muttered.

Before. His gut knotted at the word. Bree was a civilian, not someone who should be at crime scenes. The first time when she'd been a suspect, he'd been impressed with her ability to keep focused and help his investigation. The second time—the knot in his gut flared as if someone had set a match to kerosene. The second time was all the fault of that damn spy who'd gotten his hooks into her.

Matthew Tugood—or whatever his real name was—deserved to be locked away or, if James had his way, shot for dragging Bree into, into … whatever it was the man did. James swallowed his anger, washed it down with a swig of coffee, and turned back to Bree.

Her brows drew together, and a puzzled frown creased her face.

"What is it?" he asked, worry taking the space where his anger had resided.

Bree looked up from her notes. "The backscratcher. Quint had a collection of antique, um …" she paused. "Let's just say, creepy things. Among them was a backscratcher shaped like a tiger claw. Or at least that's what I assumed it was."

"And you think …" He let his voice trail off, letting her fill in the blanks.

"I suspect it was used to inflict the scratches on Quint's body. The amount of blood suggests—to me, and you can correct me if I'm wrong—that he was scratched before he died. So, someone …" She stopped and swallowed. "Tortured him." Her face paled into an unhealthy shade of gray.

"Good info. We'll check on it," James said briskly, hoping to draw Bree's thoughts away from the path they were taking. "Anything else you think I need to follow up on?" *Please, let there be something else.*

The tension in his gut eased when Bree flipped back to her notebook, some of the color returning to her cheeks. She studied the pages, making occasional notes and James could almost see her erecting her mental shield. Hiding behind her scientific detachment. Good. She needed that.

"The call," she said, pointing to a line in her notebook. "Ning said Quint had texted her to come to his office. With Lucky." Bree looked up, steel returning to her eyes. "Find out if a text was sent from Quint's phone to Ning. And find out if it was sent before—or after—the time of death."

After hours of telling James everything she could recall about Quint Christenson, Ning, and the events of the day, Bree longed for a hot shower, a good meal, and an early bedtime. Instead she swung by the campus to check on Ning.

Halfway to the vet school, she remembered that Lucky was in custody with animal control. A quick phone call assured her the cub was being fed, housed, and, at the moment, kept safe.

Retracing her route, Bree arrived at the dorms. The scent of industrial cleaner, fresh pizza, and stale beer hit her nostrils the minute she walked through the door of Merveille Hall.

She flashed her faculty badge at the check-in desk then hurried past wide spaces decked out with comfy couches and tables that carved the lobby into nooks designed to foster conversation.

Colorful illustrations depicting Marco Polo and his book *Des Merveilles du Mond*—after which the dorm was named—decorated the walls. The framed photos of international landmarks and eclectic décor marked Merveille Hall as the international student dorm.

Bree summoned the elevator and headed to Ning's suite on the fourth floor. Her suitemate Tina, a tall, lithe blonde who served as Ning's peer mentor answered her knock. "Hi, Dr. Bree.

If you're looking for Ning, I haven't seen her since this morning. Is anything wrong?"

"I just wanted to stop by and say hello. How do you think she's doing?" Bree hated lying, but for now, the circumstances surrounding Quentin Christianson were being kept as quiet as possible.

"I don't know." Tina sighed and shifted her weight from foot to foot. "When I volunteered to be a peer mentor, I thought it would be cool. You know, teaching her all about America and learning about Thailand from her. But Ning," Tina twisted a long strand of hair between her fingers, "well, she doesn't seem to like me. I mean, she almost never spends the night here. How can I be a good mentor if she's never here?"

"I'm sure you're a great suitemate and peer mentor."

Tina shrugged and opened the door wider, wordlessly inviting Bree into the small sitting area. "At first, everything seemed fine. Her English was improving and I thought she was having fun, but then she started staying out all night and acting strange. I'm worried about her."

Me, too. Bree hoped her concern didn't show on her face. She scanned the tiny room until her eye fell on a framed photo of Tina with a golden retriever. "Is that your dog?"

"That's Poncho." Tina's eyes lit up and she pulled the photo off the shelf. "He's my best friend. And a champion Frisbee catcher."

"I bet if you could bring him with you to campus, you'd be inseparable." When Tina nodded, Bree continued. "That's the way Ning feels about her tiger cub, Lucky. She isn't avoiding you, she's spending time with her furry best friend."

"That makes sense, I guess. Do you think I could meet Lucky? I mean, like, if I sign a waiver or something first and promise to be careful? Maybe that would help me get to know Ning better."

Bree made a motion somewhere between a head shake and a nod that seemed to satisfy the girl. "We'll try to work something out. For now, just help Ning make some human friends." She glanced worriedly at the door leading to Ning's bedroom, then, on impulse, pulled a business card from her purse.

"Here's my number. I'll make sure Ning is okay for the night, but if you need something, you can call me at any time. The ringer is off when I'm teaching, but I check messages."

After saying goodnight, Bree left the dorms. Once back in the privacy of her car, she called Fiona Fancier's line. The attorney answered on the first ring. "Bree," she said, her voice congenial with only a hint of reserve. "I was just about to call you. I've taken Ning under my wing for the night. And maybe tomorrow, if she needs me. I want to make sure the police don't try to badger her."

She paused. "I could offer my services to you as well. For a nominal fee to demonstrate attorney-client privilege, of course. Unless," she let the word hang in the air, "you've already retained an attorney."

"Ah, no, I haven't. That is, thank you." Clearly Fiona didn't know about Bree's work as a consultant with the Plainville PD. Something Bree intended to keep from her colleagues at the university.

"In that case, here is some free advice. You don't have to talk to the police. About anything. Ning told me about the awful scene in Quint—I mean Dr. Christianson's office. It must have been as upsetting to you as to her. Such a sweet girl. So tragic. I'll do everything I can for her." Her voice trembled. "Poor Quint. I can't imagine—He was a good friend. He didn't deserve to die that way."

"I'm sorry for your loss." Bree felt helpless, unable to find words of comfort appropriate to the situation. "As far as Ning is concerned, finding a body is certainly upsetting, but shouldn't she try to go about her normal day as much as possible? Sleep in her own dorm?"

"Maybe tomorrow. I've already given her something to help her sleep. Don't worry, as the university legal counsel, I'm going to do everything I can to get us all through this ordeal. I promise to keep you posted on Ning's condition."

CHAPTER 6

C ontent that Ning was in good hands, Bree finally dragged herself home. She phoned an order in to Chong's Chinese for delivery, took a quick shower, and settled on the couch with Sherlock. The orange tabby leaned against her body, sliding down until he lay plastered against her thigh. With a sigh of contentment, he laid his head in her lap.

"Missed me, did you? I think it's good to be home too." Bree stroked him from head to tail and was rewarded with a resounding purr. "You are one lucky kitty," she crooned. "You have a good home, and you aren't a suspect in a murder case. No reason to be jealous of that big old tiger cub now, is there?"

A twitch of his tail indicated that the mention of the tiger cub was not welcome. "Like her or not, she's in a lot of trouble. I'm not sure I'll be able to save that kitty." Despite Lucky's inability to have killed Quint, the authorities might still insist on putting her down.

"If only Ning had listened to me and kept Lucky in the cage. At least she called me rather than running from the scene. That could have been more trouble." She kept her voice pitched low and soothing so as not to disturb Sherlock.

When the food arrived, she dropped a kiss on Sherlock's head and gently slid away from him to answer the door. "Chong's delivery! Good evening, Mrs. Bree Watson. Shrimp-chicken-beef combo and shrimp fry rice." The delivery man grinned and passed her a bag of food. His grin widened when he glanced down. "Oh, hello, kitty. How is big boy today?"

Sherlock mewed in reply, tail moving in what Bree thought of as "happy kitty" mode. The man knelt and produced something from his pocket. "I bring you something special. Little bit shrimp for my best friend."

The morsel disappeared instantly. Sherlock rubbed his paws on the man's knee and chattered using a unique combination of mews and chirps. The delivery man responded in kind and produced another few bits of shrimp. "Okay, kitty. No more. Next time. Bye-bye." He ruffled Sherlock's fur and stood.

"Thank you." Bree passed him a sealed envelope containing a tip. "Everything smells delicious."

"Welcome, Ms. Bree Watson. See you next week?"

Bree nodded, slightly embarrassed that the local Chinese delivery store knew her so well, then said her good-byes and took the food inside. Once settled on the couch again, she fed Sherlock bits of shrimp from the fried rice and picked through her own entrée. The sticky-thick sauce clinging to each bite reminded her uncomfortably of the murder scene.

Poison—the weapon of choice in the previous murders she'd solved—wasn't as likely to make a witness or detective's stomach lurch as the bloody scene she'd witnessed today. She gave up trying to eat and pushed the container away.

Ten minutes later, her phone rang. Bree stared at the unfamiliar number but decided that even a call from a telemarketer was preferable to ruminating about a murder scene. "How can I help you?" she asked briskly when she answered the call.

"Oh, I was just wondering how Chong's compared to the Pad Thai we shared." Matthew's voice, soft and seductively sweet, poured over the connection.

Despite her anger at him, Bree felt herself softening. She forced a note of steel into her voice. "Hey. What's up? How's your work with Sasha going?"

He made a noncommittal sound. "I'd rather talk about you. You looked tired when you came home."

"Checking up on me?" She understood the need for security cameras in her condo entry way, but the thought of being watched left her edgy.

"Maybe I just missed you. Is that so hard to believe?"

"Is that why you bugged my hallway?"

His sigh sounded tired. "No, I did it to keep you safe. If you'd had adequate condo security—"

"—some stranger would be monitoring my movements instead of you. We've had this discussion before."

"Bree, the alarm tripped so I knew someone was in your condo. And honestly, I wanted to see a friendly face. It's been brutal over here."

"Sasha running you ragged?"

The line went dead. Obviously Tugood didn't want to talk about his everything-old-is-new-again partner. *Damn. Why couldn't she stop obsessing over Sasha? So what if the woman had once posed as Tugood's make-believe wife? But Bree knew as well as anyone how the line blurred when playing Matthew's love interest. At least for her.*

The phone rang again. "This line isn't secure," he said in clipped tones and hung up immediately. Thirty seconds later, a new call came in, from a different number.

She accepted the call without hesitation. "Hello?"

"First, I hired a new IT guy to help with our tech surveillance. I'm counting on you and Shoe to take him under your wings. Shoe has the details." A muttered conversation and the ring of an old-style cash register sounded in the background.

"Now, that's out of the way. Let's talk about you." The warmth returned to Matthew's voice. "What has you looking so ragged? If it's your so-called boss Troy, you know you don't have to put up with him."

"Not Troy. Just so you know, I took a contract teaching chemistry at Terrance University for a semester. It keeps me out of the office." She filled Matthew in on Quint's request and her decision.

"Let me guess. The job turned into more than you expected. And Quentin Christianson turned out to be a slimy character who's making your life miserable. If you don't like it, cancel the contract and take some time off."

"I can't." Bree took a deep breath, trying to steady the quiver she heard in her own voice. She put the phone down and turned on the speaker option. Sherlock skittered away. "It's a long story."

"I have time." When she didn't answer, he tried again. "Anything I can help with?"

"It's … Quint … is … dead." She heard his sharp intake of breath on the other end of the line. "Ning discovered the body. He was covered in claw marks."

Silence stretched for a bit before Matthew spoke. "How are you holding up?"

Somehow his single-minded focus on her first, regardless of the other details, gave her comfort. "I'm okay. But I've never seen a head wound up close before. There was a lot of blood."

"Where were the claw marks?"

As she described the scene, her analytical side came to the fore. Instead of *feeling* emotion, she recited evidence. And as she did, interlocking pieces of the puzzle came into clearer focus.

"The broken glass wasn't near the curio cabinet," she said suddenly. "At first, I thought it came from a broken pane in the cabinet, but the glass was between the body and the door. I told the PD to take an inventory of the cabinet to see if anything was missing. Quint might have walked in on a robbery." She shuddered as the image of the tiger claw backscratcher flashed through her memory. Not likely.

"Forget about robbery for a minute," Matthew said, echoing her thoughts. "Did you walk through the glass to get to Ning and the tiger?"

His line of reasoning startled her. Bree thought back to the moment she entered the room. She'd seen the glass, but immediately dismissed it at the look of panic on Ning's face. "I might have. When we left the room, the crime scene techs had cleared a path for us. I don't think I disturbed the evidence. Why? What are you thinking?"

"I'm thinking that if a tiger walked through broken glass and cut its paws, the PD might mistake the blood on its paws for blood of the victim. Make sure they match the samples."

"I already told the PD that Lucky doesn't have claws."

Matthew's bitter laugh crackled across the line. "And the PD never makes mistakes, is that it? Trust me. Pinning the death on the cub is a quick and easy way out of a dilemma. A murderer could walk free if someone wants to take a shortcut. Besides," he paused to clear his throat, "Ning and you would be devastated."

Her heart melted a little. "I didn't think you knew her well enough to care. Thank you." A troublesome thought hit her. "Please don't tell me you did anything illegal regarding bringing the cub to the States. Something that a check into the cub's paperwork would reveal."

The blaring of a car horn on the other end of the line muffled his words. "... would think you could trust me. I've got to go. I'll call later. Bye, Watson."

After cutting off the call from Matthew, Bree busied herself putting away the barely touched food and getting ready for bed.

Hours later, even after her tossing and turning had caused Sherlock to abandon his spot next to her in the bed, her mind still replayed the scene in Quint's office. But no amount of time helped her figure out what—if anything—the grisly movie looping through her imagination was trying to tell her.

Bree put water into a tea kettle to boil for oatmeal and poured herself a cup of strong black coffee, hoping it would wash away the remains of her restless night. Despite sleeping poorly, she itched to return to campus where, with a little luck, she'd be able to catch gossip from other staff members before official news of Quint's death was announced. If anyone questioned her presence on campus on a day she wasn't scheduled to teach, she'd claim to be working on curriculum issues.

The kettle whistled and she poured boiling water over a scoop of instant steel-cut oatmeal. While the oats cooked, she puttered around feeding Sherlock and pulled her crime notebook from her briefcase.

Returning to the oatmeal, she reached for the canister of brown sugar, only to discover it was empty. Instead she opened a jar of organic raspberry preserves and stirred a spoonful into the oats.

Notebook propped in front of her, she re-read the events of yesterday while enjoying her breakfast. *Quint's head*...

She looked at her oatmeal bowl, stomach suddenly churning at the sight of the lumpy pinkish goo, and slammed the notebook shut.

Perhaps going to the university wasn't the right move just yet. Besides, she'd promised Tugood she'd help orient his newly hired tech guy. She stuffed her notebook into the briefcase and decided to head to Sci-PHi headquarters before visiting the university. "Perspective," she muttered as she locked the front door and headed toward the condo garage. "I need some perspective."

At the corporate complex, Bree bypassed the employee parking lots and entered the underground parking garage reserved for executives. From there, she took a private elevator straight to the Tech Ops center in the owner's suite on the fifth floor of the business buildings. No one in the research complex situated on the other side of the jigsaw puzzle series of interconnected buildings would even know she was on site.

Except for Milt Shoemaker. He sat, long legs propped on the table in front of a bank of monitors, leaning lazily back in a rolling office chair.

"What are you doing this morning?" Bree asked as she entered.

"Good morning to you too." He slipped off the headphones he'd been wearing. "I'm listening to chatter on the national security channels to see what I can learn."

"Is that legal?" She pulled her mug from a shelf and helped herself to coffee and a cookie.

"Depends on whether our boss is who I think he is."

Tugood? "And who do you think he is?"

"Someone with clearance to listen to chatter. Obviously." Milt—codenamed Shoe by his colleagues in the spy ring—dropped his feet to the floor and stood, stretching, the saggy hem of his oversized sweater riding up almost to his hips with the movement. "Ah. Better. I've been at this for hours. What brings you to Tech Ops?"

"Matthew asked me to help with the new hire."

"Yeah. I guess Charles Angelo decided to hire an IT guy. Go figure."

The fictional Charles Angelo—inspired by the action show Charlie's Angels, Bree was certain—was the pseudonym

Matthew used whenever he stepped into the role of company owner. She liked that it showed Matthew's humorous side.

"What do we know about the new guy?"

"Not much. Tugood vetted him but wants us to start him off small. Make him think he's working for the Sci-PHi temporary agency only. Feed him limited other tasks to see how he responds." Milt glanced at the clock. "He's due to arrive in half an hour."

As far as Bree knew, only she, Shoe, and Nate had been recruited from her former company to join Matthew's inner circle of agents. He'd transformed the remaining personnel into employees of the Sci-PHi scientific staffing company.

Now she and Shoe were being invited to recruit and approve new team members? A flicker of pride warmed her chest and a smile tugged at her lips. She must be doing something right if Matthew trusted her to train a recruit. *Take that, Sasha.*

"Before we transform Tech Ops into a run-of-the-mill corporate IT hub, I have an idea I want to run by you."

"Go for it."

She attempted to look mysterious and ended up smiling instead. "It's more of a hunch than an idea. Remember the meeting I attended with Zed in the Pacific?"

"You mean this one?" Shoe punched a few keys and the left-hand monitor played a recorded clip of the footage her necklace cam had captured at the meeting.

"Yes, that one." *Grr.* Just because Matthew Tugood was an experienced operative and Milt Shoemaker had military experience he didn't talk about didn't mean Dr. Bree Mayfield-Watson was a lightweight.

I'll show them I'm as effective as any operative—even Sasha—when it comes to deductive reasoning and following leads. Without Matthew directing my every move. She sat in the vacated office chair and took control of another monitor.

"We used Zed's interest in the new energy sector research to hook him on my supposed breakthrough in storing and transporting explosive natural gas compounds."

"Yeah. So?"

"So, a terrorist interested in alternative energy may also be interested in controlling access to traditional energy. Sixty percent of the transfer of physical energy—i.e. crude oil—still takes place via ships." She pulled up a global map highlighting shipping routes. "And each ship has to pass through one—or more—of eight chokepoints worldwide."

Shoe leaned over her shoulder, all teasing gone from his voice. "An attack at any one of these points," he traced a finger between Malaysia and Singapore near the location of the Strait of Malacca, "could disrupt everything."

"Exactly. We've been chasing Zed thinking his endgame had to do with alternative energy. What if it's really about controlling all energy?"

Shoe's low whistle felt like praise. "Good work, Bree. What does Tugood think?"

"I haven't run it by him yet." She chewed the inside of her cheek, wondering why she wanted to impress Matthew so badly. "I'm working from a rough hypothesis at this point. I plan to spend a few hours digging into it before I head back to campus for—"

An ear-splitting buzz and flash of the computer screens drew their attention to the main elevator monitor. A young man with bleached blond hair cut in a shaggy mop looked from the keypad to his phone before entering a code to start the elevator.

"Looks like the new guy's here."

Together Shoe and Bree activated the protocol to disguise the cutting-edge Tech Ops center as a simple video surveillance hub of a modern complex.

He flashed her a grin. "Time to put on a show."

⚜ ⚜ ⚜

The elevator doors slid open, revealing a beach bum. Baggy board shorts hung past his knees, skimming a bare calf sporting what looked like a shark biting through flesh. Bree had to give the tattoo artist credit—the three-dimensional effect was as evocative as it was startling. He thrust out a hand.

"Dr. Watson, I presume?"

Bree grasped the offered hand, glad he had a firm grip. Her gaze traveled over the ink showing a tentacle wrapped around his wrist and disappearing into his sleeve. "I'm impressed," she said.

"Don't be," the beach boy countered. "I was told to meet a Dr. Watson and a Mr. Shoemaker today. You don't look much like a mister to me. Ergo, you're the doctor." He nodded to Shoe. "Mr. Shoemaker."

"We're pleased to meet you, Mr...." Belatedly Bree realized she hadn't gotten his name.

"It's Grant. Grant Mitchelson. No mister for me." He followed them down the short hallway and into the Tech Ops room. "I'm not much for formalities. Told your boy Goodie that when we met."

Goodie? Behind Grant, Shoe held two fingers in the air. Two. To. Tugood. "So, when did you meet Mr. Tugood?"

Grant shrugged. "I met Goodie maybe five?—six?—months back while I was surfing in Maui. Your man Goodie's got mad board skills for an old dude. Didn't peg him for a corporate type though." He ambled over to the monitors and looked at the surveillance cameras over each of the building entrances.

"Your system's pretty basic," he said, plopping down into a chair and playing with the camera angles. "No offense, but given the whole enter-a-secret-code-to-get-the-elevator-to-take-you-to-the-executive-floor thing, I expected more. Not that I'm complaining."

He swiveled to face them. "Goodie offered me a sweet salary and plenty of time off to ski, surf, climb, and train."

Shoe snagged a chair and straddled it, leaning on the back and facing Grant. "What are you training for?"

"Extreme sports, mostly. Got my sights on a spot at the American Ninja Warrior tryouts."

No wonder Tugood was impressed. Now to see if his mind was as toned as his body. "What would you suggest to upgrade our systems?" she asked.

"Depends on what you want to do with 'em. So, I looked up Sci-PHi and for a company that needs to attract customers, you don't have much of a digital footprint." He stood and walked to a window overlooking the back side of the corporate campus.

"Sci-PHi isn't nearly as interesting as what it used to be. Chemical Industries Corporation," he said using the former name of the company, "had a lot of public information available about it. Starting with how its flagship product sunk the whole corporate armada. And continuing on to how a murderer bypassed a security system with nothing more than an umbrella."

"What?" Bree was halfway across the room before she stopped herself.

Grant kept his eyes trained on the landscape outside the window, but Bree could see her faint reflection in the glass as well. "Mind you," he said "that wasn't public information, but if you knew where to look it was all there in the written confession.

"Bypassing security was as simple as walking up to the camera under cover of a golf umbrella and giving it a good, hard poke with the metal tip of the umbrella. Shattered the camera. Kept the murderer off the video."

"How did you learn all of that?"

"Like I said. I know where to look."

Behind her, Shoe made a sound that expressed appreciation, if not approval. "In that case, how would you suggest overhauling our security?" he asked.

Grant turned toward them and leaned against the windowsill, hands buried in the pockets of his board shorts. He crossed his ankles, toying with the heel of his boat shoes as he talked.

"For the staffing company, you need to be sure the basics are in place. Strong passwords. Digital firewalls. Cameras that make sure people aren't making off with the office staplers. A second set of cameras trained on each door if you want to avoid people sneaking in beneath umbrellas."

He stopped playing with his shoe and looked up at them, straightening slightly. "For the forensics contracts, you also need to meet more sophisticated chain-of-custody requirements for handling your data. I can whip up something that will leave your competitors in the dust."

"You know about our forensics contracts?" Bree hadn't thought that work was public knowledge.

"I've done my homework, Dr. Watson." Grant moved away from the window into the more shadowed confines of the Tech Ops center. "Any half-decent hacker could not only access the names of all your clients but could also change the data in the reports. Want me to show you?"

"That won't be necessary," Shoe said quietly, moving between Grant and the keyboards of the main computer system.

Grant shrugged, the movement careless yet somehow graceful. "As for whatever it is you're hiding behind that lame security system interface you showed me earlier, I'd need to spend a few hours investigating before I could make recommendations."

Bree stifled the urge to suck in a breath, doing her best to remain calm despite Grant's eerie surety that they were hiding something. "If you were a pizza delivery man, how would you benefit from a pair of scissors?" she blurted out, trying to both change the subject and get a feel for the man behind the hacker in front of her.

"Huh?" Grant turned to her in puzzlement. "Is that a typical interview question? Or one of those supposed tech job puzzles?"

"Assume it is," Bree replied. "What's your answer?"

"Well," he rubbed his hands through his hair, massaging his scalp and shaking his head like a shaggy dog. "I suppose if I was an honest pizza man, I'd use the scissors to cut coupons for the customers to use." He grinned at her. "Or to brandish about in hopes of scaring my customer into giving a better tip." The grin turned evil. "Or to do away with a customer who didn't give good tips."

Bloodthirsty, creative, and not bound by traditional rules.

"Tell me about your family," she countered.

"My dad's an accountant working himself into an early grave. Mom's supporting his efforts. My oldest sister's an intern at Loyola University medical center, studying nephrology. My middle sister is a suburban soccer mom, married to a younger version of our dad. I'm more interested in making memories than in making money. Life's too short, you know?"

"If my fingerprints were found at a crime scene," Shoe began, "how much would you charge me to remove them from the crime lab records?"

Grant pulled an office chair to him and sat, his gaze wavering between Shoe and Bree. "First, thank you for assuming I could do it. I can. Second, if you don't know by now that I'm not in this for money, then we're all wasting our time.

"If you need a fixer to clean up after a crime, I'm not your man. If you need a cobbler to create a fake ID, I might be your man—if your reasons are good. If you need help making the world a little better and right some wrongs, I am your man."

He stood and walked to the door. At the threshold, he paused and turned to them. "The question is: what do you need from me? Once you figure that out, Goodie knows how to get in touch."

Between interviewing Grant Mitchelson and pursuing her theories about Zed and potential activity at chokepoints and in oil pipelines, Bree didn't make it to her office at the Terrance University campus.

Early the next morning, she kissed a sleepy Sherlock good-bye and headed to the animal control compound to check on Lucky. She groaned at the sight of a cluster of signs on the lawn outside of the facility, each bearing a SWAP logo and the words "Free the Tiger" printed on them.

At least she'd arrived before the members of the Suburban West Animal Protection group gathered to protest in person. Still, as annoying as SWAP was, it didn't hurt Lucky's case to have the high visibility group campaigning for her.

After a short discussion with the attendant, a call to James to confirm her consultant status, and a bribe of chocolate peanut-butter cupcakes, she was allowed inside to visit Lucky. The cub cowered in a mournful heap at the back of a clean, but cold, enclosure. A bowl of water and an overflowing bowl of kibble sat near a slot in the cage just large enough to fit the food through.

"I just wanted to let you know, ma'am, that the animal isn't eating." The attendant shrugged. "Maybe kibble doesn't appeal after the taste of human flesh."

"Nonsense." Bree knelt by the food slot and retrieved the bowls. At the sound of her voice, Lucky lifted her head and mewed as pitifully as Sherlock sometimes did. The little cub made her way slowly, unsteadily toward Bree.

"I want some fresh water for the cub and a cup of hot water for me," she instructed the attendant. When he'd gone, Bree reached in and stroked Lucky. "You poor baby. I'll get you out of here as soon as possible." The cat rumbled in an exaggerated tiger-purr and pushed her head farther into Bree's hand.

"I know, baby. You miss Ning. She misses you, too. We all do." When the attendant arrived with the fresh water, Bree pushed it into the cage. Then she emptied most of the kibble from the other bowl and moistened the remainder with the hot water, stirring to create a mushy gruel.

"This tiger," she said as she worked, "doesn't have any claws. She also has a condition that leads to very soft teeth. In other words, she can't eat hard food."

Bree pushed the mushy food in the enclosure and Lucky took a step toward the bowl. After a sniff or two, she began to eat. Satisfied, Bree stood and turned to the attendant. She glanced at his name tag. *Ted.* "Ted, can I ask you to do me a favor?"

"Depends what it is, ma'am."

"Sounds like you're from the south, Ted. Where?" Bree hoped making small talk would put the man at ease.

"I hail from Georgia originally. My family moved here during my last year of high school." Something in his eyes told her it wasn't a pleasant time.

"My grandma lives in Chattanooga. When I was little, I'd spend the summers with her. Everyone made fun of my *Yankee* accent. It took a long time to make friends."

Ted nodded. "I suspect the kids teased you about being stuck-up. At least they didn't assume you were dumb because of your accent."

"Kids can be cruel to outsiders." She glanced at Lucky, who had finished the moistened food and now tried to lick the now empty bowl. "This little tiger cub probably feels pretty unwanted at the moment. She misses her handler."

Ted squatted by the cage and without speaking, he used a curved tool to pull the bowl out of the cage. He added more kibble and moistened it with the remaining bit of Bree's hot water before pushing it back into the enclosure. Lucky buried her head in the bowl once more.

"What favor did you want, ma'am?" Ted asked as he stood.

Bree smiled at him. "I was hoping you'd help Lucky by moistening her food for her. And maybe talking to her a bit during the day. She's used to human company. And, as I told you, she has no claws and very soft teeth. She won't hurt you."

"The cops told me the tiger clawed a man to death. But if what you say is true..."

"It's true," Bree reassured him. "I know that she has to stay in your care until she's cleared. The vet school at Terrance University will be sending over a specialist to describe her situation. Until then, can I depend on you to keep her safe?"

"My sister had a cat once. Gave it a special bed and toys and everything." He cleared his throat and stared at Lucky while he talked. "It's probably different, but do you suppose this tiger would like a bed? And maybe a stuffed mouse or something?"

"I think that would be a grand idea." Bree gave Ted one of her cards. "Call me if Lucky's situation changes. Or if you just want advice. And next time I come, I'll bring some more treats. I love to bake, but don't want to eat everything I make."

"Girls," Ted said, giving her a wink. "Always too worried about what they eat. But I'll be glad to do my part by eating anything you want to bake."

After a few more minutes, once Bree assured herself that Lucky was in good hands, she left to check on Ning, glad Fiona was no longer keeping the girl from her routines.

Too bad Ning's troubles couldn't be solved by a cupcake and a few kind words.

CHAPTER 7

O n the drive to campus, Bree mulled over ideas to keep her chemistry students engaged. The Chemistry Concepts class fulfilled a science credit for general students, although many came in thinking it would be hard and irrelevant. She'd scrapped the dry recommended curriculum in favor of one of her own creations, but still wanted to give her students something more.

She also wanted to do something special for the introductory chemistry class she taught for science students. Thinking that her Sci-PHi colleagues might help, she voice-dialed her friend Kiki.

"Hey, stranger!" Kiki's upbeat voice sounded over the music in the background. "I miss seeing you at the office."

"You miss me or my baking?"

"Both, to be honest. How are you coming on the Periodic Table of Cupcakes challenge? I haven't seen any new entries lately." The giant periodic table that her friends had given her hung in Bree's kitchen. They'd challenged her to come up with a flavor combo for every elemental symbol on the table. All 118 of them. Although including unstable new elements seemed a bit overkill.

"I've renamed it the Periodic Table of Treats to give myself a chance to make more than just cupcakes. You know how much you love my brownie recipes." Bree took Kiki's laugh for agreement. "I just finished creating a cupcake to fill the spot for lead. With a molecular symbol like Pb, it was easy."

"Peanut butter, of course. Too easy. So why haven't you brought a sample in for me to taste?"

Bree slowed and stopped at a traffic light. "Point taken. I'll whip up a batch before next Monday's staff meeting. Speaking of which, I hear music in the background. When did Troy approve that?"

"He didn't. But he also doesn't come up to the analytical labs often enough for me to worry about it. Besides, Norah sends me a text alert if she knows he's on his way."

"Thoughtful of her. Listen, I wanted to ask a favor. Would you be willing to come to the university to talk to my freshman chemistry class on the science behind forensic analysis?"

A timer went off in the lab and Kiki asked Bree to hold for a minute. Certain analyses needed to be carefully timed so Bree concentrated on pulling into the university faculty lot while she waited. She switched the call to her Bluetooth headset and walked toward the administration building.

"Hey, sorry about the wait," Kiki said when she returned. "I had to sign the chain-of-custody paperwork and log in another batch of rape test kits. Anyway, I'd be happy to speak to your classes. What do you want me to talk about?"

"We can discuss the details later, but mostly I want them to challenge the 'CSI Effect.' You know—where people think any scientific puzzle can be solved with 100 percent accuracy in an hour. And your presentation has to be entertaining," she added.

"Geez, no pressure, Bree." Her friend sounded intimidated, although with Kiki's multicolored spiked hair and her younger-than-her-years attitude, Bree doubted she'd have trouble meeting the criteria.

They made plans to meet later. Bree cut off the call and headed into the administration building. She ignored the elevators and chose to walk up to the third floor where Fiona's office was housed in the new section of the building.

Halfway up the stairs, she met Miriam Cook coming the other way, her cheeks red and her brow puckered. "Of all the boneheaded, nefarious—" She looked up. "Oh, Bree. Sorry you caught me muttering. I've just come from a meeting. What brings you by?"

"I needed to stop at the legal office to pick up some paperwork," she hedged. "Is anything wrong? Can I help?"

"It's just a minor irritation." Miriam waved her anger away. Her voice dropped to a whisper. "Did you hear about Dr. Christianson? He was found dead in his office yesterday."

Clearly Miriam didn't know the whole story. "What have you heard?" Bree asked, feigning surprise and deflecting the need for giving away any information.

Miriam shrugged. "I only know that one of my international students was in his office when he was discovered. In fact, it was your young friend, Ning." She shook her head. "Fiona called me this morning, although she should have called last night. I'm responsible for them."

"Is that what has you upset?"

The red in Miriam's flushed cheeks deepened. "A little. But mostly, it's that Max Edelston has been appointed interim VP of student affairs."

"Who is he? I haven't heard of him."

"Neither has anyone else! That's the problem. Apparently, he's Quint Christianson's nephew. He's served on the board of trustees, but the man hasn't set foot in a classroom—ever!—or in the university except to pose for the cover of our brochure. I doubt he knows anything about running a university."

"But if he's a trustee ..."

Miriam shook her head. "You'll see. There's a staff meeting called for this afternoon in the administration building conference room." She stared at Bree through narrowed eyes until Bree felt sweat run down her back. Then, Miriam sighed.

"I'm probably making too much out of this. Let's wait until after the meeting. Then if you want to talk more, we can go for coffee. Maybe it will put things into perspective for me."

"Sounds like a plan." Bree checked her watch. In thirty minutes, she needed to be in class. "Let's catch up after the staff meeting."

After saying good-bye to Miriam, Bree hustled to Fiona's office to check on Ning, but found a thirty-something man in a smartly tailored suit sitting across from the attorney. Fiona waved Bree in with a manicured hand.

"Bree, I'd like to you meet Max Edelston, our new interim VP of student affairs. Max, this is Bree Mayfield-Watson."

Max rose and politely offered a hand. "I'm sorry to meet under such bleak circumstances."

The dark sweep of Max's hair was artfully arranged to hide a widow's peak. His eyes, dark and piercing, gave Bree a once over. "How long have you been with Terrance University?"

"I just joined this semester."

"Bree has agreed to teach introductory chemistry," Fiona added.

"That's ambitious," Max said, narrowing his eyes. "Not a subject many would care to take on."

Bree offered him a tight smile. "Having a PhD in chemistry and years of teaching and research experience helps."

"Oh, so you are a veteran? Where did you teach before Terrance University?"

"Dr. Mayfield-Watson is contracted through Sci-PHi, a scientific staffing company." Fiona adjusted the scooped neckline of her tight-fitting black sweater. Max's gaze flicked to study her décolletage, momentarily lighting with interest before turning back to Bree.

"If you find university life suits you, you may want to consider joining us on a more permanent basis. Let's talk after the semester."

After you prove your worth.

Bree ignored his unspoken implications and focused on Fiona. "Ms. Fancier, may I have a word with you?"

Fiona rose, leaning forward slightly as she held her hand out to the new VP. Her height made is easy to position her cleavage in Max's line of sight. "Max, thank you for stopping by. I look forward to working with you." She accented a throaty laugh by licking her lips and her hand lingered in Max's for a hair longer than Bree considered normal.

For a competent professional, Fiona played the femme fatale very well. After closing the door, Fiona walked back to the desk. Her slim fitting skirt, high heels, and scooped neck top made her look more like she was going to a party than to a law office.

Although for once, her jewelry was subdued. She'd traded dangling earrings and breast skimming necklaces for simple diamond studs and a thin chain with a single gem nestled in the hollow of her throat.

"You seem rather taken with Max," Bree observed.

"Max? Heavens no." Fiona resumed her seat. "I admit that attractive women have a certain, shall we say, edge, when dealing with some men. A woman in a man's field has two choices. Either blend in or stand out. I'm sure you know what I mean."

Despite Fiona's smile, Bree suddenly felt dowdy in her serviceable slacks and sturdy shoes. "Working in the lab doesn't go well with easily damaged clothing. Although I did once dye my lab coat pink in graduate school."

"Well, there you have it. You do know what I mean."

Bree didn't waste time figuring out if it was a compliment or an insult. "How is Ning faring? I'm concerned about her."

"She's fine, but a little rattled. So many of our international students live in places where they are taught to fear and distrust the police. I can't tell you how many little dust ups I've had to smooth over in my years. Everything from traffic tickets to fear of deportation because they cut in front of an officer at the donut shop checkout line. But as for Ning, I took your advice and sent her back to her classes today. I'm sure she'd appreciate a call."

"That's great news. I made some calls about the tiger, too. So far, she's being held by animal control."

Fiona's heavy sigh interrupted Bree. "I am worried about how attached Ning is to that animal. It's going to be difficult for her when they put it down."

"I'm not sure that will be necessary."

"You know as well as I do that it will be. The poor girl spent more time trying to tell me the vet school would protect the tiger than she did helping me come up with a line of defense for herself. No matter what kind of research they are doing on that cub, the police will never let a killer animal live."

"Why would Ning need a line of defense?" Bree asked, getting to the critical part of the conversation. "She walked in to find the victim dead."

Fiona shook her head. "Let's hope you're right. In the meantime, you need to support my advice and not let her near the police. I haven't had a student deported yet and I don't intend to start with Ning."

Fiona's phone rang, and she answered, asking the caller to hold. She put the phone on mute and turned to Bree. "I need to take this call. I'll see you at the staff meeting this afternoon."

Bree checked her watch as she left the office. *Shoot*! For the second day in a row, she'd be running across campus if she wanted to get to her class on time.

This Sci-Spy contract was turning into more of a workout than running from villains.

❧   ❧   ❧

Bree scanned the faces of her Concepts in Chemistry class and was met with too many blank stares. "Can anyone give me a practical example of an acid-base neutralization reaction?"

A few hands popped up. Bree called on one student. "The baking soda and vinegar volcano my little brother did in science fair."

"Very good. Anyone else?" When no one else replied she flipped on the PowerPoint slide she'd prepared for class. An illustration of a frying pan and a cartoon fish popped up. "Who can tell me the name of the compound that creates a 'fishy' smell?"

"Fish guts." In the back corner of the room a knot of football players high-fived their leader who snickered at his joke. Bree caught the eye of Josh Gibbons slumped in his seat, looking uncomfortable.

Tough crowd. "Wrong," she answered, pushing a button on her phone to simulate a game show buzzer. "The answer is a chemical called an amine. It's a basic chemical. So, what might you use to counteract—or neutralize—the amine?"

Throughout the class, murmured answers came from several students. "Whoever said 'acid' is correct. In addition to smelling bad, basic—or alkaline—compounds in cooking provide bitterness. Cooking with acids not only destroys the smell from alkaline compounds, it also mutes the bitter flavors. Two common kitchen acids are vinegar and lemon juice."

A few heads lifted from their laps where their smartphones were hidden. Bree pushed her luck. "If you are cooking with fish, rinsing your hands in lemon juice afterwards will remove the fishy smell from your hands."

She flipped to the next slide, a recipe for batter fried fish. "This recipe is missing an ingredient. Anyone want to guess what it is?"

Dredge fish fillets in a mixture made from:

- 2 Cups flour
- ½ tsp salt
- ¼ tsp pepper
- ¼ tsp garlic
- 1 ½ Cups _____

Some students shouted acid, others water, still others different liquids. "You're all partially right. I'm going to add 1 ½ cups of an acidic liquid to enhance the flavor and counteract the amine smell. The liquid," she paused dramatically, "is beer."

Cheers erupted from the athletes in the back.

"When you add beer to a batter, in addition to acidity, it has foam, or carbon dioxide. This gas bubbles out of the mix and when exposed to high temperatures—say hot oil used for frying—the bubbles cause the batter to be light and airy. So, there you have it. A practical application of chemistry to cooking."

She flipped to the last slide. "The recipe is available on my page of the university website. If anyone wants extra credit, try the recipe, making one batter with beer as the liquid and another with water as the liquid. Report back to me on which batter you prefer—and show photos or video of you doing the work. The experiment will be worth fifty points toward your final grade."

Instead of scurrying out of the class, many of the students were taking down her information. "A bonus of twenty-five extra points will be given to any student who finds another recipe that includes acid-base neutralization as a key component," she added. "Good luck!"

After dismissing class, Bree waited to talk to several students who lingered to discuss their questions about cooking and chemistry. Josh joined the fringes of the group, hanging back until the others were gone. He looked over his shoulder before addressing her. "Dr. Mayfield-Watson? Which branch of chemistry studies medicines and drugs and stuff?"

"You might be thinking of pharmacology. To enter an advanced class like that you'd first need to take general and organic chemistry. You'd need the regular freshman chemistry course, not just this one."

"Hey, dweeb!" one of the football players poked his head into the classroom. "Stop sucking up or you're gonna be late to practice."

Josh flinched at the harsh tone. "Thanks, Doc. I was just asking for my brother. He's interested in that kind of stuff. But I will try the cooking experiment. I could use the extra credit. And it would impress my mom. Bye." He raced up the stairs just as the other player poked his head back into the room.

"Coming," Josh yelled, his voice high and tight as he hurried to the door and slipped from the room.

CHAPTER 8

Bree found Ning in her dorm suite, alone. Obvious relief swept across her face when she opened the door. "*Khun* Dr. Bree. Come. I make us tea." Ning ushered Bree inside and bustled about the room fussing with water and tea leaves, refusing to talk until they sat side by side with steaming mugs in hand.

To Bree's eye, Ning seemed thinner. Dark circles ringed her eyes, hinting at restless nights. She waited until Ning had settled and taken a sip of tea before speaking.

"I saw Lucky today. She misses you but otherwise is doing fine. I talked to the police department about her needs. They understand that she couldn't have harmed Dr. Christianson."

Ning sagged in her chair. The tense lines around her mouth and eyes eased. "Thank you, Dr. Bree. Mrs. Fan-cee-eh say Lucky has to be made to sleep forever for hurting Dr. Christianson. She did not listen when I say it is impossible."

"She was just more worried about you."

Ning shook her head. "She make me stay at her home. Tells me not to talk to police. Do you think this is wise?" She clutched her cup until Bree thought the sturdy pottery would break.

"To be honest, no. I'd prefer you talked to Detective O'Neil. I can arrange for you to meet with him in private if you like. I'll stay with you the whole time."

"Mrs. Fan-cee-eh will not be happy."

"She doesn't need to know."

Ning looked up, not quite meeting Bree's eyes. "She is my attorney," she said enunciating the word carefully. "She say I must have her with me anytime I talk about Dr. Christianson. Even with you."

"Like I said, she's trying to protect you. But you can decide whether to take her advice or not."

"I don't want to be sent home. My family would be so ashamed." She swallowed and blinked to hold back tears. "Please help me, Dr. Bree. Mrs. Fan-cee-eh thinks I killed Dr. Christianson. That Lucky killed him."

Bree gave up trying to maintain a distance. She took the mug from Ning's hand and wrapped her arms around the girl. Ning buried her head in Bree's shirt and sniffled quietly. "No one thinks you killed Dr. Christianson," Bree said calmly as if she were addressing Sherlock or Lucky. "You wouldn't hurt anyone. We're all here for you. Ms. Fancier's just doing what attorneys do—assume the worst and explain why that didn't happen."

Eventually Ning calmed. "The best thing you can do is to continue going to your classes and keep busy with your work. I'm sure the vet school needs help with some of the other animals."

At the mention of animals, Ning sniffed again. "I miss Lucky."

"I know. But I'll make sure she's well cared for. And I'll ask when you can visit. Meanwhile, I have an idea. Do you like dogs?"

"I like."

"Tomorrow is Saturday. Why don't I pick you up early and take you somewhere special? You can invite your suitemate if you want."

The Barkery would be just the place to lift Ning's spirits. Situated near Bree's condo in the pedestrian shopping area of downtown Plainville, the dog treat bakery run by Bree's friends

Horace and Wendy Clark featured quirky, pet-related fun. If the Clarks and their dogs couldn't ease Ning's depression, nothing could.

Bree and Ning finished their tea and finalized plans for tomorrow. When Ning's suitemate entered the room, Bree said her good-byes and left knowing Ning was in good hands.

Bree treated herself to a brisk walk across campus, inhaling deep breaths of crisp, fresh autumn air. She picked up the pace until her mind ceased its internal chatter and her subconscious relaxed.

She let her thoughts drift back to the murder scene without dwelling on any specific aspect. Eventually even that train of thought stopped and she simply enjoyed the brilliant splashes of early red and yellow foliage amid the mostly green campus trees.

A cardinal chirped in the distance. The chime of the clock in the campus bell tower indicated she'd lingered too long. She quickened her steps and hurried into the staff meeting.

Raised voices carried along the corridor as Bree approached. The thick, hot air in the crowded room slammed into her like an invisible force field. She pushed her way through. The smell of stress-sweat, stale perfume, and fresh hair spray permeated the windowless room, a sharp contrast to the fresh outside air.

Coach Fleek stood, hands braced on the elongated conference room table. "The athletic department spent good money on that freakin' animal and I'll be damned if I let it go to waste."

"The vet school funded the cub and you know it. Our research—"

"Just because you're a *doctor*," Coach Fleek accented the word with air quotes as he sneered at the head of the vet school, "doesn't make you special."

"By special," literature teacher Heather cut in, her face as red as her pixie cut, "he means able to pee while standing and willing to risk your neck for a touchdown."

"Jealous much, you hippie freak?"

"Of a Neanderthal like you?"

Fiona opened a binder, pulled out some papers and stalked up to the coach, interrupting his argument with Heather. She slapped a form in front of him. "My office, eight a.m. Monday."

"And you—" she turned to Heather in the same breath and also presented her with a form, "my office ten a.m. Monday."

Suddenly, the room plunged into darkness. "Everybody needs to calm down." Max Edelston's firm voice sounded from the doorway. "The next person to speak without being recognized is getting an official reprimand in their file."

"His file," hissed a voice in the darkness.

"Bit—"

"Am I clear?" Edelston asked in a tone that shut down the opposition. A low murmur filled the room followed by silence. He flicked the lights back on and returned to the front of the room. "That's better."

Bree slid into a seat near the door and studied the warring occupants. Coach Fleek and Heather eyed one another with distaste bordering on hatred. The coach's face and neck flushed a deep purple-red, making Bree worry the vet, Dr. Melody Warthan, might need to perform CPR on a two-legged patient.

Miriam Cook scribbled furiously in a notebook, avoiding eye contact with everyone while the history professor, the economics assistant professor, and the math teacher all shrank in their chairs, trying to appear invisible.

No one noticed Bree as she jotted notes for herself in her crime journal. She listened for any mention of Quint Christianson and his unnatural death.

At the head of the table, Edelston cleared this throat, demanding attention. "I know everyone is distressed at the news of Dr. Christianson's passing. He was a pillar of the university community."

The looks of the people around the table told Bree a different story.

"We don't know details of his death—" Edelston continued.

Heather's hand shot up. When he didn't acknowledge her, she jumped to her feet and wiggled impatiently.

"Yes, Ms. Beauchamp?"

"It's Professor Beauchamp. Among other duties, I advise the student paper. My reporters have evidence that Dr. Christianson had claw marks on his body."

A horrified gasp went up from the group. "The blame is entirely due to the fact that the athletic department coerced the vet school into allowing a wild tiger to roam the campus," she continued with a glare at the coach.

"The tiger couldn't possibly—"

Miriam raised her hand and spoke, softly but quickly, cutting off Dr. Warthan's objection. "The tiger was in the care of one of my international students. Not quite the same as roaming free. However, they did leave the vet school at the behest of the athletic department."

"That's a lie." Coach Fleek shoved his chair back from the table and hefted himself halfway out of it before reconsidering. "The meeting was called by Christianson. He was always supportive of the athletic department. *He* knew who paid the university bills."

Another round of squabbling erupted, but Bree's attention fixated on the existence of crime scene photos taken by a student reporter. She thought the police had kept the reporters at bay, but one student must have slipped past them. James and his team at the PD needed to know about this new development.

"QUIET!" Max's face darkened as he shouted for attention. "Professor Beauchamp, get those photos and make sure the originals are deleted. No one except the Plainville PD is to have access to the photos until further notice. And no one is to talk about this unless they are given permission by the police. Understood?"

Heather nodded, but Bree wasn't convinced she'd comply. When they'd met at the staff mixer, Heather had struck her as a free spirit who would resist strong arm tactics. She might, however, be willing to help a friend—Bree—and a needy student—Ning. Bree made a note to approach Heather after the meeting.

She made a second note to speak to Dr. Warthan immediately, letting her know that the cub's lack of claws and soft teeth were facts that the police department didn't want widely known for the time being.

"Coach Fleek," said Edelston, "I'm fully aware of the importance athletics plays in university life—both for the students and for our funding. As acting VP of Student Affairs, I'll be happy to discuss any issues you have. Privately. After this meeting."

He looked around the room. "The same goes for all of you. The business of the university is training young minds so they can be thoughtful, productive members of society. Academics and critical thinking skills are the foundation of our offerings.

"Over the next weeks, I'll meet with each of you privately to discuss the needs of your departments. Feel free to come to me with questions or issues as they arise. No one," he paused to look each faculty member in the eye, smiling only when his gaze landed on Fiona, "and I mean no one, is more important than anyone else."

The history teacher raised his hand. "Is the tiger still on campus?" he asked, looking as if he was about to be fed to said tiger.

"No. The police department has taken custody of the cub."
He raised a hand, palm out, to stop an outburst from Coach Fleek
before it happened. "When and if the cub is released, we'll discuss appropriate future precautions."

Mr. Edelston dismissed the meeting and escorted Coach out
of the room, gently inquiring about the football season's pros-
pects and effectively removing him from further confrontations
with Heather.

Bree hurried to the front of the room for a quiet word with
Dr. Warthan. By the time she had finished the room was empty.
Outside in the corridor, Miriam and Heather huddled together,
talking in hushed tones.

Heather motioned Bree over to them with a friendly smile.
"You were awfully quiet in there. I hope my argument with
Coach Dick didn't leave you with any bad impressions. He just
brings out the worst in me."

Bree laughed it off. "Trust me, I know all about antagonistic
coworkers. I could tell a few stories. But I did want to ask a favor
of you."

"Of course." Heather rubbed Bree's arm in a friendly gesture. "What's up?"

"You probably already know that Ning—one of Miriam's
international students—found the body. She called me, and I
called the police. Right now, she's terrified. It would really help
if you could keep those pictures of the body out of the public eye.
For Ning. And me." Bree raised her brows in question, hoping
she looked imploring, rather than demanding.

Heather waved the comment away. "Don't give it another
thought. I promised my reporter a byline and a juicy lead later
if she kept the story under wraps for now. And I had her delete
the photos from her phone. The photo files are locked up on my
computer. I'll keep them safe." She extended a hand, little finger
outstretched. "Pinkie swear."

Bree made her first ever pinkie swear and breathed an internal sigh of relief. The pictures wouldn't stay out of sight forever, but she may have bought a little time for the detectives.

"Now," said Heather, "Miriam and I have decided to invite you to share a cup of coffee at *The Underground*—our off-campus coffee house. If you're up for it."

CHAPTER 9

Bree kicked off her shoes the minute she entered the condo. The overstuffed couch with its inviting pillows and a snoozing Sherlock tempted her, but she knew better than to sit for even a minute.

She stopped to give Sherlock a kiss on her way to the shower. He opened one eye, sniffed her clothing and hissed. Bree backed away. Sherlock could be such a baby sometimes.

As she peeled off her clothes and tossed them in the hamper, she wondered if he'd hissed at the lingering scent from her visit to Lucky this morning or if he was reacting to the scents from the tension-laden conference room.

Sherlock's reaction aside, she wanted to wash the grime of the day away and energize herself for the night ahead. She soaped up with an energizing grapefruit and spice shower gel, but skipped the shampoo suspecting that she'd be washing the scent of smoke out of her hair in the morning anyway.

Both Heather and Miriam warned her that the club only offered coffee and whatever snacks—*wink, wink, nod, nod*—people brought to share. If the establishment was like other student hangouts, the winks and nods probably hinted at underage alcohol and other forbidden items.

Inspired by images from the 1960s movies her mother adored, Bree dressed in dark leggings, flats, and a long tunic-style top. During her stint undercover as "Cat Holmes, undergraduate," she'd discovered the comfort of tunics and leggings. Not that she chose to wear the baby blue and pinks that formed her undercover disguise, nor even traditional beatnik black. Burnt orange and gold suited her mood.

She swiped on mascara and ran a brush through her tangled hair, fluffing it before fishing in her jewelry box for a pair of understated CZ earrings. Her nail snagged on a spy cam necklace she'd worn on missions with Matthew. She palmed it, and reaching behind a nest of chunky, geometric shapes, flicked on the switch for the recording device.

Her conscience nagged her as she slipped the chain over her neck and adjusted the length for the optimum video capture angle. The police department couldn't use covert surveillance evidence, and her use of the camera might invalidate anything she learned in the investigation.

Besides, using the camera fell into the gray areas of operations Matthew used rather than the realm of by-the-rules James. What did using it say about Bree's moral scale?

She shushed the nagging voice and opened the control app on her phone. A few clicks later, the device was set to email regular video and audio file bursts to her Sci-Spy computer. The police might not be able to use the information she gathered, but *she* could use it to review and document her investigations.

Sherlock's plaintive meow drew her back to the living room. This time he rubbed his head against her sweater and purred in contentment rather than hissing. "Good thing my sweater and your fur match, or I'd be a mess, you big baby." She cooed and fussed over him, alternating between petting the cat and fixing a sandwich before calling James.

"Detective O'Neil."

"It's me. I talked to Ning today and she's agreed to meet you and tell you what happened."

A chuckle snaked across the phone. "She's not the only one you sweet-talked today. Ted over at animal control can't stop raving about you. In another day, your tiger will be as spoiled as that menace of a cat at your home."

"Sherlock isn't a menace." Bree fed the orange tabby a bit of ham from her sandwich. His rough tongue rasped across her fingers, licking away all traces of salty goodness. "He's a very smart boy, aren't you, baby?"

"Great." James sighed. "Now I'm relegated to second place after the cat. Or maybe third place after the tiger and the cat. I didn't hear any news about the precinct getting cupcakes—only the animal control division."

"Don't worry, I'll be sure to double the recipe for my next batch. You'll get your share." They chatted for a few more minutes with Bree filling him in on the latest developments on campus. "Before I forget," she said, "you need to know that someone on the student newspaper supposedly took photos of the crime scene."

James cursed, interrupting her narrative.

"Don't worry," Bree said. "I immediately spoke to the faculty advisor—that's Heather Beauchamp—and she assured me she had the situation under control." Bree told James about the steps Heather had taken to manage the situation.

"Good job. I'll contact Heather."

"I told her it was the best way to protect Ning, and me," Bree added. "Heather is distrustful of authorities, so tread carefully, James."

"Good to know. I'll turn on the charm and keep the bullying to a minimum."

Bree heard the tension under his forced joviality. "For what it's worth, I believe Heather would do anything to protect the students. Especially ones she sees as vulnerable, like Ning."

"Anything? Including murder?"

The accusation hit Bree like a sucker punch to the gut. "Isn't that a bit of a stretch, James?"

"Maybe. Maybe not. You know as well as I do that nice people can do bad things. I never assume anyone in an investigation is innocent."

"Except me. Right?" The laughter she'd expected didn't follow her comment.

"Even you were a suspect when we first met," James said. "For what it's worth, I'm glad you weren't the killer. I'd be even happier if you'd give up trying to investigate."

Bree held her tongue while silence filled the airwaves. "We both know that isn't going to happen," she finally said softly. "But I promise to be careful. And I also promise to fill you in on any and everything I know tomorrow after we finish talking to Ning."

"What about now? I could come over tonight, if you like. Or we could meet for coffee. I could be there in half an hour." The warmth in his voice made it clear that he wanted to do more than just discuss the case. "If I can't stop you from investigating, at least I can keep you close to me while you do."

Bree fingered her necklace absently, wondering why she continued to keep him at arm's length. "I wish we could, but I promised to have coffee with some of the other teachers." *In a place that wouldn't welcome a police presence. Wink, wink. Nod, nod.*

The Underground, true to its name, could only be accessed by a narrow, twisting flight of stairs tucked near the back entrance of a bookstore catering to epic fantasy and cult fiction. Bree half expected to see a pair of eyes peer at her from behind a sliding peephole and wondered if she needed a password to enter.

Instead, in answer to her knock the door opened a crack, spilling light into the stairwell. "Professor Beauchamp invited me," she stammered when the student simply stared at her.

A smile split his face and dark eyes nearly obscured by a curly mop of deep brown hair lit up. "Mrs. Heather, your friend is here," he called, addressing the room behind him. The door opened wider and Bree blinked as she stepped into a brightly lit room.

Exposed brick walls painted in shades of white, yellow, blue, and red reflected light from assorted lamps scattered throughout the room. Heather waved at Bree from one end of a bar built from painted cinderblocks and layers of polished wood.

"Quite a place you have here," Bree said as she threaded her way through the mismatched couches, chairs, and tables.

"*Disarray by design.* It's a combination of donated, discarded, reclaimed, and a lot of elbow grease." Heather waved her hands as if presenting a luxury rehab project on TV. "The art students created the paint designs, the theater majors shored up the furniture, and the engineers made sure all the coffee makers work."

"Cheers. And welcome to *The Underground.*" Bree turned at the sound of a familiar British accent.

"You remember Nigel from the faculty mixer, don't you?" Heather asked as she indicated the tall, slender blond with artfully styled hair who slid behind the bar.

"Of course. Professor Beauchamp referred to you as a talented barista."

"Right-O." He winked at Bree and nodded to the assorted cluster of coffeemaking implements on the bar. "I can create a work of art using everything from this old percolator to the espresso machine. So, what do you say? Fancy a coffee? Or maybe a cuppa?"

Heather raised a brow and gave him a teasing smile. "Want to translate that into American English for our guest?"

"It's all right," Bree interrupted. "Between reading Agatha Christie mysteries and my own travels, I know he's asking if a want a cup of coffee or a cup of tea."

"Then, my well-traveled and well-read patron, which do you prefer?" Nigel gave her a brilliant smile.

"I'll take the cuppa. Lady Grey, if you have it."

"Let's sit over here," Heather said leading her to a futon against a back wall. "We can enjoy our tea and chat."

As they settled in and Nigel brought their tea, a young woman with a razor-sharp pageboy cut and a melodic Jamaican accent started singing on the makeshift stage. Bree didn't recognize the song.

"Abigay is an engineering student by day and a songwriter by night. She's developed quite a repertoire." Heather nodded to the singer. "Like so many others, she sometimes feels out of place and alone at Terrance U.

"For as long as I've been teaching, I encourage the new students to express their feelings through song, poetry, or writing. It teaches skills in written language and gives them a creative outlet."

She fished her cell phone out of a pocket, scanned a text, then turned to the door where Miriam Cook appeared. She waved the other teacher over. "A couple years ago, Miriam had the idea to create a coffee house atmosphere where the students could perform their art. Things took off from there."

Miriam stopped by the bar, gave an order to Nigel, then settled in near Bree and Heather. "What do you think of our experiment?" she asked Bree.

Before she could answer, the singer stopped and another student took her place on stage. Bree recognized the young man who had opened the coffeehouse door for her.

"My poem is entitled *The First Year*."

Alone. Alone. Long way from home.
In dark of night, I cry; I moan.
A fine bit chipped off my soul.

Away. Away. At end of day.
No one to greet me. Nothing to say.
I cry. I moan. A fine bit chipped off my soul.

Bit by bit. Day by day. Still I stay.
Soul frays away. Chips grind to powder.
Despair takes root. Sorrow cries louder.

Alone. Alone. Long way from home.
In dark of night, I cry; I moan.
A fine bit chipped off my soul.

"Are they all like this?" Bree whispered, feeling a wave of compassion for the young poet. "He sounds so distressed."

"Homesickness is difficult, especially at that age," Miriam replied. "It can impact anyone, but our international students are even more prone to it. For most, it's their first time away from home. Many don't have the money or time to go back for visits. Some find it too expensive and difficult to call or even video chat.

"Add to that the challenges of a new culture, a strange language, and prejudices—both innocent and antagonistic—from other students, and it can become overwhelming."

Miriam accepted a steaming café latte from Nigel and took a long sip. "We do what we can to help. We also offer counseling if we suspect deeper depression."

The poet began a new verse accompanied by a lone student snapping his fingers from the audience. Soon others joined in the snapping and the quiet clicks gained volume.

"That's the other students showing support for him." Heather shrugged her slim shoulders. "I have no idea who started it, but it's become a tradition at *The Underground*."

The poet smiled and moved to a more upbeat stanza as the snapping continued.

"The coffee house is wonderful." Bree kicked off her flats and curled her feet under her on the futon. "But I remember you saying something about it closing down and reopening." She watched both Miriam and Heather closely.

The teachers exchanged worry laden glances. Finally, Miriam spoke. "When Heather and I first approached Dr. Christianson, he fully supported the idea of a coffeehouse. We opened *The Terminal* on campus grounds. Later," she frowned, her eyes darkening with anger. "Let's just say that last year, he closed down the project without warning."

"That's putting it nicely." Heather's foot tapped on the cement floor, the staccato rhythm fast at odds with the snapping fingers in the background. She turned to face Bree. "Someone—and I personally blame Dick Fleek—influenced him to pull our funding. Luckily for us, the bookstore owner let us use his space in exchange for some basic repairs on his cellar."

On stage, Nigel thanked the first poet then adjusted the microphone for his taller frame. "I present to you, *The Underground Anthem*," he said simply.

Fancy a coffee? Fancy a tea?
Whatever you fancy, share some with me.
Want cream or sugar? Bring something to barter.
Your life can be easy, or very much harder.

A shilling, a dollar, an athlete, a scholar,
Fancy free for a fee; fancy free for a fee.

Fancy a whiskey? Fancy a beer? ...

Finger snapping immediately accompanies his poem and several patrons of the coffeehouse joined in, murmuring the verses sotto-voce, like churchgoers at prayer. The voices rose as they repeated the word chorus of "fancy free, fancy free."

Bree shut out the sound of the poem, swept her hair behind her ears and tried to focus on Heather and Miriam. "Why would Dr. Christianson pull your funding?"

Heather gave her a hard stare, her eyes narrowing in anger. She pointed to Bree's pierced earlobe. Her mouth formed a bitter line. "I guess you weren't part of the diamond stud club long enough to understand."

CHAPTER 10

"The diamond stud club?"

"Heather and I both hoped you'd been the one strong enough to break the mold." Miriam shrugged, her cheeks flushing. "After all, you have a PhD, years of outside experience and spunk. But if Quint could get to you, he could get to anyone."

"Trust me, Quint is—was—a master at getting what he wants." Heather picked at a cuticle in rapid, restless movements. When a dot of blood appeared, she stopped and looked at Bree. "How long were you sleeping with him? And more importantly, what did he use to get you to agree?"

A hot stab of anger flashed through Bree, leaving her light-headed. "I wasn't sleeping with Quint Christianson. And in the short time I knew him, believe me, the issue never came up. But," she softened her voice and looked at the other two teachers, "I can understand that he might have tried in time."

After all, he'd spent much of their initial interview staring at her cleavage. A woman who didn't have Bree's experience deflecting inappropriate stares and fighting her way up in a male-dominated profession might well have allowed his overtures to turn into something more invasive.

"But your earrings ..." Miriam prompted.

"... are inexpensive CZ that I treated myself to last Christmas."

Silence fell on the little group. Across the room another student took the stage and finger snapping reverberated around the trio of teachers.

"I'm sorry," Heather said at last. "It's just that, for all the rest of us, these earrings represent a symbol of being bullied by Quint."

"He gave them to us each as a special present." Miriam took a drink from her mug and cradled her hands around it. "Quint had a way of making you feel like you were *the one*. The one he'd been waiting for. When he gave me my diamonds, I thought they meant something."

"Tiny studs for a tiny spitfire. That's what he said to me." Heather's eyes snapped as if they were, indeed, aflame. "When I first saw Miriam with her earrings, I put the pieces together. By that time, I'd gotten tenure and thought Quint's harassments were behind me."

"Eventually, Heather and I—and all of the others we could find—made a pact. To wear the earrings so that we'd never forget how Quint demeaned us. I think we managed to warn a few teachers away from his machinations, but they never stayed at TU for long."

Bree shifted so she could watch both teachers. "So, he's been harassing all of the female staff? In exchange for job security?"

"And now," Heather set her coffee cup on the table with a thud, "you know why he pulled the funding for the coffee house. Because when neither Miriam nor I would dance to his tune, he retaliated."

As details of the story unfolded, each woman seemed to feed off the other's anger.

"I'm glad he's dead." Heather's cold announcement stopped the conversation. She turned to Miriam. "Don't look at me like you aren't."

"I'm glad he's gone too. But if I'd been the one to do him in, I'd have used poison. Not something brutal."

"Not me. He had it coming. I'd have clawed lower and removed his ability to harass anyone, if you get my drift."

The hairs on Bree's neck stood at the casual, vicious pronouncement.

"What," Miriam hesitated, "what did the body look like?" She addressed the question to Heather. For whatever reason, even though she was Ning's sponsor, the general public didn't seem to know Bree had been at the murder scene. She wasn't about to enlighten them and put a crimp in her investigation, either.

"Forget I said anything." Heather waved the comment away as if it was an annoying fly. "It's in the hands of the police, where it should be."

A soft, but insistent, tap on her cheek, followed by another, and another dragged Bree from a pleasant dream.

Meow. Sherlock gazed at her expectantly. The cat had no concept of Saturday. Or of sleeping in. But he made up for that with persistence. Bree gave up trying to sleep and swung her legs over the side of the bed.

"Okay, okay, I'm moving." Sherlock raced ahead of her as she padded barefoot into the kitchen. Once the cat was fed and the coffee brewing, she headed to the shower to shampoo the smoke from her hair and rinse the sleep from her eyes.

By ten when she'd finished her household chores, Bree settled in with her third cup of coffee and her computer, Sherlock curled by her feet. As she processed the video and audio files from last night, she opened a battered notebook. "When in doubt, go back to basics. Time to pull out the crime notebook." Sherlock shifted, looping one paw across her ankle and resting his head on her bare foot, but otherwise gave no response.

"What? Not helping me with my investigation this time?" She wiggled her toes and smiled when a purr rumbled through the giant tabby's furry body. "I guess I can't rely on you to have all the answers."

She scanned her notes on the crime scene, frowning at the page. Crossed out sections, arrows inserting new bits of information, and general disorder created a scrawled patchwork of conflicting data. In the past, she'd created her notes on the crime scenes as she encountered them. The scientific cataloging of details calmed her mind and kept panic at bay.

This time, her hands full with Ning, a cowardly tiger, students and reporters crowding the scene, and the police immediately swarming the area, she'd simply committed the details to memory.

She puzzled over her multiple notations regarding the glass at the site. It hadn't come from the curio cabinet doors. It was between the body and the door. But was it also around the body? And did it matter?

"My thesis advisor would have my head for performing an experiment and recording the results from memory after the fact," she grumbled to the sleeping cat. "In the hours between the event and discussing it with James, who knows how many critical details I forgot or twisted to try to make them fit together?"

Was she losing her scientific edge as she drew deeper into the spy world? Or was she learning a new set of observational skills?

She took a slug of the still hot coffee and pushed her doubts aside. *Observe. Record. Then hypothesize.* Flipping to a clean page, she started a table of suspects. Who had motive, means, and opportunity to kill Quint?

Ning found the body. She had no past with Dr. Christianson, no reason to want him dead. If she had murdered him... she'd done a clumsy job of it. No checkmarks against any critical indicators followed her name in the table.

Coach Fleek. Burly. Strong enough to inflict a head wound on his boss. But why? They'd argued. Over the cub and the quarterback? Or something more? Coach had shown a nasty streak at Mr. Edelston's staff meeting. And a calloused disregard for anything except the athletic department and his team's winning streak. Opportunity? Check. Means? Check. Motive? Bree, the scientist, refused to let her growing dislike of the man color the facts. She put a question mark in the motive column.

Heather Beauchamp.

Miriam Cook.

Bree slid her foot out from under Sherlock's sleeping form and paced across her kitchen. Both women had reason to hate Quint for his abuses and manipulations. Either could have visited his office without raising suspicions. She hurried back to the notebook. *Check class schedule and timeline.*

Miriam's timid demeanor argued against her having the strength or will to bash someone over the head. Or did it? Bree recalled the teacher's anger over Max Edelston's appointment to the interim VP position and settled for a question mark in the means column.

Heather was another story. *I could hold my own against any man.* The diminutive spitfire had bragged about her prowess at the staff mixer. She'd backed up her talk in the confrontation with Coach at the staff meeting.

Bree reluctantly put a checkmark in the means column for Heather. Followed by a note asking if someone of her height could really have inflicted a death wound on someone as tall as Quint.

Who else? Fiona Fancier's office was on the same floor as Quint's. Bree remembered how Fiona had clung to Quint before heading to the faculty mixer. They'd been close. And she'd been distraught over Quint's death. So, while she had the means and opportunity, she lacked any obvious motive.

On the other hand, Quint's widow, Pamela Christianson, had plenty of motive. At least if she knew about Fiona, Miriam, Heather and any other of Quint's affairs. Motive-check. Means—check. Opportunity?

He likes a good work-wife balance. Miriam's words echoed in Bree's memory. Would anyone have noticed if Pamela visited her husband at work? She noted the question in the opportunity column.

Bree's stomach growled. She headed to the fridge, opening it to scan the shelves while she racked her brain to think of other suspects. Instead of suspects, her mind created grocery lists.

She slammed the fridge door. Everyone on staff was a suspect. She listed all the people who'd attended the staff meeting, but without more information, she couldn't do anything else. Time to switch gears. She ripped out a page and shut the book.

Her stomach growled again as her pen hovered over the page. *Milk. Butter. Eggs.*

CHAPTER 11

The sound of the doorbell startled Bree almost as much as the sight of Sherlock hurtling his bulk toward it at top speed. Tremors shook the floor in the wake of his footfalls.

Abandoning her grocery list, she followed the mewling cat and opened the door. Ning and her suitemate, Tina, stood in the hallway, laden with packages.

Ning dropped her bags inside the door and knelt, scooping up Sherlock. "Hello, pretty kitty," she murmured, burying her face in the thick orange fur. Sherlock's contented rumble filled the air.

"So much for her excitement over seeing you." Tina winked at Bree then passed her some bags. "All Ning could talk about this morning was shopping so she could surprise you with a home-cooked Thai dinner. Her menu sounded so good, I almost canceled my date for tonight."

Together Bree and Tina lugged the bags to the kitchen while Ning cooed over Sherlock. Rice noodles, curry paste, sweet and spicy chilis, limes, basil, lemongrass, coconut milk and more soon crowded the counter.

"It looks like the two of you shopped for an army. Where did you find all this?" Bree asked as she stashed chicken, shrimp, tofu, and eggs in her formerly empty fridge.

"It's amazing what you can learn online. Did you know we have a Pan-Asian grocery fewer than ten miles from campus?"

Tina wrinkled her nose. "Ning was in heaven shopping for her spices and ingredients, but the fish tank at the seafood counter—ugh!"

"If you think that's bad, you should try shopping on the streets of Thailand. The markets are crowded with everything imaginable. Most of it—including the smell—is farm-fresh and ready to eat. No preservatives. Unless you count salt or vinegar."

"Ning says you've traveled lots of places. How many countries have you been in?"

"Twelve? Thirteen?" Bree shut the fridge door and faced the girl. "To be honest, I'd have to count the stamps on my passport to be sure. It's all a blur at times."

"I don't even have a passport." Tina looked up from studying the swirling Asian script on the label of a spice jar. "Yet. That's one reason I volunteered to be a peer-mentor in the international dorm. Professor Cook says there's more than one way to learn about the world."

Professor Cook. Miriam. "Are you taking classes with her this semester?" Bree asked.

Tina's blond curls bobbed in acknowledgement. "Last year I studied Europe and South America. This year, I'm doing India—"

"*Khun* Dr. Bree," Ning stepped into the kitchen, Sherlock draped over her shoulder like twenty pounds of limp noodles, "can I give the pretty kitty a bath?"

"I don't think Sherlock likes water." *And I don't like his reactions when he's annoyed.*

"No. He like. Come, I show you."

"Let's wait until another time," Bree hedged. "My friends at *The Barkery* are expecting us. We don't want to disappoint them."

In truth, although she'd told Horace and Wendy Clark to expect a visit from them, she hadn't specified a time. But the ruse worked. Ning swung the cat from her shoulders and deposited him on a kitchen chair where he purred while enduring—enjoying?—a belly rub.

Soon after Sherlock had come to live with her, Bree had learned–after a bloody swipe from his back claws—not to touch his vulnerable belly. Yet Ning did so easily and was rewarded with a docile sigh and purring. Maybe her magic touch could convince him to happily submit to a bath. Bree decided not to push her luck.

Instead, she put away the remaining groceries and herded the girls out the door and down the stairs. A short walk later, they arrived at the pedestrian shopping area and entered *The Barkery.*

Typical Clark chaos greeted them in the warm confines of the pet bakery and grooming salon. A middle-aged woman with three dachshunds dragged Wendy from one "party room" to another, claiming each dog preferred a different venue for their "birthday" party, and requesting a discounted price. Another customer browsed various pet sweaters while Rookie, one of the resident *Barkery* dogs, sat patiently nearby, gaze glued to her bag.

Bree stifled a laugh. The beagle had been adopted by the Clarks after his drug-dog training conflicted with new medical marijuana laws in his former hometown. His ability to sniff out narcotics had helped her catch a killer. Unsuspecting customers cooed over his silent attentiveness to them, unaware the dog was really signaling the presence of illegal substances.

"Rookie. Out," she said, giving him the signal that released him from his task. He trotted over, tail wagging in the air.

"Aren't you the sweetest thing?" Tina crouched near the dog and let him bathe her face in sloppy kisses. More than one of the college girls needed pet therapy today.

Bree nodded to Horace and Wendy then watched as Rookie shuttled between the two girls, his body quivering with happiness. When his customers left the shop, Horace flipped the door sign to "closed" and released his other dogs from the living quarters behind the retail area.

Krupke and Mrs. Krupke, shaggy dogs of indeterminate breed, bounded out to join Rookie in bestowing kisses on the girls. "Mind your manners," Horace rumbled over the din, and all three dogs dropped to their haunches and presented a paw to the girls.

"So cute." Tina reached to take an outstretched paw.

"This," said Horace, "is Krupke. He's the head goose-chasing dog for the *D.O.G.* business."

At Tina's puzzled look Bree added, "that stands for *Dog on Guard*. Local businesses hire them to keep the Canada geese from getting too comfortable on site. Mr. and Mrs. Clark own *D.O.G.* as well as *The Barkery* and *The Groom-N-Room*."

"No need to be formal, Doc Bree," the lanky store owner chided. "Call us Horace and Wendy." He quickly introduced both other dogs as well. "We're glad you stopped by to visit."

Wendy appeared over his shoulder, a plate of treats in her hands, which she passed to the girls.

"It's for the dogs," Bree said quickly before Tina could take a bite.

"Cupcakes for dogs?"

"Pupcakes, actually. The main ingredients are …" She lifted a brow in Wendy's direction.

"The red velvet pupcakes are chopped liver, brown rice flour, pumpkin, and my special recipe."

Tina broke off a piece, sniffed it, and held it out for Rookie. Ning did the same for Krupke and Mrs. K. Once the dogs finished their treats, Horace praised them and told them they were free to play. As if on command, their perfect manners disappeared and the roughhousing resumed.

Wendy ushered the guests into one of the party rooms and produced mugs of tea and a plate of cookies created for human consumption. The girls dug in, making short work of the cookies.

"So, which of you is from Thailand?" Horace asked, his blue eyes twinkling in his weathered face as his gaze darted between the blond and her dark-haired companion.

Both girls burst into giggles. Finally, Ning answered. "I am."

"And where is this tiger of yours I hear so much about?"

Her smile drooped and Ning's eyes fell to the floor. "Lucky is in jail. For murder." She paused, searching for a word. "Framed," she added.

"Lucky will be released soon," Bree said, praying it was true. The sad look Ning gave her didn't hold much hope.

"If Doc Bree says Lucky will be released, you can trust her to do everything in her power to make it happen. Meanwhile, I have a bit of a problem I think you could help me with. We've taken in a new orphan."

Horace excused himself and the muscles in Bree's neck tensed. The kind-hearted Clarks were known for taking in anything with fur and a need for love. At least so far, their strays had sported fur rather than scales.

A sad wail, like a baby's cry, drew her eyes to the door. Perched on Horace's shoulder sat a small monkey, spiky black hair framing a face with eyes and muzzle rimmed in a startling white fur. "This is Miss Peepers."

He urged the monkey from his shoulder only to have her twist in his embrace to lock her tiny arms around his neck, face buried in his shirtfront. "She's a mite shy at first," he said, stroking her back and speaking softly. "It's okay, baby girl. These are friends. Nobody is going to hurt you."

Miss Peepers peeked over his arms then ducked her head back to the safety of Horace's checkered shirt. "She belonged to my great-uncle Edward," Wendy said softly. "He brought her back from one of his military posts in the Pacific. Later, he trained her to help him as he aged. By the time he was confined to a wheelchair with M.S., Miss Peepers had become one of his primary caregivers."

"I've heard about organizations that train monkeys as service animals," Bree said. "But I've never met one."

"Only a few such organizations existed," Wendy continued, "and most were plagued by controversy. When Uncle Edward passed on, we tried to find one to take Miss Peepers, but the few that are still around refused to adopt older animals they hadn't trained."

"So now she's our girl. Aren't you, missy?" Affection warmed the rough edges of Horace's voice. "We're going to take good care of her." As the easy conversation flowed, Miss Peepers gained confidence, sneaking more glances at the guests until it became a game of peek-a-boo between the monkey and Ning.

Eventually, Miss Peepers let out a squeaky little chirp and climbed from Horace's arms to grasp Ning's outstretched hand. A tiny fist curled around Ning's index finger. The capuchin chirped, Ning answered in soft, melodic Thai and Bree wondered, once again, at the girl's connection to the animals she worked with.

"Looks like Miss P found a new friend." Horace's grin split his face, making the deep wrinkles around his mouth and eyes look as if they, too, were smiling.

Wendy reached across the table to remove the now empty cookie platter. "Do you think you and Ning could ask someone from the vet school to take a look at her, Bree? Horace and I have done our share of research, but most vets don't know much about the care of exotic animals."

Bree bit her tongue to keep from asking questions she didn't want answers to. With the Clarks, it was best not to look too closely. If anything about Miss Peepers was illegal, Bree didn't want to know. At least not until she could enlist the help of her sorority sister from the Brookfield Zoo.

"I take Miss Peepers to the pet school," Ning announced. "The pet doctors are very good."

"Vet," Tina murmured. "Short for veterinarian. Animal doctor."

Ning shrugged and resumed her conversation with the monkey as they chattered in capuchin and Thai. "I take. Pet School will help."

CHAPTER 12

If James O'Neil found it strange to be sitting at Bree's table watching a capuchin monkey comb through Sherlock's hair while a Thai whirlwind whipped up Pad Thai and Panang Curry in her kitchen, he didn't show it.

That was one of the many things Bree liked about James.

"I think I'll delay asking about your day," he said as he sipped a beer, "and tell you about mine instead."

His voice dropped, and he cast a wary eye at the kitchen where Ning chopped vegetables in a staccato rhythm, unconcerned with the two of them for the moment. "I have updates to share with you." He rubbed the spot between his eyes.

"And it's not good news?"

"It's news. Just not helpful news. First, we were able to verify that a text was sent from Quint's phone to Ning near the time of his death."

"But you can't be more specific."

"I have a hypothesis." A ghost of a smile lit his face when he used her favorite word to describe his thoughts on the matter. "Blood smears were found on the fingerprint reader of the phone, making it likely Quint's print was used to unlock it post mortem."

"Then you'll also be able to see the killer's—"

"—fingerprints?" he finished for her. "No, we didn't. Just smears that could have come from a stylus. Like I said it wasn't helpful news, unless reaching a dead end is helpful."

Bree buried her head in her hands and bit back an exclamation of frustration. James's hand rested on her shoulder, giving it a light squeeze.

"There is one possible lead. The crime techs found this at the scene. What do you make of it?" He pushed a small, sealed bag across the table. Inside, a brilliant cut gem winked at her through a blood-encrusted smear.

Dread crawled into her belly and curled there like a snake. "Is it a diamond?"

James shrugged. "Diamond. CZ. Cut glass. We won't know until after it's been examined. We do, however, know that the blood on it is Dr. Christianson's."

"Any DNA?"

Another shrug. "Crime labs are backed up and DNA analysis isn't a department specialty. Nor is it a priority when it would be so easy to pin the incident on the tiger already in custody."

A sizzle of meat hitting a hot stir-fry pan filled the kitchen. "You know Lucky couldn't have done this," she whispered, hoping Ning couldn't hear over the noise of her cooking.

"I know. For what it's worth, my superiors aren't too pleased with me for putting that in my reports. They hoped for a neat end to the investigation by now." He raked a hand through his hair, causing the sandy blond ends to stand in disarray. "Instead they have no suspects, an enraged athletic department threatening civil action if they don't get their tiger back, and a brewing public relations nightmare on their hands."

"What are you going to do?"

James rolled the beer bottle between his palms, his brow furrowed. "Swallow my pride," he said at last. "Maybe bend a few rules, for the sake of putting a killer behind bars."

"Bending rules isn't your style."

"You're right. It isn't." He sighed. "Luckily for me, I have a way around this that doesn't bend rules. Much. I have a consultant with access to a forensics-lab-for-hire."

"Are you asking me to use my resources to help you out?"

James nodded. "I'm asking you to use your resources. *All* of them. Requesting a contract lab to fast-track a DNA analysis isn't so much bending a rule as taking a parallel path to getting answers. So," he cocked his head, "will you help?"

Bree closed her fist around the sample. "Consider it done."

She stashed the sample in her purse to take to the Sci-PHi labs and returned to a table laden with more food than the three of them could eat. Fragrant chilis, the tang of fish oil, and the scents of succulent stir-fried chicken and grilled shrimp scented the air.

Ning smiled as she slid into a chair. "I make Pad Thai with shrimp, Panang Curry with chicken and sticky rice. My family recipe."

Before Bree could sit, Miss Peepers raced into the room and swung her lithe body onto the chair beside Ning, her shyness forgotten as she eyed the food. Bree took the remaining chair next to James, across from the odd duo.

James spooned helpings of both entrees onto his plate and closed his eyes in appreciation after the first bite. "This is wonderful," he said to Ning, flashing a smile and turning on the charm. "Where did you learn to cook like this?"

While James did his best to charm Ning out of her fear of authorities, Bree focused on the food. Rich coconut and chili broth coated sliced, melt-in-your mouth white meat chicken, leaving more than a hint of warmth behind when she swallowed. Carrots, chunky bell peppers, and tender mushrooms added texture and richness to the dish.

Across from her, Miss Peepers fingered bits of chicken and shrimp from a small plate Ning kept filled for her. Bree noticed chopped bits of fruit and nuts in addition to the other food and wondered if Ning had found them in her kitchen or if the Clarks had sent them in a goody bag along with the monkey.

She helped herself to a spoonful of peanut and green onion topped noodles from the Pad Thai platter and squeezed a wedge of lime over the serving. The grilled shrimp with its slight char and the mild peanut, garlic, and lime of the sauce contrasted nicely with the spicier curry.

Beside her, conversation flowed easily. Ning had lost some of her rectitude and was entertaining James with stories of her family restaurants where she'd spent her childhood chopping vegetables and washing dishes.

"As much as I enjoy your stories," James said, laughing as he looked around the table "I really do need to bring up the elephant in the room."

"Elephant?" Ning's brow creased but her body remained relaxed.

"It's an American phrase for something no one wants to talk about," Bree supplied.

"Yeah, I shouldn't have said it when what I really meant was the monkey in the room." James nodded to Miss Peepers then offered her a slice of carrot from which he'd licked off the curry sauce. Her little fingers grasped the offering and she nibbled it with enthusiasm. "What's her story?"

Ning launched into the account she'd learned from the Clarks, leaving out details and making up others in their place, but essentially getting the gist of it correct. James peppered her with questions about the habits of monkeys while keeping Miss Peepers supplied with vegetable bits.

"She like you," Ning said to James. After a quick glance at Bree, she added, "I like you too."

The atmosphere in the room shifted.

"I'm glad," James said softly. "I like you, and I want you to know that you can trust me." As if to emphasize the truth in his words, Miss Peepers slid out of her chair, scampered under the table, and hopped onto James's lap.

Ning nodded to the monkey. "Miss Peepers has friends now. She not so alone. Like me." She looked at Bree, a sheen of tears in her eyes. "Like Lucky."

"I stopped by to check on Lucky before I came here tonight," James said. "She's made some new friends too. Look." He fished his phone out of his pocket, found a photo and slid it across to Ning. The photo showed the holding area where Lucky lived. The cub snuggled in the middle of a heap of blankets, surrounded by an array of toys that would make Sherlock jealous. Next to her sleeping form, Ted, the animal control worker, squatted, stroking her fur.

Ning blinked rapidly as she slid the phone back to James.

He took the phone and smiled at her. "Thanks to Dr. Bree's help, and confirmation by the vet school, I've been able to arrange Lucky's release. But I think you're going to have to let Ted, here, come to visit her once in a while."

"Oh, yes." Ning's smile lit the room.

"Before she comes home," James said gently, "I was hoping you could tell me about what happened that day on campus."

"Mrs. Fan-cee-eh won't like." Ning pushed her plate aside. "She tells me not to talk to the police."

"I know. And I know she's just trying to protect you. But you can trust me. Someone killed Dr. Christianson and tried to make you and Lucky take the blame for it. I'm not going to let that happen. But I need your help to find the real killer."

Under James's skillful, gentle questioning, Ning began to tell her side of the story. While they talked, Bree cleared the plates and set the kitchen to order, keeping one ear trained on the conversation between James and Ning, ready to intervene if needed.

Yet somehow, with Miss Peepers and Sherlock acting as buffers, Ning opened up to James, easily telling her story of the dreadful day. By the time she finished, the kitchen was neat, the leftovers stored, and the conversation turned again to light topics.

Hours later, after Bree settled Ning and Miss Peepers in the guest room for the night, she had a few quiet moments with James. They sat side-by-side on the couch and when his arm went around her, she snuggled into the embrace instead of resisting.

"Looks like you made quite an impression. Did you learn anything new?" She rested her head on his shoulder.

He settled deeper into the couch and clasped her free hand in his. "Ning's story didn't differ much from yours."

"But there were some differences?"

He shook his head. "Not differences. Additions. Ning reminds me of the foster children I met through outreach programs."

A gush of warmth hit her, and she gripped his hand tighter. "I didn't realize you volunteered for a foster program. Do you still work with them?"

"Children in the system are used to being shuttled from place to place. They learn to make the best of every situation but be ready to move at a moment's notice. So, they don't make many lasting relationships. Basically, they have trust issues."

"You seem to have gained Ning's trust."

He nodded, studying their entwined hands. "Ning is different. She has a family and a positive history with relationships. Her initial distrust for me is simply based on my role in law enforcement. She just needed to know there was a human behind the uniform."

Bree waited, wondering where the conversation was headed. Back to relationships? Back to her and James? Or elsewhere?

Minutes ticked by, broken only by Sherlock's soft snore.

"Ning doesn't like or trust anyone at the university—outside of you, some of the vet school personnel, and her suitemate," James said eventually.

Bree tugged her hand free and twisted to face James. "It's always hard for students to adjust. But there may be a way for her to make more friends. Miriam Cook and Heather Beauchamp sponsor a coffee house designed with the exchange students in mind. She can meet others there."

"You can try, but," James frowned at her, "I get the feeling Ms. Cook intimidates her."

"Miriam?" The timid professor Bree knew didn't fit that bill. A trickle of unease slid down her spine. Was Miriam hiding more than a decade-old affair with Quint Christianson? Was she more or different than what she appeared?

"Apparently," James continued breaking into Bree's thoughts, "she pushes the international students to acclimate—which is part of her job—but Ning isn't one to be pushed."

"Anything else I should know?"

James ticked off items on his fingers. "She feels cowed by her attorney, hates Coach Fleek, and is afraid of the football players." He shook his head with a smile. "All of which seem pretty normal to me, given the position she's in. I think the best thing we can do for her is to get Lucky back and get Ning involved in caring for him and attending her classes. The girl needs a dose of normalcy."

A screech and banging on the guest room door followed by a sharp command in Thai, interrupted the companionable conversation.

"Somehow," Bree said, "I don't think normalcy is in the cards for any of us, anytime soon."

CHAPTER 13

In the months since her former employer—Chemical Industries Corporation—had been turned into a scientific staffing company and Troy had been appointed as head of the department where she worked, Bree had never looked forward to his mandatory Monday morning staff meetings.

Until today.

Bree set her coffee aside on the counter and faced Miss Peepers. "Give," she commanded, holding her hand out to the monkey. Confused—or simply ignoring the command—Miss Peepers turned Bree's spy camera necklace in her hands before popping the faux gem into her mouth.

"No!" Bree lunged before she could stop herself, not wanting the monkey to chew through a battery cable and hurt herself.

Miss Peepers scampered away, swinging up to the top of the bookshelf. But at least she stuffed the necklace into a small pouch she carried like a messenger bag instead of chewing it.

Bree scooped a glob of peanut butter from the half-full jar onto her index finger. "Come," she coaxed, holding the treat out to the monkey.

A minute later, after climbing down to lick away the treat, Miss Peepers perched on Bree's shoulder and combed her fingers through Bree's hair. The gentle, almost ticklish sensation of being groomed by a primate made Bree smile. She retrieved her coffee and stroked the monkey's tail while the grooming continued.

Ning removed the necklace from the distracted animal's satchel and stashed it a kitchen drawer before handing Miss Peepers a baby rattle festooned with bells and sparkling gems. "She is curious."

"Don't let her curiosity get her into trouble," Bree cautioned, transferring the monkey to Ning's shoulder. "Remember, Horace and Wendy told us she understands a list of commands and knows how to behave among humans. She's just testing her limits with us."

"No stealing, little girl." Ning ruffled her charge's fur. "We go to the pet clinic now?" she asked Bree.

Bree glanced at the clock, dismayed to see it was nearly half past eight. "First I have to stop by the office. Will you and Miss Peepers be all right in the car alone for a few minutes?"

"Yes. Fine." Ning bundled herself into a jacket more suited to winter than a mild autumn day, and cajoled Miss Peepers into a coat of her own.

Once upon a time, during her life as a service animal, Miss Peepers had learned to wear a bright vest while working. Wendy had explained that the monkey still enjoyed wearing clothing—as evidenced by the duffle stuffed with her wardrobe.

"Ride?" Ning asked, and Miss Peepers jumped into a backpack style carrier which Ning looped over her shoulder.

A short ride—and a ton of monkey chatter—later, Bree heaved a sigh of relief as she pulled into the Sci-PHi parking lot.

A screech filled the car as Ning tugged on the leash attached to a harness around the monkey's hips. Miss Peepers gave up on her quest to climb into the front seat and settled for racing from one back window to the other, chattering in excitement.

Between phone calls to the vet school, multiple visits to *The Barkery*, and around-the-clock surveillance of Ning and the monkey, her weekend had passed in a blur. Only a few more minutes and she could officially get back to the relative peace of teaching reluctant students and investigating a murder.

Staff meetings never looked so good.

Bree stepped off the elevator and entered the second-floor labs of the complex in time to see her friend Kiki striding toward the stairs. "Kiki," she called, "do you have a minute?"

"No, and neither do you if you want to make it to the meeting on time." Kiki paused mid-stride and pivoted back to Bree. Her lips widened in a mischievous smile "Then again, I don't have anything against making Troy wait for a while. What's up?"

"I have a sample to drop off. The police department asked me to facilitate an analysis."

"Does that mean you've been hanging out with Detective Hottie?" She winked at Bree, her eyes dancing with delight. "Something tells me boss-man Tugood should hurry back here if he knows what's good for him. Unless, of course, you don't want him to..."

The suggestive tone heated Bree's cheeks and she cursed the fair skin that let her blush so easily. "For the last time, Kiki, I do not have something going on with either the detective or the boss." At least, nothing she understood, let alone knew how to move forward.

"Are you sure? You sound a little like you're trying to convince yourself, not me." Kiki's laughter shook her shoulders and caused her burgundy and gold spiked hair to shimmer like leaves in the autumn sunshine.

"You're young, Bree. Don't waste your thirties buried in work. Live a little. Take it from a friend who's got at least a decade on you—the career will always be there. A chance to find that special someone might not."

A smile tugged at Bree's lips. Although she wasn't in the market for a relationship, some of Kiki's carefree nature always lifted her spirits and made her reevaluate her life choices. "Point taken. But for now, the only man I need is Nate. Is he in?"

Kiki jerked her head in the direction of a walled off office at the back of the labs. "He's holed up checking ways to improve detection limits on our equipment. The lucky dog doesn't have to sit through Troy's meetings like the rest of us."

"You could get promoted to senior research fellow if you'd give up running the forensics contracts. You'd be out of Troy's reach."

"And leave the rest of you to deal with his ego alone? Not today." She looked at her watch. "Speaking of which, you'd better hustle if you want to chat with Nate before the meeting. Shall I save you a chair?"

Bree agreed and hurried to Nate's office. He looked up when she entered, his gaze sharpening when she closed the door.

"Mornin', Bree. I take it this isn't your average social visit?" His southern drawl, so reminiscent of her grandmother's Chattanooga accent, slid over the words like hot grease on a burger patty.

She shook her head. "Official business." She handed him the bag containing the blood encrusted stone. "The Plainville PD needs a DNA analysis on this. It was found at a crime scene I'm working with them."

"Well…" he drew the word out as he peered at the stone "since we both know the Sci-PHi forensics team isn't equipped for DNA analysis, I take it this is an off-the-books project?"

"Let's just say I convinced Norah to log it as a blood typing sample for the PD, but in reality, I need your special skills."

Nate tugged at the tufts of gray hair covering his head and raised his eyes to her. "Even the spy van isn't equipped with what we need. I'll have to send it out. Any special cover story we need for it? What's your timeline?"

The two chatted about how to handle the issue, knowing that they'd need all of Tugood's spy resources to pull this off. In the end, Nate agreed to start the project and keep her apprised.

"Don't forget, Tugood is out of pocket but Shoe might have some resources." Milt Shoemaker had become a lynchpin of their covert activities. Bree suspected he and Tugood bonded over past military actions that neither of them discussed with the rest of the team.

"Good call. Now hustle to your staff meeting before Troy blows a gasket." Nate turned to the sample, then his computer, too deep into his assigned task to make small talk with Bree.

Satisfied, she hurried down to the conference room using her acting skills to look sufficiently embarrassed at being late. As grating as it was to be deferential to Troy, doing so wrapped him in a cocoon of superiority and kept him unaware of the spy business for which the staffing company was a front.

She stepped into the meeting room, but her words of apology froze on her lips. Troy cowered in the back of the room, fighting several of her colleagues for space against the wall.

"What the hell is this," he yelled when she entered, his voice almost an octave higher than normal. "Get it out of here."

Miss Peepers perched on the edge of the conference table, eyeing Troy as warily as he eyed her. Ning stood nearby, holding a leash attached to a harness on the monkey's hips. Milt Shoemaker—aka "Shoe"—calmly offered the capuchin wasabi peas which she gobbled as fast as he could hand them to her.

Norah slipped into the room and brushed past Bree, a mug of water in her hands. "Here you go, baby," she cooed holding the mug out to Miss P. The monkey ignored the drink and reached instead for a chain dangling from Norah's waist.

Bree choked back a snort when she looked at Norah. Today, her standard black and purple tee shirt was topped with a steampunk inspired bustier, complete with dangling keys, goggles, and gears. She brushed the chain out of Miss P's reach with a lace gloved hand and placed the mug firmly in the monkey's grasp.

"This breaks every rule we have in the company," Troy sputtered, his eyes never leaving the monkey's face. "I'll write you up for this one, Bree, see if I don't."

"There's no rule against a monkey on site," Norah shot back, drawing Troy's fire. "I checked."

"Pets are forbidden..."

"Service animals are allowed..."

A din of voices washed over her. Bree ignored the squabbling and pinched her lips tightly against the temptation to join Kiki and Shoe in laughing out loud over the situation.

Instead, she addressed Ning in a low voice. "I thought I told you to wait in the car."

"Yes," Ning acknowledged. "Miss Norah invited us inside. Where it is warm."

"Of course she did." Norah went out of her way to annoy Troy and Bree had given her an ideal method by bringing Ning and Miss Peepers onto the corporate campus. Curse Ning's need for subtropical heat even on a beautiful autumn day. The girl probably wouldn't have left the car otherwise.

"Ride?" Bree asked Miss Peepers while holding out the backpack. Treats forgotten, the capuchin loped across the conference table and snuggled into her carrier. Bree helped Ning hoist the carrier, monkey included, onto her back, determined to rectify the situation as soon as possible.

"I'll take care of this," she began, addressing Troy.

"Yes. Get it out of here." He turned to look at the researchers crowded in the room. "You can all leave, too. Staff meeting is canceled." Giving Bree, Ning, Miss Peepers, and the rest of them a wide berth, Troy eased out of the room and fled to the safety of his office.

Bree followed, herding her charges back to her car, hoping the look of panic on Troy's face was worth whatever repercussions he dreamed up for her.

CHAPTER 14

L   ater that morning, Bree trudged to her university office
    and dropped an armload of homework papers on her desk,
pleasantly surprised that her Concepts in Chemistry students had
completed her recipe challenge.

After a quick trip to the ladies' room and a stop by the vending machines, she settled down to grade the papers and wait for
any students who chose to come to office hours.

Ten minutes into the chore, the words blurred in front of her
eyes. As she reached for her can of Diet Coke, her phone vibrated
in her rear pocket, startling her like a prod from a frayed electric
cord. She jumped, scattering the stack of homework pages across
the floor.

The words *Your Boyfriend* flashed across the screen. *Damn.
Why didn't I change that back after the last mission?* The cover
story had been thin at the time and was nonexistent now. Matthew
was her boss, nothing more. Despite what she'd once hoped. She
took a breath to calm her thumping heart then answered the call.
"Hello, Matthew."

"Bree." His voice sounded more tired than she'd ever heard.
"Don't. Bait. Troy."

All sympathy fled at his brusque words. "I don't know what
you mean."

His sigh reverberated over the connection. "It's nearly midnight here. For the last hour and a half, I've listened to Troy rant

about wild animals, unauthorized visitors, insubordination, and every other crime you can imagine. All of which he lays at your feet."

That was fast. She conjured the image of Troy's face after the morning meeting, but it wouldn't come into focus.

"He threatened to report the situation to everyone from the company president to the new owners if I didn't get you under control," Matthew continued.

"You *are* the new owner."

"The secret owner," he stressed. "The secret owner who needs to keep Troy as department head so we can go about our business. We stroke his ego, and he runs the day-to-day business without asking questions we don't want him knowing the answers to."

"I know that," Bree snapped, tired of Matthew's tone. "I was the one who suggested him—"

"Do you? Because ten minutes ago he was ready to turn in his resignation. Putting us right back at square one in terms of finding a department head we can manipulate."

"Look, what happened today was an accident. I'm sorry. I didn't deliberately try to antagonize Troy. This time."

The silence on the other end of the line stretched, until Bree thought she'd lost the connection. A breathy sigh indicated she hadn't. "I know Troy can be an ass. I understand the temptation to needle him. But I have to be able to count on you to pull it back in control before he reaches the breaking point."

The exhaustion in his voice drained the last bits of anger from her. "For what it's worth, I did tell Ning to stay in the car with the capuchin."

"Capuchin? Troy made it sound like King Kong was rampaging through the building. I honestly couldn't make heads or tails of it."

"I'll make it right with him. Maybe I should write an official letter of reprimand for myself and send it out on company letterhead. From the owner."

His chuckle lightened the mood. "Not a bad idea, Watson. Give yourself a two-week suspension while you're at it."

"That's a harsh punishment, boss."

"No, it's giving you time away from Troy while you handle your university work and solve a murder. Harsh is what I'll do if Troy quits because of you."

"What—" Bree took a swift gulp of Diet Coke to ease the dryness in her throat, "—what do you mean?"

"If we lose Troy, I'll promote Kiki to department head and you'll face your worst nightmare. Lying to your best friend."

Matthew's threat reverberated in Bree's mind long after she'd helped two students struggling with her Concepts in Chemistry class. Even long after she'd proctored the Advanced Chemistry laboratory class. And still later, after she'd had her dinner and settled at the kitchen table, Sherlock at her feet, laptop open.

The absolute worst part of the spy business was keeping secrets from family and friends. The thought of hiding even more from Kiki than she did now caused an uncomfortable tightness in her chest. One that lodged next to the lump of guilt she'd carried since seeing Troy's stricken face that morning.

Her earlier petty laughter stabbed at her conscience. She'd gained enough skill in reading people to know Troy hadn't been annoyed. He'd been afraid.

Bree unleashed the anger she felt at herself in the reprimand letter from the fictional Charles Angelo, company owner. Even the reference to the Charlie's Angels franchise of spy movies didn't cheer her as she hurried through the letter and sent it off to placate Troy.

Next task: dislodge Sherlock from where he lay snoozing in the middle of the yet-to-be-graded homework papers. "Come on, baby, time to move." She hefted his body to his feet and he scrambled for purchase on the papers, sending them flying before plopping back down.

"Seriously, cat. Move." She lifted him to his feet again. No luck.

Finally, she opened a bag of treats and dropped crunchy tartar-removing salmon bites into his bowl. Sherlock moved.

Bree hustled to gather the papers, lifting the sloppy heap to the table. As she bent to retrieve the last few, Sherlock raced to the pile and pounced. His sharp teeth clamped around a plastic bag amidst the pages.

Bree grabbed for a corner of the two-inch square of plastic, wrestling it from Sherlock's grasp. He jumped back with a hiss, his fur standing on end, making him look like forty pounds of angry kitty. He sneezed then raced from the room.

Reddish-brown powder spilled from the torn pouch onto her hand, filling the air with a bitter-tasting residue. She stashed the mangled plastic and powder in a larger zipper style bag then washed her hands and rinsed her mouth.

Behind her, Sherlock continued his rampage of the condo, jumping from couch to table to counter and back again with more energy than he'd ever displayed.

Bree turned the sealed bag in her hand. Smudged printing beneath a black pawprint logo identified it as Tiger Powder.

She looked closer. Tiny punctures near the top of the original bag made Bree suspect it had been stapled to one of the homework papers. But which one?

Bree turned back to Sherlock, who had moved from the living room back to his dinner bowl. She reached to pat him and received a swipe and a snarl. Whatever he'd gotten into from that pouch affected him.

She filled his water bowl and watched for the next hour as he went from mania to his normal, sleepy self, only deciding against calling the vet in the late hours of the night when he slept deeply but peacefully.

Someone had taken great pains to get the Tiger Powder to her. Now she needed to figure out why, who, and what, if anything, it had to do with Quinten Christianson's murder.

In the morning, when Bree woke to find Sherlock his normal, cranky self, she heaved a sigh of relief. With no scheduled classes to teach and a self-imposed exile from the corporate offices, she lazed around in her pajamas enjoying her morning coffee while grading the extra credit papers from yesterday.

While many of the students had thrown themselves into the task of doing kitchen chemistry, one set of papers stood out. Primarily because while all had minor differences in the cooking techniques and the observations, they all looked exactly the same.

She lined the nine papers up next to one another. The font, paragraph style, and line spacing looked as if a single master sheet had been copied and shared among the nine students. Individual lines had been scratched out with handwritten changes penned onto the sheets to make them appear different.

Bree plucked two of the samples from the lineup and looked closely at the handwritten changes. Identical looping letters, sloping to the left of the page stared back at her. She looked at the names on the papers.

Tanner White.

Josh Gibbons.

Damn. She scanned the names atop the rest of the papers, imagining her classroom layout and putting the names with the faces of the cluster of student athletes in her class.

Yesterday, after class, Josh had run down the steps, hands full of homework papers. He'd looked distracted, hustling away as quickly as possible, muttering under his breath about being late for practice. None of the other team members had waited for him.

Bree gathered the nine offending homework samples, shaking her head in dismay. Josh had seemed to be a promising student. Curious. Bright. Staying to ask questions about—

About pharmacology. Or in his words "drugs and stuff."

She rifled through the pages again, this time searching the upper corners of each page. All, except one of the homework sets contained a single staple in the upper left corner.

Josh's paper contained two staples. Flipping it over, she spied a sliver of plastic clinging between the metal clamp and the paper.

Now she knew who.

Time to find out what. And make a hypothesis about why.

Her first stop after leaving the house was *The Barkery*. The aroma of vanilla and cinnamon coffee scented the air. Muffled barking mingled with the jingle of the bell over the door as Krupke and Mrs. Krupke raced to greet her, Rookie loping along behind.

"Good morning, my friends," she said, dropping to her knees to pet the wiggling trio. She rubbed ears and accepted kisses, then pulled the tiger powder from her bag. Rookie immediately dropped into a sitting position, alerting to the scent of narcotics.

"Good boy, Rookie," she murmured, rubbing his head and praising him before giving him the command to release his alert. She dropped the sample back in her bag just as Horace came through the door in the back of the shop.

"What's all the commotion out here?" His grin split his weathered face, its curves mingling with the sunbaked wrinkles making his whole face smile. "Them dogs is actin' like they ain't seen you in a month o' Sundays. Shake 'em loose and come on back for some fresh coffee. Wendy just pulled scones out of the oven. Apple. My favorite."

"They're all his favorites," Wendy called from the back room, her voice laced with laughter.

Bree gave the dogs one last pat and followed Horace, the lure of fresh coffee and scones too tempting to ignore.

"How's our little Miss Peepers doing?" Wendy asked as she handed Bree a cup of coffee. She gestured to the cream, sugar and, more importantly, plate of scones.

"Ning took her to the clinic yesterday. I imagine we'll get her bill of health sometime this week. Meanwhile, Ning and Miss Peepers seem inseparable."

"It does my heart good to know. The poor thing was so distraught over losing Uncle Edward. We were lucky to be able to rescue her."

Bree sipped the hot coffee. "I'm surprised he didn't make provisions in his will for her. Lots of people remember to take care of their pets."

"Don't get me started on his will." Wendy grabbed her mug and headed back to the coffee pot. "I never saw a more snarled mess. He went to—and I quote—a 'boutique' law firm. *Specializing in caring for all of your unique needs*, according to their letterhead."

"They weren't even in business by the time the old man died. Had been closed down for bankruptcy or some such," Horace added.

"I heard it was malpractice. But the will still stood. Uncle Edwards's assets—what little there were—were funneled into a charity no one had ever heard of. And Miss Peepers was set to be auctioned off. Horace, bless him," Wendy placed a kiss on his cheek, "offered the executor a hundred bucks for her and we skedaddled out of there."

"And good riddance to the Fine and Fancy law firm."

"It was Fancy Finance and Estate," Wendy corrected.

"Fancy Finance. The name should have made Uncle Edward think twice."

Wendy rolled her eyes. "He didn't give a fig about the name. He just said the pretty, young attorney made him feel special."

Horace snaked his arm around Wendy's waist and gave her a squeeze. "You make me feel special. Together, there's nothing we can't handle."

Bree gave the lovebirds an indulgent smile, then finished her coffee and returned home to pick up pans of coconut cupcakes she'd whipped up with the leftover ingredients from Ning's Thai dinner feast.

Second stop, the police station. James wasn't in, but she left some cupcakes with a note for him.

Third stop, animal control. She hurried past the SWAP protesters, not making eye contact. The sounds of their chanting "free the tiger" faded to a dull murmur once she entered the building.

Inside the animal detention area, she chatted with Ted, learned that Lucky would be released into the custody of the Terrance University vet school within the next twenty-four to forty-eight hours, and dropped off more cupcakes.

By late morning, she entered the Sci-PHi corporate headquarters through the underground parking lot and made her way to the owner's suite via the private executive-only elevator, assured that no one noticed her.

"Hey, Grant." He looked up from his keyboard at the sound of her voice, blinking as if waking from sleep. "I brought cupcakes."

"Your cupcakes are wreaking havoc on my training," he grumbled as he grabbed one and crammed half of it in his mouth. "But so worth every extra sit-up and mile I have to run to make up for them."

The compliment was all the more powerful for the grudging way in which it was given. "Thanks, Grant. Listen, I need your help with a special project I'm working on with Matthew."

Excitement lit his eyes. "So, I finally get to do something other than keeping the corporate office supplies safe?"

"It may not be much more exciting." Bree pulled a flash drive containing the video she'd taken at *The Underground* from her pocket. "I have a series of video files that need cleaned up. Specifically, I need to isolate the audio portions of it. The area was noisy, and I don't want to miss any of the conversations."

"So, it's for a video blog?"

"Something like that." Bree pulled up a chair and decided to let Grant in on some confidential information. "While I was working under contract with a local university, a senior staff member was murdered. I'm investigating."

"Duuudeette." Grant took the drive from her. "That's intense. How'd you get involved?"

"Wrong place, wrong time," she said.

"And Goodie's okay with you looking into a murder? Is that part of his gig?"

Bree shook her head with a slight smile. "All you need to know for now is that I need to have every bit of information you can get extracted from those files."

He looked as if he had further questions, but he shrugged them off with a lift of his shoulder. "On it, boss."

Five minutes later, Bree left Grant clicking away on his keyboard and slipped into a back section of the Tech Ops center, deep in the shadows of a bookcase. At the push of a hidden button, a panel in the wall slid open. She hurried into a second, hidden elevator, which connected directly to Matthew Tugood's office on the second floor of the complex.

More bunker than traditional office, this was her typical means of entering the Tech Ops center. Under the guise of reporting to her boss in his office, she had freedom to come and go as she pleased.

Today, she sat at Matthew's desk and called Nate, asking him to join her there. A brisk knock announced his presence before he opened the door to the office.

"What brings you here today? I heard from Kiki that you were on some kind of probation for bringing a monkey into the office yesterday."

"Hence the reason I asked you here, rather than coming to your lab."

Nate settled in a chair in front of Matthew's desk. "I suspect this is just your way of playing possum," he said in a thicker-than-normal southern drawl. "Seems to me like you mebbe don't want to face Troy for a couple of days."

"Actually, it's worse than that. He was ready to quit after yesterday. Matthew threatened to put Kiki in as department head if Troy bolted. So, we came up with the reprimand from Charles Angelo as a way of calming him down."

"That boy let his promotion go to his head." Nate shook his own head sadly. "He wasn't ready and he's floundering. You and Matthew might-could have done a better job of finding a department head than Troy."

"Maybe. But it's done. And I need to lie low for a while. But I also need some help with the Christianson murder case." Nate's bushy gray eyebrows raised, but he said nothing. "Someone left this sample of 'tiger powder' for me to find. Our favorite drug dog already confirmed my suspicions, but I need you to find out more about it."

Nate sniffed the sample, then tasted a tiny bit of it.

"Careful, Sherlock got into it and ran crazy for a couple hours. I suspect it's a powerful stimulant."

"The cat okay now?" Concern shadowed his eyes. Nate had a soft spot for both animals and humans in trouble.

"He's fine. For now, I just need to know about the powder."

"And the DNA sample you left for me yesterday. Looks like I'll be burning my midnight oil at the RV."

Bree smiled at the reference to the mobile lab the Sci-Spy team used for their work. Nate had outfitted it with state-of-the-art analytical equipment, all camouflaged as high-end cabinets in the RV they used for covert work. "You love every minute you spend in that lab. Don't try to tell me otherwise."

"It's a mite more sophisticated than anything we have in this old place," he said with a smile that lit the room. "I can do just about anything in that RV."

"Except DNA analysis," Bree interjected.

"Except that." Nate grinned at her. "In any case, what I do in the van is a whole lot more interesting than anything I do around here." He shoved the sample into the pocket of his lab coat.

"Any other news on the Pacific front? Or is Matthew still kicking his heels up with that former partner of his?"

Bree gritted her teeth and turned away from Nate. She booted up her computer, intent on delving into the shipping angle on her research on Zed. "You know Tugood," she said tossing the words over her shoulder as she focused on the screen. "Need to know only. And we don't."

CHAPTER 15

The next afternoon as Bree watched over a series of experiments her advanced lab students were performing, Coach Fleek barged into the lab, banging open the door.

"Hey, little lady," he said, his voice reverberating off the high ceilings and stone lab benches of the room, "I was hoping we could have a chance to talk."

Chatter in the room, always subdued, dropped to a fraction of a decibel. "It's Dr. Mayfield-Watson." Bree said as she reached into her lab coat pocket and drew out a spare pair of safety glasses. She handed them to Coach. "While you're in my lab, you'll need to wear safety glasses."

Coach waved them away with a wide grin. "No need. It'll only take a minute." He stepped closer and Bree widened her stance, planting one foot forward into his path, effectively stopping his encroachment.

"I wouldn't let you in the lab without glasses any more than you'd let a student on the field without an athletic protector. Safety first, for both of us." She held the glasses out again, pretending not to notice she poked him in the chest with them.

They stood eye-to-eye for a tense minute, then Coach gave her a curt nod. "I'll just wait outside and walk you to your office after class."

He turned on his heel and trudged out the door, shoulders tensing when a smattering of students in Bree's class broke into applause.

"Ladies and gentlemen," she said loudly to regain control of the room, "you have fifteen minutes to finish your experiment and put your lab supplies away. I suggest you focus on your work."

The students finished their projects, but as they filed out of the room after class, Bree received nods of approval, covert thumbs-up signs, and one murmured "thank you."

Coach, on the other hand, paced the hallway, cracking his knuckles, looking as annoyed as a caged cat. "I've got a free hour if you still want to chat," she said.

"Thanks. Dr. Mayfield-Watson."

Bree ignored the grudging tone and lightened her own to diffuse the tension. "It's Bree, when we're not in front of students. I'm sure you understand how important it is to maintain a sense of order in a classroom—or on the field."

Coach swiveled his head and gave her a long, silent look, not breaking his stride. Finally, he nodded. "Understood." A few steps later he spoke again. "I like you. You've got spunk. And good sense."

A memory of his confrontation with Heather at the staff meeting flashed through her mind. Heather had challenged Coach—but had earned his ire rather than his admiration. Spunk without good sense?

They arrived at her office and entered. "What did you want to see me about?"

Coach dropped into a chair, the wooden frame creaking at the sudden force of his bulk. He spread his legs and leaned forward. "Our first main season game is scheduled for Friday. We've promised the fans a tiger. We don't have a tiger."

Coach looked at her expectantly, the cracking of his knuckles the only sound in the silence. Bree watched his hands, mesmerized by the restless pulling and cracking. Goose bumps raised on her arms when she noticed his diamond encrusted ring was missing from his right hand.

"What are you going to do about it?"

Bree jumped at the harsh words, her breath freezing in her lungs. "Do?" *About his missing ring? Or about the loose diamond found at the scene of the crime?*

"Yeah. You brought the girl with the tiger to Terrance U. I'm counting on you to get it back."

The tiger. Bree exhaled and drew in a fresh, easier breath. "As it happens, I checked with animal control about the cub yesterday. Lucky should be released into the care of the vet school today or tomorrow."

"So, he can appear at the game Friday night?"

"You'll need to speak to Dr. Warthan, but I'm sure she'll clear the cub to attend the game."

"Fine." Coach rose. "Thank you for your time."

"If you have another minute, there is a matter I need to discuss with you." Bree waited until Coach turned back to her before continuing. "There have been reports that some of your players harassed the cub and her trainer. The animal and the girl both need to be treated with respect."

Coach shrugged. "Boys will be boys. What do you want me to do about it?"

"I expect you to teach them respect. And restraint. Good citizenship, as well as good sports training." Bree rose as she spoke and leaned forward, dominating as much space as her smaller body could.

Again, tension crackled in the air between them.

"I'll have a talk with my team," Coach said, ending the standoff. "In return, I *expect* you to make sure my boys get passing grades in your class. Capeesh?"

Without another word, he turned his back on her and strode out the door.

Dealing with Coach left Bree exhausted and frustrated enough to reach for the emergency stash of Thin Mints she kept in her desk drawer. Thank heavens her extended clan of cousins had several members in the Girl Scouts.

As she munched on a cookie and sipped a cup of tea, Bree pulled her crime notebook out and turned to the page of suspects, making notes next to the names of those who could have potentially lost a diamond in Quint's office.

Coach, Miriam, and Heather topped the list. Each had conflict with Quint. Coach, she knew, had been in Quint's office. Of course, he could have lost a diamond from his faux Super Bowl ring before Quint was murdered.

The ladies, on the other hand, had both sported their diamond earrings well after the time of the murder. But that didn't, in Bree's mind, put them in the clear. Every costume jewelry store on the planet sold tiny "diamond" studs like the kind Miriam and Heather wore. Without analyzing the earrings, Bree couldn't verify whether they were real or fake.

Which brought her to the topic of DNA. Would DNA be present on a diamond from a ring or earring? Unfortunately, even a rush test took time.

Frustrated, she reached for another cookie. Common sense stopped her just in time and she sealed the bag she stored them in and stashed the goodies away. Instead she focused on a concrete task she could accomplish. She dialed the vet school.

"Dr. Warthan?" she asked when a woman answered, "it's Bree Mayfield-Watson in the chemistry department."

"Oh, Dr. Mayfield-Watson. Pleasure to talk to you. How about we dispense with the formal titles? What can I do to help you, Bree?"

The warmth in the woman's voice put Bree at ease. "I called to see if you'd heard from animal control and if our cub had arrived yet. I'm sure Ning will want to be reunited with her as soon as possible."

"I've no doubt she will. Listen, if your class schedule permits, why not pop over to the vet school and we can go to the commissary for a break? I'll fill you in on everything that's happened this week. It's a lot and I deserve a slice of French Silk pie for surviving as well as I have." Laughter followed.

"Sounds like a plan." They set a time and Bree cut off the call. She'd only communicated with Dr. Warthan sporadically, and always with a crowd of people around. Like at the staff meeting. She looked forward to getting to know another scientist on the university staff.

Too bad this wasn't only a social meeting. Bree closed her eyes, thinking about what she wanted to learn from Melody Warthan. Planning for how she'd divulge—and receive—information. And wondering if Melody belonged to the diamond stud club.

On her way across campus to the vet school, Bree stopped by the administration office to request an updated class schedule. "I've misplaced mine," she said with a smile.

"I can print a copy of your schedule," the student worker at the desk replied. "Easy."

"If you don't mind, I'd like to have a copy of the master schedule. Several of my students claim to have conflicts with other classes. I need to verify if that's correct."

The student frowned and glanced at the clock. "The master schedule would be hundreds of pages. I can't do that. My shift ends in fifteen minutes."

So much for getting everyone's schedule. "Most of the conflicts appear to be with the English and the International Studies departments." She limited her request to Heather and Miriam's class schedules, and the student complied. Bree stuffed the schedules into her bag and left the office.

Instead of heading to her car, Bree decided on a brisk walk to the vet school. While it might not negate all the calories from the Thin Mints, it would be a buffer against them—and against the possibility of French Silk pie.

She walked, her pace increasing until her breath came in deep, regular, lung-filling puffs. Her mind calmed even as her blood pulsed with the exertion. Bree tugged at the sagging waistband of her pants, realizing that since she'd given in to Tugood's suggestion she run—or briskly walk—more, her clothes had gotten looser.

Not a bad trade off—a clear mind and trimmer body—without feeling like she was on display at the gym. Of course, she didn't intend to stroke Tugood's ego by telling him.

Fifteen minutes later, she arrived at the vet school commissary in need of a cool drink. She declined the mile-high chocolate cream pie that Melody selected in favor of a commissary fall special—apple nachos, a concoction of crisp slivers of Granny Smith apples drizzled with caramel and white chocolate topped with crushed walnuts and pretzel bits.

As Melody slid into a seat across from Bree, she scanned the woman's hands and ears. Only a slim gold band decorated her hands. Her ears, neck, and wrists were free of jewelry. Although with the exotic tilt to her dark eyes and the creamy, warm skin tones that only came from blending of multiple ethnicities, Melody Warthan didn't need jewelry to accent her natural beauty.

Melody reached up and released a hair clasp, sending waves of silky black hair cascading over her shoulders. She rubbed the back of her head with long, slender fingers, sighing in contentment. "Ah, much better." She smiled at Bree. "It feels good to let my hair down."

"Literally, that is," Bree added as she scooped up a gooey apple slice.

"Literally and figuratively. You have no idea how nice it is to have another scientific-minded female on staff to chat with." She picked up her fork and sliced off a tiny bite of chocolate pie. "Don't get me wrong, I love the vet school, but the number of female doctors, professors, and even vet students at Terrance U. is well below the median for most schools of our size."

Median. Bree munched her apple thoughtfully. Few people in her life knew the term and she immediately appreciated Melody's comment.

"So more than half of the vet schools in the country have more female staff and students?"

"Actually, seventy-five percent of the vet schools in the country have a greater number of female students and staff than Terrance U. I'd been raising the issue with Dr. Christianson before he died," Melody said, licking a bit of chocolate off her lips, "but any headway I might have made died with him. I'll have to start over with Max Edleston."

Bree took the opening. "Had you made much progress?"

"No. As much as Dr. Christianson talked a good game, when it came to gender and ethnic diversity, he didn't always follow through." A shudder went through her slender frame.

"Did he ..." Bree hesitated, then plunged forward at Melody's questioning look. "Did he ever make inappropriate advances toward you?"

"He tried once, early in our association. But after my husband picked me up at his office, I think Dr. Christianson decided there was easier prey to be had." Melody smiled. "Let's just say my husband is big. Really big. I wasn't about to tell Christianson that Marcus is a softie. It served my purposes to let him think Marcus was prone to jealous rages."

Interesting. So, Melody was no stranger to pretending to get what she wanted. Bree filed the impression away to examine later. "Have you heard of the diamond stud club?"

Melody froze, fork midway between her plate and her mouth. She lowered the bite of pie and nodded. "It wasn't a coincidence that I arranged for Marcus to pick me up that day at Christianson's office. I'd been warned by some established teachers to take care around the VP. Why do you ask?" Her brow crinkled in concern. "Did Christianson try something untoward with you?"

"No." Bree shook off the memory of how Quint seemed to prefer talking to her chest than her face. "I work in a male dominated field. I learned early on how to avoid that kind of behavior."

Melody smiled and took a sip of tea. "I knew you were a kindred spirit. Trust me, they're harder to find than a brown-skinned professional at Terrance University."

"Speaking of hard to find, you said the animal control returned Lucky to the school."

"Earlier today. The officer, or whatever he was, nearly teared up when he released the cub to me. I ended up telling him he was welcome to visit her anytime."

"That must have been Ted." Bree laughed and shared the story of how she'd won Ted over. "I have a feeling he'll take you up on the offer."

"As soon as he left, and I assured myself Lucky was in good health, I notified Ning." Her smile turned misty. "The reunion of those two was a sight I never thought I'd see. I love animals and it was always a given that I'd go on to be a vet. But never, in my wildest dreams, did I think I'd be doing research on rare animals.

"And I couldn't begin to imagine the depth of the human-animal bond I'd see between species that weren't traditionally seen as pets. It's made me rethink some of my preconceptions, I can tell you that."

"What do you mean?"

Melody licked the final crumbs off her fork and pushed the pie plate away. "For starters, I was always taught that it is cruel to remove an animal from its natural habitat. But in Lucky's case, she couldn't survive in the wild. And while she'll never be a traditional pet, the way she's bonded with Ning is simply incredible."

The vet shrugged. "I'd attribute it to the fact she was orphaned and adopted by Ning and the other trainers, except that Miss Peepers seems to have bonded just as strongly with the girl. And I know they just met recently."

"Ning definitely has a special touch with animals. She even wanted to give my cranky cat a bath. Sherlock," she said as she pulled out her phone and paged through her photos, "isn't the most trusting of cats. Yet here he is minutes after meeting Ning." She passed the photo of a limp, content Sherlock draped over the girl's shoulder. Bree shook her head and returned Melody's shrug. "Go figure."

They chatted a bit further with Melody asking about Sherlock's current vet and how Sherlock and Bree ended up together. Bree finished her iced tea and apple nachos then wiped her fingers.

"Before we go to see Lucky," Melody said, "there are some irregularities with Miss Peepers that I need to discuss with you."

"Is she ill?"

"No, she's perfectly healthy, but she is also highly unusual. As I indicated before, I'm not a fan of people keeping wild animals as pets. In the case of the capuchin, I suspect she wasn't obtained under legal circumstances."

Bree stared at the doctor, wondering just how much trouble Horace and Wendy Clark could be in regarding the monkey. Deciding it was best that the vet know the whole story, she told Dr. Warthan what she knew.

"I suspected something like that." She reached out and covered Bree's hand, her voice low as she continued. "I can help. I know ways around the legal restrictions. I normally wouldn't do it, but, again, Miss Peepers is highly unusual."

"Thank you."

Melody Warthan leaned back in her chair with a smile. "My pleasure. Do you know that it's nearly impossible to toilet train a monkey of any kind? It's just not in their nature."

"I hadn't known. But it doesn't surprise me." She thought back to the day she and Ning took Miss Peepers to the vet school. "I guess I thought monkeys wore diapers. But I don't remember seeing them on Miss Peepers."

"That's because you didn't. I tried to put a diaper on her and she ran from me with Ning in pursuit. She stopped dead in her tracks when she saw one of the vet techs coming out of a staff bathroom. Next thing I know, Miss Peepers was perched on the toilet relieving herself." Melody shook her head. "Darndest thing I ever saw."

"If you knew my friends at *The Barkery,* you'd be less surprised. They have a way with animals. I guess Wendy's great -uncle Edward did too."

"It takes hours of patience and persistence to train any animal, and it's easy to see the ones who were trained by harsh methods. Bottom line? Like Lucky, Miss Peepers would be far less healthy and happy without human interaction than she would be with it." Melody rose. "Come on. Let me show you."

CHAPTER 16

B ree followed Melody past boarding areas filled with every breed of cat and dog she'd ever heard of—plus good old-fashioned, mixed-breed pets. "This wing is dedicated to our small, domestic animal studies. In other words," Melody said flashing a smile, "pets."

"Good afternoon, Dr. Warthan." A passing vet student greeted her politely. Melody nodded in return.

"That's one of our new interns," Melody explained. "He specialized in large animals, mostly horses, although he's birthed a calf or two in his day. Most of the domesticated large animal studies take place in the complex next door. That simply leaves our exotic animal rooms."

The maze of hallways started to look more familiar to Bree. "I know about your research with Lucky and the tiger genetics. When I first got involved with Lucky's transfer, I was told you had a thriving exotic animal research program. Given what I've learned recently about Dr. Christianson, I'm surprised he championed your work with exotic animals. The studies were your initiatives, weren't they?"

Melody twisted her hair and secured it with the clip, her brisk movements those of a detached professional. Her tone was clipped when she replied. "Frankly, I doubt anything would have come of my push for exotic animal research if it hadn't been for the athletic department. Much as I hate dealing with people like

Coach Fleek and his ilk, it was the coach and the athletic booster club that convinced Dr. Christianson and the university trustees to invest in Lucky."

They turned a corner and Bree saw the door to the holding area where she'd met with Ning and Lucky before. "Now I know where I am."

"Yes. The times you visited Ning before, you came through the back entrance, not through the school itself. Let's see how our two exotic babies are doing."

"Two?" The question had barely left Bree's lips when she neared Lucky's enclosure and understood. Ning curled on her cot, reading a book, Lucky next to her. And combing through Lucky's fur, like a miniature hair stylist, was Miss Peepers. The capuchin lifted her fingers to her mouth, sucked briefly on them and, with a wrinkled brow, returned to grooming the tiger. Just as she'd done with Sherlock days before.

"Looks like she's disappointed that Lucky doesn't have fleas."

"*Khun*, Dr. Bree." Ning looked up at the sound of Bree's voice, her face alight with happiness. "Lucky and Miss Peepers like each other."

"I can see that." Bree smiled at the sight, noticing the girl didn't budge, lest she disturb the sleepy cub.

Dr. Warthan, however, didn't mind disturbing the trio. She opened the door and moved to the cub's side, stroking her fur and gently working her way toward the paws.

Miss Peepers screeched and loped across the area, stopping to swing on the bars at the front and door of the cage. Then she raced to the back corner where Bree spied a child's potty-training setup. To her amazement, the capuchin climbed onto the seat and did her business.

"Goodness," Bree said, turning to Melody, "Miss Peepers seems almost human, although with fewer privacy issues."

"You have no idea," Melody replied. She stood. "From the looks of it, Lucky is ready to go to her first football game on Friday. Ning, do you understand what is involved?"

Ning nodded. "I take Lucky in her cage," Ning made a face "and Mr. Coach gets money for people looking at her."

Dr. Warthan chuckled. "Exactly right. Except all you need to do is stay with Lucky on the sidelines of the game. Your job is to keep her calm and happy despite the noise of the game. At halftime, her cage will be rolled out onto the field so people can see her. For the second half of the game, she'll go with you to the private boxes."

Ning shook her head. "Lucky hate the cage. A box is worse. I not let her go into a box."

"It's all right," Bree said, hunkering down so she could look Ning in the eye. "A box is a special, private room where people pay a lot of money to watch the football game. It's like a room in a fancy restaurant, except it has a view of the football field."

"Once you are in the box," Dr. Warthan explained, "you'll have a very important job to do."

Ning nodded. "Keep Lucky calm and happy, despite the noise in the box."

"Yes. But you'll also be able to talk to the donors—that is the people in the box—about how important Lucky is to the vet school and how important it is that humans take care of the world so tigers can thrive."

"Oh! Yes. I tell them about Lucky being born and abandoned by her mother and how we took her to the tiger sanctuary in Thailand. And how she came to the pet school."

Dr. Warthan turned to Bree. "Ning is a natural. She'll charm the donors, and if we're lucky, we'll get some more support for the exotic animal clinic. I'll join her to help talk about the program, but she and Lucky will be the stars of the show."

"I'll be there too," Bree promised. Watching out for everyone involved.

By the time Bree left the vet school, shadows were lengthening on the campus. As much as she loved glorious autumn days, she hated to see the daylight hours slip by so quickly. A glance at her phone told her it was nearing six o'clock. She inserted her Bluetooth headset, dialed Nate, then stashed the phone.

"Well, if it isn't Dr. Watson," he said, picking up on the first ring. "I expected a call from you soon."

"Am I that predictable?"

"No. I was fixin' to call you if you didn't call me first. With the money our boss invested in my RV lab, I figure those analyses always take priority. Besides, I can't resist a puzzle."

"So, you know the identity of the Tiger Powder?"

Nate laughed. "I guess I'm the predictable one. I got right on the analysis last night. Turns out to be a mighty interesting compound. Mixture, actually."

"Stop trying to draw it out, Nate. Just tell me what you found." Bree passed under the shadows of a copse of trees, shivering as she lost the heat of the autumn sun.

"Turns out infrared analysis was a bust. I had to fire up the HPLC columns and do good old-fashioned GC-MS. You taught your students about that yet?"

"I teach chemistry to football players. Chromatography of any kind is out of their league, let alone high-pressure liquid chromatography and gas chromatography-mass spec. For that matter, it's been a decade since I studied either of those in depth."

Nate snorted into the phone. "Kids these days," he grumbled. "Guess I'll have to stick around a while longer and put off my retirement. Anyway, back to your problem. Turns out that powder was a mix of what looks to be cocaine and anabolic steroid derivatives. Both mixed with lime to dissolve in water."

"So, you think it's a performance enhancing drug?"

"That'd be my guess. Couple of other interesting compounds were in there too. Sugar. And some kind of what I think is cherry flavor. Leastwise, I'm not sure since my molecular library doesn't contain too many food substances."

Bree sucked in a breath. "Wow. That gives a whole new meaning to drinking the Kool-Aid. Looks like I'll be watching for more than just the tiger's welfare at Friday's football game."

Ahead, the administration building loomed. A group of people descended the stairs. Bree squinted, making out the tall silhouettes of Max Edelston and Fiona Fancier along with the more diminutive shape of Heather Beauchamp. "Listen, Nate, something's come up. I need to get off the line."

"One last thing before you go. I checked into DNA testing. It's unlikely we'll be able to pull anything from the gemstone you gave me. I just wanted to let you know."

"Thanks." Bree cut the call off and pulled the earpiece out, stashing it in her pocket as she arrived at the admin building. She caught up with the group at the foot of the stairs.

"Hey, Bree." Heather was the first to greet her. "Isn't it great? Max and Fiona just agreed to host a faculty training seminar on sexual harassment. Clear your calendar."

Privately Bree dreaded yet another mandatory training, however necessary. "That's wonderful news," she said out loud, pleased to note no sarcasm entered her voice.

Heather turned to Max. "I was thinking we could—"

"If you'll both excuse me," Fiona interrupted, glancing at her gold wristwatch, "I have another appointment."

"I'll walk with you." Bree took advantage of the situation so she could head home herself. She fell into step alongside

Fiona, walking in companionable silence enjoying the view of the sun low in the sky. "You must be swamped. I can't imagine preparing for a harassment training is much fun."

"It's standard stuff I've done dozens of times." Fiona's heels clicked on the pavement and Bree wondered if her conversational attempt would die. "The thing is Professor Beauchamp doesn't seem to understand the law cuts both ways on this type of thing."

"What do you mean?"

"Simple." Fiona stopped in her tracks and turned to Bree. "Most people assume men harass women in the workplace. And while that's often true, the reverse also happens." Her lips quirked in a semblance of a smile. "I've reprimanded women more than once regarding harassment."

An image of Fiona slapping forms in front of both Coach and Heather at the staff meeting flashed through Bree's mind. Had that been a prelude to an official harassment reprimand? And if so, was it an isolated incident? Or part of a pattern?

"I hadn't thought of it that way," Bree said as they resumed walking.

Fiona was silent until they reached the cracked asphalt of the parking lot. "How is Ning doing?" she asked suddenly. "I'm worried about her."

Bree filled her in on Ning, leaving out her talk with James as well as the adventure at *The Barkery* and Miss Peepers. She finished by saying how happy Ning was to see Lucky again.

"They didn't put that animal down?" Fiona's eyebrows rose to her hairline and her lips pursed in thought. "I'm surprised. That puts a new spin on things."

Bree slowed to a stop as they reached Fiona's car. "Why?"

"Nothing I can talk about. It's an attorney-client thing." She looked at her watch again. "Speaking of which, I promised Pamela Christenson I'd stop by this evening. We need to discuss Quint's estate disbursement. Max can't move into the vice president's office until it's settled. And Pamela wants to plan a memorial service for Quint."

Max may want to move into Quint's office, but until the police cleared the area, no one was gaining access. Which was another topic Bree needed to discuss with James when they next spoke.

She filed the thought away and continued her conversation with Fiona. "Were you handling Dr. Christianson's estate? I thought you were an employment attorney."

Fiona opened her briefcase and fished in it for her car keys. "I'm an employment attorney now," she said, her eyes not meeting Bree's gaze. "And a legal voice for the students. But I came to the university with over a decade of experience in the private sector, handling all aspects of the law. Flexibility is the key to my success."

She clicked the button to unlock her car and stashed the briefcase inside. "Now, if you'll excuse me, I have a client to meet."

CHAPTER 17

By the time Bree made it home, it was nearly six-thirty. She fed Sherlock and scanned the fridge for something for herself, settling on a salad. As she assembled the ingredients, she dialed James and put him on speakerphone.

"O'Neil."

"How was your day?"

"Long. I'm pulling a second shift at the PD tonight. How about you?"

"Just made it home from campus. I had a couple of things I wanted to talk to you about that might be pertinent to the investigation."

"I haven't eaten yet, either. How about coming to the PD and joining me for dinner? I'll order in something. Your choice, my treat."

Bree considered the salad veggies and decided they'd keep for another day. "Deal. Surprise me with what you order."

She cut the call, changed into jeans and a light sweater, then headed to the living room to cuddle with Sherlock for a few minutes before leaving. As expected, he'd gulped his dinner and was curled in his favorite spot on the couch.

Bree switched the TV on, locating a local news channel. Most of the programming focused on the upcoming Terrance University Tigers game. An image of Tanner White—star quarterback for the team—flashed onscreen and Bree sat straighter, earning her a mew of displeasure from Sherlock.

"What do you want our viewers to know about the upcoming game?" An interviewer thrust a microphone in Tanner's face. The quarterback pushed sweaty hair off his forehead. His eyes shifted to the side where other players were jogging off the practice field before turning back to the camera.

"I just wanted them to, you know, know that we, we're all, you know, practicing hard and expect to kill the competition." He pumped a fist in the air with a sudden surge of energy. "TIGER POWER!" he shouted. Others on the team joined in the chant.

As the chorus of "tiger power" grew, the camera zoomed in close, and Bree caught the dilated pupils and unfocused gaze on Tanner's face.

A second later, the camera was blocked by a meaty hand. "No more interviews today," said the voice of Coach Fleek. "My players need their rest."

The station went to a commercial break and Bree, with one last stroke of Sherlock's soft orange coat, headed out to meet James.

At the Plainville police department front desk, Bree flashed her consultant credentials and was buzzed into the main bullpen. James rose from his seat at a desk across the room when he saw her enter.

Bree crossed the nearly deserted room to greet him. After a somewhat awkward one-armed hug, they settled into their respective chairs. "Why the need to pull double duty?" she asked.

"It happens—the difference between a uniform who's paid by the hour and a detective who's on salary is that only one of us gets paid overtime. And it's not me." He rubbed a hand over his face. "On the other hand, I get a peaceful, quiet room to work in and occasionally a friendly face to keep me company."

The desk sergeant popped her head in and waved a huge shopping bag at James. "Order's up, Detective. And for the record, I miss the eggrolls."

James crossed to the door and took the bag. He reached into the bag and tossed her a small sack. "This order of extra garlic knots should cushion your disappointment over losing out on egg rolls."

"Thanks, boss." She took the bag and headed back to the reception area.

James turned to Bree. "Okay if we go to our usual spot?"

"Fine by me." The first time she'd shared dinner with James in the privacy of the interrogation room, icy currents of edgy energy had made the evening uncomfortable. Since then, she'd come to view it as simply a private space—provided James adjusted the lights in the interrogation and viewing rooms, to allow them to see out of the one-way glass and no one to see in.

Tonight, when they arrived, James excused himself to get drinks from the vending machine while Bree unpacked their food. Spicy garlic and cheesy aromas drifted from the bags. Bree opened two piping hot containers of baked ziti smothered in marinara sauce, a bag of garlic knots, and two side salads. Packets of grated cheese topping, salad dressing, and butter completed the feast.

"What do you think? I was in the mood for something hearty and *Mama Marinara's* fit the bill."

"The smell is to die for." Bree's stomach rumbled in appreciation. She grabbed a can of Diet Coke from James and took a seat opposite his chair.

Conversation took a back seat—if random "umm" and lip-smacking noises punctuated by the occasional "that's good" counted as conversation—until they polished off the salads and dug into the entrée.

At last, James sighed and pushed his empty food container aside after wiping every last bit of sauce up with a garlic knot. "The only thing that would have made that meal better would be a glass of wine. And maybe a comfier room. Either way, I feel better."

Bree licked her fork clean and set it down, covering the rest of the entrée so she could finish it later. "Very nice. And a good change from Chong's Chinese, no matter what the desk sergeant says."

James took a swig of Mountain Dew and leaned back in his chair. "Over the phone, you said you had some new information for me. What have you learned?"

"For starters, I've got my labs looking into the gemstone you gave me. We're not sure they can pull DNA off it, but my guess, we'll at least get partial information."

"That's better than what we have. Christianson's blood type was almost as common as dirt. Which is to say O positive. *Only*," he said, making air quotes around the word, "about thirty-eight percent of the population has it."

"Only." Bree snorted. "So, there's almost a two-in-five chance that the killer shares his blood type. Not very helpful. I'm not sure the DNA test will give us much more information. But I did spend some time thinking about everyone I know who had access to Quint and also was known to wear diamonds of the approximate size of the ones you found."

She shared her list with him, focusing on Coach and the Diamond Stud Club members, and mentioning the vet school personnel as well. He took all the information down on a legal pad he'd brought with him into the room.

James rubbed his forehead. "If what you've learned about Quint's harassment is true, there could be many other 'diamond stud club' women, as you call them. We'll need to widen the investigation."

He pulled a pen from his shirt pocket and drew a line through Pamela Christianson's name. "We can cross her off the list. She has an alibi covering the time from the night before the murder till the time she was notified of her husband's death. She, her sister, and a dozen friends booked a weekend at a private spa where they dined on celery sticks and artisanal water while taking salt scrubs and other stuff I didn't understand."

Bree pulled out her own crime notebook and drew a line through the question mark in her "opportunity" column near Pamela's name. Beside it, she made a note detailing Pamela's alibi.

"I also learned tonight that Fiona Fancier is handling Quint's estate. She claims that Max Edelston is pushing her to finish up matters so he can move in to Quint's old office."

"As for the office, the crime scene techs released it earlier this week. The university should have been notified. I'll make sure they were."

"Did you find anything of interest?"

"We found too much. Besides the diamond chip I gave you to analyze, we found fingerprints of just about everyone on staff—including you. And debris on the carpet tracked in from all corners of the university."

He made a face. "If you dig deep enough into any carpet, you'd be amazed at what you find. Dirt. Dust mites. Hair bits—again from everyone on campus, or so it appears. Given that all of them had legitimate reasons to visit Quint's office, none of that evidence points to anyone."

"I used my position at the university to get the class schedules of both Miriam and Heather for the time window during which Quint was killed." Bree removed the printouts from her bag and scanned them. "Bummer. Another dead end. Neither of them were scheduled to teach at the time. Meaning they could easily have dropped by Quint's office and killed him."

"Other than the harassment issues, do we have any motives?"

"Jealousy might have been a motive for Pamela, but her alibi checks out. The other teachers-turned-lovers strike me more as victims than as the jealous type."

"Things aren't always as they seem," James reminded both of them.

"We also have the argument Ning heard between Coach and Quint. Unfortunately, she didn't know what it was about. But coupled with his missing championship ring and the evidence of enhancement drugs, I'd say he has things to hide."

"Whoa. Back up. What missing ring? What drugs?"

Bree shook her head, massaging away the beginnings of a headache. "Sorry, I'll blame that on food overload. I thought I'd told you already." She began with Coach's visit to her lab and office regarding the football team and ended with her discovery of the enhancement drug.

"If Quint learned about the drugs and confronted Coach about them, it would give Coach motive to silence him," James began, his slow speech indicating he was thinking aloud.

"On the other hand," Bree took up the narrative, "if Quint and Coach both knew about the drugs, they could have argued over any number of things. How to hide the scandal. How to split profits. How to pay suppliers."

James sat up in his chair and pinned her with the look of an experienced interrogator. All at once, the walls closed in on Bree and her breath grew tight in her chest. "You used to have a much less devious mind," James accused. "It might help us now, but I hate that you can look at the seedy side of life so easily. One more crime to lay at the spook's door."

A surge of energy roused Bree, pushing away her apprehension. The tightness lessened and she drew in an easy breath. "Don't blame it all on Tugood. You had a hand in it too. As did I."

James slumped in his chair again. "I'm sorry for my part in destroying your innocence," he said, his voice tinged with sadness.

"It isn't your fault. If we must assign blame, put it on the person who murdered my former boss and framed me. That's the one responsible for my loss of innocence."

"Amen," James agreed. "For what it's worth, you're right about the possibility of Quint and Coach both knowing about the drugs."

Both sat, scribbling notes and trying to regain the easy camaraderie of earlier in the evening. As Bree flipped through her notebook, a question popped into her mind.

"James, did we ever get a full inventory of the curio cabinet?"

He shook his head. "We never located a list of items in the cabinet—which isn't in itself unusual—but we did dust the shelves and assured ourselves that nothing appeared to be out of place, with the exception of the tiger-claw backscratcher you told me about. The placement of the other artifacts is consistent with a typical display, and no smudges were found on the shelves."

When she didn't reply, he prompted her. "What are you thinking?"

"When Quint first showed me his artifacts, he mentioned being interested in 'local remedies' that his international students shared with him. What if the drugs used by Coach and the team fell into that category?"

"Meaning they were legal imports?"

"No, meaning they were bribes paid by students who wished to enter the university." Bree shoved her chair back and paced the length of the small room, images and thoughts whirling in her mind as she replayed her first day in Quint's office.

"Something about Ning's arrival annoyed Quint. He hadn't been 'kept in the loop' as much as he wanted. He also mentioned gifts students gave him from their homes."

"Gifts are a long way from bribes, Bree."

She reached the end of the room and paced back to the center before answering. "Not if you saw the value of some of the items in the case. I mean, some of them, like the medieval torture instruments, were just creepy, but others were crusted in gemstones."

"All right, then." James added items to the list on the legal pad in front of him. "I'll request information on the international students and cross reference them to their places of origin to see if what pops up. Looks like we're in for some old-fashioned police work involving lots of interviews."

"We?"

He looked up from the pad and pointed his pen at her. "Yes, we. As a consultant, I'd like you to be involved in the interviews."

"I'm willing to do whatever you need, but wouldn't it be more effective for me to stay on campus and just observe?"

James tapped the end of the pen against the table, restless bursts of sound to accompany his thoughts. Finally, he let out a huge sigh. "As much as I hate to admit it, I do need you to remain anonymous. Which means we'll have to take a page from your spy-craft manual." He motioned to the window of the observation room behind him. "You can watch from in there and communicate with me via earpiece."

They cleared up the remainder of their dinner and strolled back to the bullpen, discussing who to interview and what strategies to use.

When she was ready to leave, James accompanied Bree to the door. At the threshold, he cupped her cheek in his hand. He gazed down at her, hints of conflict swirling in his blue eyes.

"Bree, whatever happens, I need you to know that I value you. Both for who you are and for the work we do together. But as much as I value your insight and skill, I wish to the depths of my soul that you had never been plunged into the murkiness of these investigations."

Chapter 18

Before Bree left for campus on Thursday morning, she called home. Her father answered on the first ring.

"Hello, sunshine. How are things with you?"

"Doing fine, Dad. I just hadn't talked to you or Mom in a while." She poured herself a cup of coffee and absently stirred in cocoa powder.

"Speaking of your mother, she's already at work. Her first clients come at eight-thirty and it's nearly that now. You used to be an early bird too. What happened?"

"Dad, I was never a morning person. I just had to be at work early in the morning. As it happens, I'm still working the university teaching contract, so my days start a little later."

"You're not cheating your employer by shaving off time, are you?" His voice sharpened. "I wouldn't like to think my daughter was slacking off."

Bree thought of the hours she'd put in chasing terrorists, being ready to jump into a mission at a moment's notice, and conversely, Tugood's oft repeated instructions to take time off. "No, Dad, I'm not slacking off. In fact, my boss tried to give me a few days off and I couldn't take them because of the university contract."

"I should have known as much. Sorry for jumping on you, sunshine. Your call just surprised me, that's all. It's not like you to call in the middle of the morning."

Calling *eight-thirty* the middle of the morning was overstating it a bit, but Bree let the comment slide. They chatted for a few more minutes, falling into an easy discussion of the thermodynamics of global warming, the feasibility of transforming plastic waste into useful materials, and the overall state of scientific literacy.

"How do you like university life?" Dad asked, changing the subject. "Because if you're thinking of making a career switch, I want you to know that your mother and I will support your decision, one hundred percent."

"I hadn't really planned on making it permanent." Bree took a sip of her coffee, dreading the turn in the conversation that she knew was coming.

"I don't like the idea of you working for that staffing company," he said flatly. "A scientist of your caliber shouldn't be doing grunt work. At the very least, you deserve to have your name on the papers you write. You should be directing research, not acting like an extra pair of hands in someone else's lab."

The coffee in her stomach soured and Bree swallowed a lump of disgust. If her family knew how important her job was, she was sure they'd be proud. Almost sure, at least. But being an analyst and sometime operative for a covert agency wasn't the sort of thing she could share with them much as she wished otherwise.

"I like my job, Dad," she said softly. "Really. The challenges are always changing and, believe it or not, I'm making a difference."

"That's for today. But tomorrow, if you change your mind, how will working at the staffing company look on your resume? What kind of job will you be able to get the next time around?"

Bree didn't have an answer. At least, not one that didn't involve lying about her job, her boss, and her future. She settled for silence.

"Promise me you'll think about it, sunshine."

"I will, Dad. I will." Bree invented a set of office hours she didn't have, told her father she loved him, gave her love to her mother and cut off the call. Before she said something she absolutely, positively shouldn't.

On the drive to campus, her phone rang. Bree pushed the Bluetooth connection in the car. "Mayfield-Watson here."

"Dudette, you seriously need to get a shorter name." Grant Mitchelson's voice boomed through the speakers and Bree adjusted the volume.

"I'll take that under consideration."

"Cool. You are a chill dudette. I just called to let you know I've separated those video and audio tracks you brought me. I sent them to your email. It isn't perfect, but if you want more enhancements on specific parts, you know where to find me."

"Excellent. Thanks."

"No sweat. Hey, Mr. Shoemaker told me to start running diagnostics on individual computers in the company, but he was real weird about it. Said I should tell folks that some dude by the name of Angelo ordered it. Do you know who he's talking about?"

"Yes, I do." Bree slowed for a stop light while deciding on her course of action. "Charles Angelo is Mr. Tugood's boss. He's the one who told us to hire an IT expert."

"Oh. My bad. I thought Goodie was the main man around here."

He is. And he isn't. Unless and until Grant was read into the entire spy ring, she wouldn't tell him Tugood's secret identity. "Mr. Tugood reports to a boss just like the rest of us. But he also runs special projects. The work you do with Mr. Shoemaker or me falls under that division. You aren't to share that information with others."

"Got it. I don't know you or work with you. Or Mr. Shoemaker. I also don't know anything about the stuff that requires a secret code to get into the elevator."

"That's right," she agreed.

"So, in other words, it's like this floor of the building is the bat cave—only upstairs—and Goodie and Shoemaker are Batman and Robin. Which makes you—who exactly?"

"Wonder Woman." *Take that, surfer dude.*

"Riiiight. Wonder Woman. W-squared. That's your new name. W-2. Lots better than Mayfield-Watson."

"Look, Grant, just follow Mr. Shoemaker's lead and work on the computers."

"Will do, W-2. The silver surfer following Robin's lead. Aloha."

Bree pulled into the parking lot and exited the car, wondering if Matthew had seen enough in Grant to justify the level of crazy the kid brought to the team. And what Shoe would do the first time Grant referred to him as "Robin." As she'd told her dad, life at Sci-PHi was many things—but never dull.

Today, campus took on a festive air. The oval swarmed with students, faces painted with orange and black strips, fist bumping one another and generally engaging in crazy antics. Banners advertising tonight's pep rally and bonfire draped several of the campus buildings. The team logo emblazoned sweatshirts, tee shirts, miniature footballs, signs, and even jewelry. Terrance University rivaled her mother's Buckeyes and her father's Wolverines when it came to team spirit and pride.

Bree snapped a few photos as a smile tugged at her lips. If she did stay at the university, she'd add yet another team to the rivalry her mother and father had fostered over the years. She uploaded the photos and texted Mom and Dad with the message, *Go Tigers.*

"I see you're catching Tiger Fever," said a voice behind her. Bree turned to find Miriam Cook dressed in a knit Tigers sweater and paw print earrings in place of her normal diamond studs. "Even the most hardened academicians fall prey to it. Don't expect too much of your students today or tomorrow."

She flashed a smile, more carefree than Bree had seen yet from the teacher. "If they don't actually cut class, their minds will be AWOL. After the first game, things calm down until the end of season championship games."

"Thanks for the warning." They headed toward the administration building together.

"I suppose you've already made plans to attend the game," Miriam said, "but if you haven't, I'm sure we can find room for you in the block reserved for the international students."

"Wow, your students have their own block of seats?"

"It's part of the immersion program. While they're in the States, I like to make sure they experience more than just work and study. Most are actually fascinated by 'American football' as opposed to the football they're familiar with."

Bree smiled, feeling carefree herself. "Otherwise known as soccer."

"Exactly. I likely won't have the same attendance problems you will today since I'm devoting all of my class time and my office hours to explaining the ground rules of football."

She pulled a sheet of stapled pages from the messenger bag on her shoulder and offered them to Bree. "In case you're not a football fan, you might want to bone up on the basics. If you sit with us, I guarantee the students will spend a portion of the time asking you to explain what happened on the field."

"Thanks." Bree accepted the sheets. "My parents were both degreed professionals, but college football season was still a lively time in our house. My mother is a graduate of The Ohio State University, and my father is a University of Michigan alum who bleeds blue and gold."

"Oh, heavens! Even here in Chicagoland, we know how deep that rivalry runs. I'm surprised you aren't a child of a broken home."

They chatted for a few minutes as they made their way to the staff mailroom. Bree's box was stuffed with information on student activities surrounding the game. And a bold lettered announcement of a mandatory sexual harassment training for the staff. "Looks like Heather fast tracked the training. I wonder if Fiona has time to prepare. It's set for Wednesday."

Miriam made a face. "I love Heather to death, but she can go overboard. I hope this isn't one of those times."

The hairs on Bree's neck raised, sending a prickle of awareness down her spine. "You mean like the argument she had with Coach at the last staff meeting?"

"Those two are old news. But, yes, that's an example. She goes out of her way to raise his hackles, then attacks when he takes the bait." Miriam lowered her voice. "Between you and me, I sometimes wonder if she didn't do the same with Dr. Christianson. Not that it excuses what he did."

Her left hand went to her earlobe and she paused awkwardly, fingering the tiger paw earring as if she didn't recognize it. A faraway look crept into her eyes. Bree wondered if Miriam was reliving her own experiences with the vice president and felt a tinge of guilt at prodding for more information. But a murderer needed to be brought to justice.

She placed a hand on Miriam's arm, and the restless movement stilled. "Believe me, whatever happened, it wasn't your fault. Using a position of power to demand favors is a reprehensible act."

"It is. But it happens. I'm grateful Heather took me under her wing and helped me navigate the situation. I was still learning the ropes, but she'd gotten tenure a short time before I started at T.U. I think it made her bold. I sometimes wonder if she didn't make things worse with Quint—I mean Dr. Christianson. For herself and for others."

The sound of the outer office door opening startled Miriam. "Sorry," she said quickly. "I've said too much. I'll see you at the game tomorrow." She hustled away before Bree could ask any more questions.

CHAPTER 19

As Miriam predicted, attendance at Bree's advanced chemistry class was light. She considered calling off tomorrow's Concepts in Chemistry class, especially since many of the students were athletes, but remembering her suspicions about cheating, she decided against it. She'd use the time to give extra credit to students who actually wanted to be in class.

Just as her office hours were ending, James called, asking her to come to the station to prepare for interviews. She shut down her computer, stashed her work, and headed across campus to her car. The oval was eerily quiet after the morning's activity, but she attributed that to activities surrounding the pep rally and bonfire.

At the PD, James ushered her into the observation room and showed her how to communicate with an earpiece he fitted into his ear. "You can feed me information if there's something you think I should ask."

Bree nodded, more comfortable with the hidden communication than she cared to admit to James. She settled into her chair and watched him enter the interrogation room. "Bring back any memories?" she teased as he arranged the table with his notepad and pen.

"Very funny." He turned to the glass and pointed at her. Or rather at where he thought she was.

"I'm in the other chair, James." Knowing that he truly didn't see her somehow made her more comfortable with the upcoming interviews.

Moments later, James left the room and returned with Fiona Fancier, both carrying cups of coffee. "Thank you for taking time to meet with me today, Ms. Fancier."

"Is it usual at the Plainfield Police Department to gather information in the interrogation rooms? Or am I under some kind of suspicion?" Fiona sipped her coffee and looked at James through cool eyes.

"Nothing like that." James sat at the table, put his coffee down and stretched his legs out. "We're a small department, but even so, I find the noise of the bullpen annoying. Especially at this time of day. I sometimes retreat in here to get a little privacy. It's definitely quieter. But we can go back to the bullpen if you like."

He half stood, and Bree imagined he was giving Fiona the raised eyebrows, friendly puppy dog look she'd seen him use to disarm interview subjects.

It must have worked.

"No need." Fiona waved his offer aside. "As long as we're clear." She flashed a smile and a length of leg highlighted by her miniskirt and stilettos as she sank into the chair opposite James.

She brushed her hair behind one ear, setting a sparkling earring swaying before withdrawing a gold pen and slim notebook from her briefcase. "I'm happy to help in any way I can with your investigation. Assuming that it doesn't conflict with my attorney-client privileges."

"Privileges? I understand you are the attorney for Miss Phailin Sintawichai—more commonly known as Ning. Are you representing anyone else in the case?"

She looked at James, smiling before reaching to touch his hand. "Ning is a wonderful girl, Detective. I'd do anything in my power to help her. And while I know it's a bit presumptive on my part, I'm trusting you with this disclosure. I can trust you, can't I?"

"Of course." James didn't pull his hand away, but Bree caught the restless way he rolled the pen between the fingers of his free hand. The habit betrayed his nervousness at being on the receiving end of Fiona's charm.

"I'm glad." Fiona leaned forward, the scooped neck of her silk camisole pulling tight across her cleavage. "Because I want you to know that there is absolutely, positively no way that girl can be held accountable for what the tiger did, or did not, do. She may be its trainer, but she's as much a victim as anyone else in this sad case." Her eyes pleaded with him to understand.

"Of course," James replied, and Bree could imagine the reassuring smile he must have pasted on his face.

"Thank you."

James cleared his throat and extracted his hand from beneath hers. "If we could return to my earlier question, is there anyone else in this investigation that would be impacted by your attorney-client privilege?"

"You should know that I've made myself available to everyone on the university staff." Fiona leaned back a fraction of an inch, angling her body but staying close to James. "Even our contract professor, Dr. Mayfield-Watson."

Bree gasped, thankful that no one heard the sound. Except James, of course. Had he tensed his shoulders at her reaction? Or was that her imagination?

"I see," he said, ignoring her outburst like a pro. "It's just that you used a plural form of privilege."

Fiona said nothing. From everything Bree had read or seen about interrogations, the attorney's response was cool and appropriate.

"I understand you are also the attorney representing Dr. Christianson's estate. Is that correct?"

"Who have you been talking to, Detective?"

"It simply came up as part of the investigation into his death. I'm sure you understand."

No reply.

James cleared his throat. "We know that Dr. Christianson kept a set of curio cabinets in his office. The crime scene team logged all of the items in the cabinets, but we were wondering if there was a master list of the contents." He raised his hands in a helpless gesture. "It occurred to me that robbery may have been a factor in Dr. Christianson's death. You know, he walks in on a robbery and the startled thief reacts, causing his death."

"Are you saying the scene of his death was consistent with a robbery?"

"You know I can't tell you that."

"Of course." Fiona made a note on her pad. "I'd be happy to provide you with a list of the cabinet contents. As it happens, the probate court needs them to depose the will."

"Thank you. I would prefer to work with you on this rather than discuss it with the grieving widow."

Fiona's mouth tightened at the mention of Quint's wife. "Mrs. Christianson has been through a lot. Starting with the unfortunate shock of her husband's death. I appreciate your attentiveness to her feelings in this matter."

"You sound like a good friend as well as an attorney." James nodded in approval. "She's a lucky woman."

"She's anxious to be done with the whole ordeal," Fiona added, thawing a bit. "Unless her husband's death is deemed a suicide, she will be the beneficiary of a substantial life insurance policy, and an additional AD&D clause on Dr. Christianson's university supplied life insurance."

"Standard terms on accidental death & dismemberment while at work, I suppose?"

Fiona nodded. "The only thing not left to his wife was the curio cabinet and its contents. Quint felt that because the contents were gifts from our international students, that the university should have first option to buy them at fair market value."

"With Pamela Christianson as the beneficiary?"

"No," Fiona shook her head. "I'm afraid not. It was his wish that the funds be used for charitable purposes. Specifically, he wanted to help continue the university's work in bringing in diverse students."

"So, a scholarship fund?" James scribbled a note. "To an existing charity?"

Another shake of Fiona's head. "No. A new fund was to be established. And before you ask, I was asked to spearhead it in my role as university counsel."

Bree cleared her throat to get James's attention. "Is it unusual for a university attorney to do private work as well?"

"You seem to be wearing a lot of hats, Ms. Fancier. Is that normal in your line of work?"

"I made sure my university employment contract allowed me to do work on the side. I'd sold my personal business when Dr. Christianson recruited me. Most of my clients went to the new owners, but a few wanted the personal touch I'd promised them."

"Thank you. That clears things up. I do appreciate you giving me so much of your time. Before you go, do you know of anyone who would want to harm Dr. Christianson? Someone who stands to gain, like Mr. Max Edelston, perhaps?"

Fiona paused in the act of putting her notebook away. "Of course not. Everyone loved him. He instituted a great many forward-thinking policies at the university. His nephew, Max, idolized him. Any other questions, Detective?"

James shook his head and stood, gesturing Fiona to the door.

"Ask her about the diamond stud club," Bree prompted as Fiona reached the door.

"There was one last thing. Sorry. I forgot." James glanced at his notepad. "What do you know about the diamond stud club?"

Fiona paused and turned back to him. From her vantage point in the observation room, Bree clearly saw the startled lift of her brows, followed by a smoothing of her features. Fiona widened her eyes in surprise. "I have no idea what you're talking about. But if you're looking for a gentleman's club, I'm sure I'm not the right person to ask."

An hour after Fiona left, James ushered Max Edelston into the interrogation room. Again, he blamed the noise of the bullpen for making him retreat to the privacy of the interrogation room.

"No problem at all." Max took a seat, straightening his tie as if he was attending a board meeting. "What can I do to help you?"

"Tell me about your relationship with your uncle."

Max smiled. "When I was a boy, Uncle Quint was the one who took me on fishing trips and helped me build model cars at the cub scouts. It seemed like he always had time for me. My father worked in a steel mill. One of the last jobs of its kind and he took every extra hour they could give him. Which was a lot given that they were running on a skeleton staff."

"And more recently?"

"Uncle Quint was the reason I went into education. That and the poor effects of exposure my father suffered. Education was a way to earn a living while keeping healthy. Plus, I love working with young people."

"Did you expect to be given the position of interim vice president?"

A nervous tic in his cheek caught Bree's attention. "No, Detective, I didn't expect to move into the VP's suite. At least, not yet. I'd joined Terrance University's board of trustees in hope of learning more about the institution. I'd expected to be offered a chance to apply for the job when Uncle Quint retired."

Max leaned forward, looking James in the eye, his posture rigid. "Let me be perfectly honest. I expected to have a head start on the competition. Uncle Quint had all but promised me he'd advocate for my taking over his position. So yes, I take it back. I did expect to be given the position."

"Thank you for your honesty."

"But I didn't expect it to be this soon." Max slumped in his seat, his bravado crumpling. "Or this way."

James took a sip of his coffee, keeping silent. A proven technique Bree sometimes used herself. Let the silence weigh on the subject of an investigation. More often than not, they'd talk to fill it.

"I loved my uncle and aunt. To see him die this way... mauled..."

"I thought the details of the body hadn't been released," Bree said into the microphone. "How did he know the body was mauled?"

Before James could act on her suggestion, Max spoke again. "I went with her, you know. Aunt Pamela asked me to go to the morgue to identify his body." He shook his head slowly, as if dazed by the memory. "Even the scars from the autopsy couldn't hide the scratches that covered his body. It was a viscous way to die."

"I take it you don't believe the tiger cub mauled him?"

Max shrugged. "There was something malevolent about those marks. Targeted. Purposeful. So, no. I don't think the tiger cub did it. And before you ask, I don't know who had reason to do this. For Uncle Quint's sake, I wish I did." He looked up, eyes vacant.

Bree and James had run into their second dead end of the day.

CHAPTER 20

Bree juggled her program, a large soda, a hotdog, and a bag of popcorn while she carefully navigated the steps in the stadium. Band music filled the crisp evening air and cheerleaders worked overtime to get the crowd whipped up. Although still early, the stands were filled nearly to capacity.

She found the international student section easily. The block of reserved seats was bordered by a row of flags from the homelands of the students, interspersed with university Tiger Power flags. Bree found a seat near Miriam. "I'll sit with some of the students when the section fills up. For now, I need someone I can trust to watch my popcorn and soda," she said as she staked out her space.

"Good call. But where are you going so soon?"

Bree waved her hands, unable to answer around the bite of hotdog. She trained her eyes on the field while she chewed. No sign of Ning and the cub, although several pep leaders dressed in tiger costumes had come onto the field.

"I'm going to look for Ning and Lucky as soon as I finish eating," she said to Miriam. "I can't believe how crowded it is already. The game doesn't start for nearly an hour."

"Like I told you yesterday, Tiger Fever runs rampant during the first game of the season." She explained the importance of the pep club and cheerleader roles in generating positive energy for the game.

"I get it," Bree said, dusting the last crumbs of hotdog bun from her fingers. "But don't you think it's sexist to have the ladies of the pep club prancing in short skirts, thigh-high boots, and tiger tails while the men get full coverage costumes complete with tiger heads?"

"Far be it from me to disagree," announced Heather who had come up behind them. She plopped down on the bleacher and leaned so her head came between Miriam and Bree. "But on nights like tonight when it's unseasonably warm, even I'd prefer not to be bundled inside a smelly tiger suit."

"Eew." Bree scrunched up her nose. "I hadn't thought of it that way. Those things probably smell from last season's sweat."

"That or dry-cleaning fluid. Either way, it can't be fun."

Below them on the field, members of the pep club began a tumbling routine, chasing one another in a comic rendition of a tiger attack.

Bree excused herself, leaving her program, soda and popcorn in the care of Miriam and Heather, and headed toward the locker rooms. Smoke from lingering tailgaters in the parking lot scented the air, its tang reminding her of campfires and cookouts at her grandmother's home when she was a child.

She hiked past the food vendors. A smattering of SWAP protesters who'd turned their "free the tiger" fervor on the university roamed the crowd, but their chanting was drowned out by the students cheering on the Terrance Tigers. Bypassing lines of students waiting to find a seat or a bathroom and crowds of photographers, Bree finally pushed her way through to the entrance of the athletic building.

A uniformed guard blocked her way.

"Players and coaches only," he said when she tried to enter.

"I'm a staff member." Bree flashed her university ID badge. "I'm here to check on the tiger cub and her trainer."

The guard shook his head and crossed his arms across his chest. "Players and coaches only," he repeated.

"Give it up, lady," shouted a voice from behind her. "We already tried that."

Bree turned to find a bevy of reporters and photographers at her back. "Show us Terry the Tiger," one of them called. Others took up the chant.

"Terry. Terry. Terry."

"Show us the tiger."

A ruckus broke out to one side of her and the guard stepped forward to deal with it, shouting into his shoulder radio for reinforcements. Bree ducked into the complex behind him, unnoticed in the chaos and hurried past the entrance toward the locker rooms.

No sign of Ning anywhere.

She paused near the main locker room, hesitant to head into a room full of half-naked football players. Surely Ning wouldn't be in there.

"Drink up," said the familiar voice of Coach Fleek. "And mind you, don't waste it. Our supply of tiger powder has to last the entire season."

"Tell your boy Tanner not to waste it on practice," said an unidentified voice.

"Shut it, Freshman. And consider yourself lucky to even be on the team." Other voices joined him in chastising the younger team member. *That must be the quarterback, Tanner White, and his gang.* "And none of that for the water boy, either."

"I don't want any." Bree recognized the voice of Josh Gibbons. Now, more than ever she was sure he'd slipped her the sample, hoping she'd do something with it.

Coach called for silence and Bree held her breath, listening closely. "Your job is to focus on the game. The opposing team.

Not the sidelines. You hear me? Hands off the tiger and hands off the girl with him. You clear?"

Someone catcalled in defiance of Coach's order. Sniggering followed. "As if I'd want anything to do with the Asian twig," said the probably-Tanner voice. "All I need is Tiger Power!"

"Tiger power. Tiger power."

Bree slipped away, the sound of the pre-game pep chant echoing in her ears while she navigated the maze of the athletic complex in search of Ning and Lucky. She turned a corner then heard a booming voice from far down the corridor she'd just left.

"This way, ladies and gentlemen of the press." Bree peeked around the corner and saw one of the security guards, holding a tiger flag high, followed by members of the press. She opened a door into a storage room near the intersection of the hallways and waited, ears trained on the footsteps of the crowd.

When the group neared her position, she listened carefully, trying to determine if they turned at her corridor or went straight. The volume of the crowd increased, but no one passed by her position. She eased out of her hiding spot, walked to the corner and joined the crowd of reporters, no one the wiser.

Several twists and turns later, they arrived at a large room, with a garage door on the opposite wall. Inside the room, Lucky paced in a cage the size of a small parade float—complete with a miniature tractor to pull it. Looped through the bars of the cage were black and orange streamers. The four corners were topped with Terrance University team flags.

Ning stood to one side, dwarfed by the cage. Bree drew a sigh of relief when she saw Dr. Warthan and several other people from the vet school flanking the tiger trainer.

The press corps flashed a few photos while Dr. Warthan explained the importance of animal research and conservation. They listened politely, but soon became restless and threw out questions trying to redirect the conversation.

One of the streamers came loose and fluttered down, startling the cub who growled, then batted at the flying fabric. Flashes lit the semi-darkened room and the crowd went wild as Lucky played with the fabric. Ning stepped forward, holding what looked like a cat toy on a long stick. She pushed it through the bars of the cage and encouraged Lucky to play, exercising the cub and delighting the photographers.

Bree slipped away, confident that Ning was in good hands. She backtracked through the maze, returning to the bleachers to find the international student area crowded. She squeezed in, finding space between Nigel and a student from India whose name she thought was Aarav. Miriam passed her drink and popcorn up to her.

The microphone crackled to life. "And now, Tiger fans, it's time to introduce the three-year state champions, your very own TEEERRANCE UNIIIVERSITY TIIIGERS!"

The team burst from the tunnel Bree had vacated minutes earlier, racing through a paper barrier with the Tiger logo, Tanner White leading. The crowd surged to its feet, cheering and waving, a din of happy noise that washed over Bree, reminding her of the few high school games she'd attended. She joined in the cheering.

As the enthusiasm waned slightly, the band burst into a musical interlude, designed to rally the fans again. After the short intro, the announcer came on again. "Introducing our new mascot. The one! The only! Terry the Tiger!!"

The tractor pulling Lucky's float entered the arena, Ning seated behind the driver on a small platform. They circled the arena slowly, cheers erupting as they passed the stands. Shouts of "Terry" and "Tiger" wafted through the crowd, growing stronger in each section the cage passed.

Bree winced when she saw a cup hurled at the passing float. The plastic bounced off the bars, spraying Lucky with liquid. The cub reacted, jumping in a startled move, her mouth open in what Bree assumed was a growl that was drowned out by the crowd's cheer. A security guard rushed into the bleachers and led the offending student away. No more projectiles headed toward the cub.

By the time the cage returned to its place near the band, Lucky was chewing contentedly on a toy dressed in the opposing team's colors, no longer caring about the noise on the field.

Eventually the crowd settled down and the game began. Behind her in the bleachers, Bree heard low voices. She glanced over her shoulder to see Fiona seated next to one of the senior students from South America.

"What do you mean, I may not be able to graduate this year?" he asked.

"You still have some basic requirements to meet. Your academic advisor should have told you." Fiona rattled off a list of three classes.

"Can I add them this semester?"

"I'm afraid the roster is full," Fiona said, her voice sympathetic. "I'll do my best, but you may need to extend your stay by another semester. If you can't get the classes this year, they won't be offered again until next fall."

"Can I test out of them? Get credit for the tutoring I did? Something?" Panic filled the young man's voice. "My scholarship won't cover an extra semester and my parents can't afford to keep me here when my younger brother is starting classes next year."

"Your brother? That does create a different spin on things. Don't worry. We'll find some way to help you. We can try to extend your scholarship or set you up on a self-study plan or any of several other options. Come to my office next week and we'll discuss what we can do."

Beside Bree, Nigel muttered under his breath, a catchy rhyme that sounded familiar, but out of place. Over the crowd noise, she caught the words "athlete" and "scholar." Before Bree could puzzle out the rest of his words, the Tigers scored a touch-down and the crowd was on its feet cheering. After that nothing mattered but the game.

By halftime, the jubilant crowd roared with excitement. The Tigers held a fourteen-to-zero lead. Players rushed off the field, whooping, chest bumping, and generally acting like the over-zealous teens most of them still were.

Bree left the bleachers and circled the outer rim of seating, skirting the SWAP protesters as she made her way to the box seats where the wealthy alumni donors and athletic booster exec-utives would be gathered. Ahead of her, she saw Ning huddled in the Terrance University hoodie that hung on her thin frame. She paused to pull up the hood and Bree saw a shiver pass through her before she squared her shoulders and pulled Lucky's travel-ing cage through the doors that Dr. Warthan had just entered.

Bree hustled to catch up and reached the trio at the freight elevator. She slid inside. Dr. Warthan pushed the button to take them to the box on the top floor of the complex.

"How do you like the game?" Bree asked.

"Game is good," Ning replied, her voice muffled by her hood, "but cold."

"It will be warmer in the executive box. I think you'll enjoy seeing the game from that vantage point."

"And," added Dr. Warthan, "they'll have snacks. You're welcome to eat and drink while you are a guest of the athletic booster club."

"Snacks for Lucky too?"

"Yes. I arranged for some snacks for Lucky. The donors will want to bottle feed her. She's a little old for that, but she'll be fine."

Ning giggled, and Bree remembered her lesson in bottle feeding cubs. *They revert to a baby-like state when bottle fed,* the tour guide had told her. And, true to his word, the cubs became snuggly and pliant when suckling, even to the point of letting humans play with their paws.

Not that Lucky needed a bottle to become snuggly when Ning was around. The cub behaved more like a super-sized version of Sherlock than the wild animal she was.

The distance between the freight elevator and the entrance to the box consisted of a short hallway. A blast of stale, heated air left Bree gasping, but at least Ning warmed enough to remove her hood by the time they entered the box. The girl's eyes were puffy, likely from the smoke that had permeated the parking lot of ground level of the field.

Inside the box, cigar smoke circulated, making the air less fresh. Bree held back a sneeze, which emerged as a strange cough instead.

Over the next hour, donors were introduced to "Terry the Tiger," aka Lucky. Ning showed them how to hold a bottle for her, play with her, and generally interact with her, shyness fading as Ning took on the role of teacher.

By the time everyone had had a chance to pose for photos with Lucky, the cub, warm, full, and tired from her antics entertaining the crowd during the first half of the game, curled into a ball and fell asleep. Her soft, nasal snores, half purr, half growl, filled the room.

Happy donors now courted Ning, fetching sodas and snacks for her. She accepted toast points with caviar from one donor. After a careful nibble, she slipped the remainder into the pocket of her hoodie when her benefactor looked away. Chicken wings suited her tastes better. After a while, Ning relaxed, although Bree still worried about the dark circles under her puffy eyes.

"She looks exhausted," Bree whispered to Dr. Warthan.

"It's been a long and stressful day for her. Everything is new. Don't worry. I'll see that she gets home safely. And I'll personally shoo her out of the clinic and make sure she spends the night in her dorm."

"Thank you."

Across the room, a donor put his arm around Ning's shoulder to lead her to the viewing windows overlooking the field. The girl flinched and shied away before quickly hiding her reaction.

Bree stepped to the window beside them. The vantage, situated above the home goal post, showed the rest of the field spread out in front of them. The angle of the box with its floor-to-ceiling bird's eye view gave the illusion of hanging in mid-air over the goal posts. Bree stepped back, and Ning followed.

The donors swarmed them, thanking Dr. Warthan, Ning, and Bree for the visit and stopping to pet the sleeping cub. Lucky stirred, getting unsteadily to her feet, head still swaying with sleepiness. Ning rushed to her, unclipping her from the leash and moving her back into the confines of her traveling cage.

"Tell her I said goodnight and that I'll see her on Monday," Bree said to Dr. Warthan before heading to the door to get a jump on the crowds.

She reached the bleacher section near her car just as the final game buzzer sounded, in time for a clear view of the celebrations—including dousing the coach in icy water.

The Tigers won forty-nine to three.

Bree dodged the players, fans, band, and pep club members who thronged the sidelines, barely making it out of the stadium before a wave of humanity surged toward the parking lot.

She'd survived her first college football game as a faculty member. Go, Tigers.

CHAPTER 21

Saturday morning Bree woke to a throbbing headache that even caffeine couldn't cure. Thinking back over last night's game, she wondered briefly if this was how the players felt after their performance drug wore off. Which led her to chastising herself for drinking a soda she'd left unattended in the care of people she barely knew. People who might be cold-blooded murderers.

Although to be honest, Dr. Christianson's body was more consistent with a hot-blooded, spur of the moment, crime of passion. Not the meticulously plotted poison-based murders she'd seen before.

The question was which passion? A jealous lover? An angry coworker? A fed-up former victim? The jumbled, disparate pieces refused to come together into a whole picture.

Had Coach and Quint argued over performance enhancements? Over funding? Something else? Or had the killer been a woman?

She still had not reviewed the cleaned-up video files from her night at *The Underground*—which could give her clues about Miriam and Heather.

The throbbing in her head intensified, piercing her skull like ice picks. Bree popped two painkillers and lay on the couch, her thoughts grinding in useless circles.

A dip of the cushions and a soft mew alerted her to Sherlock's presence. He braced one paw on her shoulder then slid his body along hers, leaving no space between them. Once settled, he lay his head on her arm and heaved a contented sigh. Purring soon followed. Lulled by the soothing vibrations and soft sounds, Bree dozed, her tired mind resting.

Thirty minutes later she woke feeling calm. Normal. And relatively pain free. She took her time doing household chores, then fixed herself a grilled cheese sandwich with chips and settled down to review the notes in her crime notebook.

What she wouldn't give to be able to see Coach's championship ring to check for missing diamonds. She made plans to stop by his office Monday to congratulate him on the game and try to steer the conversation to his ring.

Unable to learn more from her notes, she booted up her computer to check the augmented video files and learn if Grant Mitchelson's computer wizardry made up for his irreverent quirks.

She polished off her sandwich and grabbed a second can of Diet Coke before the video files finished loading. Opening the program, she noted that Grant had transformed what was a jerky movie into a series of clips, each labeled with timestamps.

Ignoring the ones showing nothing more than the interior of her condo and car, she located and loaded the clip from *The Underground*. Three sections of information marched across the screen. The top line included individual frames from the video. Each looked clearer than she remembered from the last time she'd tried to view the file.

The second and third lines consisted of audio files, complete with tiny graphs of sound waves. One was labeled "conversation" and the other "background." After a little experimentation, Bree learned how to choose the audio track and play it simultaneously with the video.

She ignored the background noise, focusing on her interactions with Heather and Miriam as she replayed the events of the night, letting the video fill in gaps her memory had forgotten.

Heather's body language had been relaxed, easy as she showed Bree around the establishment. Her interactions with the students, including Nigel the barista, indicated familiarity and even friendship. The minute she'd received the text from Miriam, her back straightened and the tiny muscles around her mouth firmed. Why put up a wall with a woman who was a close friend and ally?

Or had the energy changed for other reasons? Watching the frame-by-frame view of the interactions, Bree recognized the source of the vague warnings in her gut that night.

Miriam, for all her friendliness, leaned slightly away from Bree, as if assessing her. The duo had spoken cautiously about Quint, their language ever so slightly halting until Bree somehow signaled she understood and supported their efforts.

Things had thawed then and the body language of both teachers reflected their growing trust in Bree. Until the fateful moment when she'd swept her hair behind her ears, revealing her fake diamond stud earrings.

Bree didn't need to see the enhanced view of the night to pick up on the rigid posture of both women. It was the audio—and the calm way both women discussed their preferred method of murder—that chilled Bree to the bone.

Heather—who picked fights and boasted of her fierce feminism—gravitated to crimes of passion.

A brisk walk around the block and some window-shopping retail therapy revived Bree, blowing the angst that gripped her. As she puttered in the kitchen, trying to re-create Ning's curry, she turned up the volume on the background audio file and listened to Nigel's cultured voice reciting his poem. The rhythm worked its way into her mind, like a snippet of song, impossible to forget.

A shilling, a dollar; an athlete, a scholar.
Fancy free, fancy free.

She recited the lines mindlessly long after the audio clip finished looping through several renditions and fell into silence. The thud of her knife as she chopped veggies seemed to echo the words. *Fancy free. Fancy free.*

Maybe she should take the advice in the words and give herself a break. Since the day she'd found Ning and Lucky huddled in Dr. Christianson's office, she'd been pushing to try to unravel the mystery and keep her friend safe. But pushing didn't always yield the desired result.

Vowing to let her subconscious mind mull over the issues, Bree planned an evening of distraction: watching old movies and catching up on the precarious pile of books by her bedside. She ignored the mystery novels, thinking they'd remind her of real life, and dove, instead, into a paranormal romance series she'd been saving.

The distraction worked. Until the moment she closed her eyes and her subconscious morphed the book characters into players in the drama that was her life. The shapeshifter in her dreams constantly transformed from James to Matthew and back again, keeping her on edge and wary of both.

Evil vampires wearing the faces of her university colleagues wafted through the shadows, fangs bared. And shackled to her leg as she tried to outrun the evil, the ghost of Quint Christianson begged for justice.

CHAPTER 22

Classes returned to normal on Monday, if hung-over football players huddled in the back of the Concepts in Chemistry class constituted normal. The only abnormality was that Josh Gibbons selected a seat in the front of the class—away from his teammates.

Bree announced an upcoming exam. "The exam will consist of problem solving and essay questions discussing the chemistry concept we've covered in class," she said, raising her voice to be heard over the groans of the class. "Grades will be based on how clearly you show your thought process, as well as whether the problem is solved correctly. And," she directed her next comments to the jocks in the upper corner of the room, "I'll be looking carefully at the handwriting on the test to be sure you've turned in your own work."

Tanner White slammed his notebook shut. "Don't worry," he said to his friends, pitching his voice so that it carried to Bree. "Coach will make sure we pass." With a fist bump to the other players, he led them from the room.

Later, as Bree entered her advanced lab class, the memory of her private meeting with Coach lingered in the lab like the sulfurous odor of natural gas. He would definitely be unhappy with her for holding his players accountable for their own scholastic achievement.

A shilling, a dollar; an athlete, a scholar.

The rhyme lodged in her head resurfaced, triggering another memory. Not of the night at *The Underground,* but of Nigel murmuring the phrase at last week's football game. He'd uttered it in response to—

"Excuse me, Dr. Mayfield-Watson, but I'm having trouble with this titration. Every time, the red turns to deep blue before I can catch the color change." A student looked at her in frustration. "What am I doing wrong?"

Bree headed to the young woman's station and looked over her notes. "Here's the problem. You're trying to do it all at once. Approach the problem in two steps…"

After lab period ended, she handed out the next assignment, answered questions and checked the room to be sure everything was in order before heading to her office for a much-needed break.

The note slipped under her office door changed her plans. Bree opened the folded sheet. Dr. Warthan left a message with the building admin after not reaching Bree by phone.

Come to the vet clinic. Ning needs your help.

Bree gathered her things and hurried to the clinic, opting to drive rather than walk. When she entered via the back door to the tiger enclosure, Lucky raced to the bars to greet her.

"Are you lonely, girl?" she said rubbing the cub's ears. "Where's your buddy Ning?"

Lucky's mew sounded pitiful. With a last pat, Bree headed to the front desk. She pulled out her cell phone—which she'd powered down while in the lab—and tried to call Dr. Warthan. Eventually they found one another in a small treatment room off the main clinic waiting area.

Ning sat in a plastic chair, her head drooping low. At her feet, Miss Peepers sat, offering her a bottle of water, patiently trying to get the girl's attention to no avail.

Beneath the sleeve of Ning's tee shirt, Bree saw purple bruises, their edges fading to deep green. Dr. Warthan stood nearby, a blood pressure cuff dangling from her hand.

"I found her like this when I came in to check on Lucky. I think she spent the weekend with the cub. I brought her here and immediately tried to contact you. She's physically fine," the doctor assured Bree with a weak smile. "At least as far as I can tell. But—" she waved her hand in Ning's direction, "she's distraught. I thought you should be here."

Bree rushed to the girl's side, wrapping an arm gently around her shoulders. "Ning? What happened?"

The girl roused at the sound of Bree's voice. "Quarterboy," she said in a low, angry tone that Bree had never heard her use. Ning lifted her sleeve. "Quarterboy do this. After game."

The garish purple encircled Ning's upper arms as if she'd been roughly shaken by a much larger person. Bree swallowed her rage and forced herself to speak calmly.

"Tell me everything."

Miss Peepers climbed into Ning's lap, hugging her neck gently. The motion seemed to soothe the girl and she stroked the capuchin's spiky, silky hair for long moments before speaking.

"After we visited the box, I take Lucky back to the game. Quarterboy sees us and grabs me. He say I should kiss him. Say I bring the team luck. Me and Lucky, who he call Terry. I say no. He kiss me anyway." A grim smile touched her lips. "I bite him for kissing me. But he angry and slap me in the face. Quarterboy is bad man."

Bree turned Ning's face from the shadows and brushed her long hair aside. She gasped at the puffy eye, also rimmed in bruises.

"He tell me to keep quiet or he hurt Lucky." Ning's eyes widened and she tightened her grip on Miss Peepers. "I not let that happen. I want to tell Mr. James the detective."

"Yes," Bree said. "we will definitely do that. First, I need you to come with me to visit Ms. Fancier. We're going to file a complaint against the quarterback, Tanner White, and the coach."

By the time the trio reached the attorney's office—Ning seemed to need the monkey and Bree didn't insist on leaving her behind—Bree had channeled her anger into creating an action plan. She settled Ning in a chair in the waiting area outside the office and headed to the door. The sound of voices within stopped her.

"The university board has decided to extend your scholarship." Fiona's voice could be heard faintly through the closed door. Bree couldn't hear the other speaker. "That is correct," said Fiona. "This is in exchange for allowing the chemistry and veterinary departments to study the chemical composition of your local arthritis remedy… No, we don't need any money… Yes, it's that easy."

Bree backed away from the door when she heard footsteps and was seated with Ning by the time Fiona opened the door. One of the students Bree recognized from the bleachers at the football game exited, shaking Fiona's hand, all smiles.

Bree waited until he'd left the area before ushering Ning into Fiona's office. The attorney shied away from Miss Peepers, but wisely didn't ask Ning to relinquish her hold on the capuchin.

In a few words, Bree outlined Ning's previous complaint regarding the football team. "I had the opportunity to alert Coach to the behavior of his players and he assured me he would handle the situation. But as you can see," she gestured to Ning's injuries, "matters have escalated."

With much encouragement from both Bree and Fiona, Ning repeated her story. Miss Peepers stroked the girl's hair, soothing her during the recitation.

"For the record, you bit Mr. Tanner White?" Fiona made a note.

"Yes. When he kissed me. Without permission."

Fiona sighed. "That's unfortunate as it could precipitate a counter claim. However, it's clear to me you were standing up for yourself."

"She most certainly was," Bree said. "And she should not have been put in that situation. She—"

A noise erupted in the room outside Fiona's door and the attorney rose to see what was happening. When Bree heard the voices of both Coach and Tanner White, she moved to stand between Ning and any further interaction with the men.

Fiona and Bree together confronted Tanner and Coach.

"Coach Fleek, you've been warned about controlling the behavior of your team members before."

"They're boys! Excited by the game. Cut 'em some slack. You know the importance of the team as well as Christianson did."

"What I know," said Fiona in icy tones, "is that any overt misdeeds on your part—or the part of your team—could end the athletic program at Terrance University."

"Then we'd be broke, and you know it."

Coach and Fiona faced off, toe-to-toe, staring in a power struggle that seemed to last for hours. Tanner slunk into the hallway, shamefaced. Finally, Fiona spoke in low tones. "We both know there are larger issues at stake. Clean up your mess. I'll expect to see you in my office in the morning."

Coach turned on his heel and stomped away, his face red, but his lips sealed. Bree breathed a sigh of relief when his footfalls receded down the hallway.

Back in the office, Miss Peepers sat perched on Fiona's desk, chewing the tip of a pen.

"My Montblanc! Give it back." Fiona forgot her nervousness around the monkey and held out her hand. Miss Peepers relinquished the pen, then dug into her bag and offered Fiona a dried banana chip in apology.

"Just get it out of here," Fiona told Bree. Her face, wan and tight, held the look of someone on the verge of fainting. "I'll file the necessary paperwork and speak to Ning tomorrow."

Before more chaos could ensue, Bree bundled Ning and Miss Peepers out of the office, across the oval, and into her car.

Instead of driving Ning to her dorm, Bree headed to her own condo, worried the girl was reaching a breaking point. She tucked the shivering Ning in a blanket and settled her on the couch with a mug of hot cocoa. Sherlock hefted himself up and snuggled beside her while Miss Peepers stood sentry on the back of the couch and combed her fingers gently through Ning's hair. The girl's shivering stopped and her eyes drifted closed, a sigh escaping her lips.

Bree turned the TV on low and found a program on the Animal Planet channel to keep the trio entertained. Her own restless energy was less easily soothed. Tension from her clenched jaw radiated up her neck and past her ears as she relived the last hours.

To keep her hands busy, she retreated to the kitchen and pulled out a large stock pot. For Bree, cooking and experimenting in the kitchen transported her to a happy place. Her chemist's version of meditation, she supposed.

Today, she focused on Grandma's chicken noodle soup, mentally reciting the recipe like a mantra. She rough chopped onions then minced onions, letting the mini food processor do most of the work. Bree blinked rapidly and rinsed her knife under cold, running water. She refused to give in to tears—even onion-induced ones—when anger suited her mood much better.

Once the onions were browned in butter and olive oil and simmering with chicken stock, Bree attacked a stack of veggies, directing the building anger at several defenseless celery stalks. With each thwack of the knife, she imagined a judge's gavel slamming home at a sentencing hearing for Coach Fleek and Tanner White.

Not that any such thing was likely to happen, she admitted as she shifted to slicing carrot rounds on a mandolin. Both might get a reprimand from the university, but she doubted any significant punishment. Still, she'd work with Fiona to be sure some follow-up took place.

She set aside a small bowl of carrot rounds and dumped the rest of the veggies into the soup pot. After wiping and drying the counter, she turned her energy to making noodles. As Bree mixed eggs, yolks, flour and salt with a bit of water to make the dough, her body relaxed.

Mixing. Kneading. All took on a familiar rhythm she'd learned in her grandmother's kitchen. From the time she was big enough to climb onto a stepstool and reach the counters, she'd helped her grandmother with the chore every chance she got.

"Thanks, Gram," she murmured as she set the dough aside to rise. Grandma's voice echoed in her mind, a memory from a safer, happier time.

"Would you look at that," Grandma had mused as she flipped past a TV cooking show. "Grown people afraid to make pasta by hand. Not like you and me, Bree. No, sir. We can do anything we set our minds to."

I can do anything I set my mind to. Including protecting Ning while dealing with criminal harassment from football players. All while solving a murder. She would find a way. Or make one.

Bree checked the broth, seasoning it with salt and pepper before impulsively adding frozen peas and corn to the mix. A couple of cans of chicken followed. When she turned back to the pasta dough, Bree discovered she had company in the kitchen.

Chirp. Miss Peepers swung herself up onto a kitchen chair and eyed the distance between the chair and the counter.

"No, no, little girl," Bree chided, distracting the capuchin with a couple of carrot rounds. "No fur babies on the counter while I'm cooking."

Miss Peepers regarded her curiously but settled down with the treats. One went into her mouth. A second went into the pouch slung over her tiny shoulder. One for now. One for later.

Bree pitched her voice low in a singsong style, chatting with the monkey while she worked. "First you separate the dough into smaller lumps," she said, her hands following her dialogue in a practiced movement. "I do this all by hand. Like my grandma. Should I roll the noodles thin or thick?"

Miss Peepers gave no answer except to reach for another carrot. Bree dusted the work surface with flour and rolled the batch until it was about a quarter inch thick. She turned the edges over, folding the dough into a loose tube which she cut into chunky strips.

Humming while she worked, Bree finished rolling and cutting the batch of noodles as the soup came to a boil. She dropped them in, a few at a time, stirring to help them cook. Once the pasta was in, she lowered the temperature to a simmer.

A hiss disrupted her concentration. Bree swiveled away from the stove, coming face-to-face with a standoff between Sherlock and Miss Peepers. The monkey clutched her bag, eyes wide. Facing off with her, the cat's tail twitched in a way that spelled trouble.

"Hey, big boy," she called, trying to distract Sherlock, "how about some treats?" She reached into the cupboard and pulled out a pouch of tuna snacks, dumping a few into a bowl she placed on the floor for Sherlock. He didn't take his eyes off the monkey, but his whiskers quivered and the furious tail twitching settled into a calmer rhythm.

Bree left the two to work out their differences while she fished her phone out of her purse. A quick check assured her Ning was still calmly settled on the couch. Bree dialed Melody Warthan at the vet school and filled her in on the events of the afternoon.

"Bree," Melody said when she'd finished her story, "don't get your hopes up about anything happening to the coach or his players."

"Surely the university will take action."

"Do you really think so?" Melody's voice held a hard edge. "Trust me, Tanner's a star player. He won't even get a single game suspension during the season. Football is king at Terrance U. Don't let anyone tell you otherwise. Just look at the hoops we had to go through to be able to study Lucky and her condition."

While Melody outlined the paperwork nightmare the university had required for acquisition of the cub, Bree wedged the phone between her shoulder and ear and mediated a brewing fight between the cat and the monkey.

Sherlock hissed and swiped at Miss Peepers when she reached her tiny fingers into his bowl. She popped a tuna treat into her mouth and he crouched low, eyes narrowed. Next thing she knew, a flurry of orange fur launched itself at the monkey, sending the capuchin scurrying to the top of a bookshelf. At least no blood was drawn.

"It sounds like you have a battle of your own going on over there," Melody commented, her voice losing some of its tension. "What's up?"

"Sherlock and Miss Peepers are fighting the next world war. I didn't think they'd get into it when I brought Ning home with me for the night. But they'll calm down. Meanwhile, I made some comfort food for Ning and I'm letting her catch up on her sleep.

"I'm worried that you're right about Tanner, Coach, and the rest of the football team. The season just started and I'm sure they'll still require Ning to accompany the cub to events."

"As if she'd leave Lucky alone with the players. But I might have a solution."

"Sending one of your large male vet interns to accompany Ning and Lucky?" Bree crossed her fingers and hoped Melody would agree.

Laugher danced across the connection. "I knew you and I thought alike. Yes, I already have someone in mind. Someone Ning has met and trusts."

The image of the young vet, specializing in large animal care, popped into Bree's mind. Someone like him would be an ideal protector for Ning. "Are you sure you can spare someone?" Bree asked Melody.

"I'm glad to help. Speaking of which, I wanted to do a bit more research on your Miss Peepers. I have some tricks up my sleeve, but it would help to know more about her benefactor and the law firm who handled his will. Who did you say it was?"

"Edward Clark. No, wait, it was Wendy Clark's great uncle. I'll have to get his last name for you." Bree jotted a note to herself. "The law firm was a small place called Fancy Finance, or Fine Estates ... something like that. I don't think they are in business anymore. How will that help?"

"I just want to see who I'll be up against if I have to bend any rules," Melody said. "Whatever you can get for me will be useful. Meanwhile, I'll work out the details regarding Ning's future appearances with the football team."

A crash sounded in the living boom. Bree hurriedly thanked Dr. Warthan and cut off the call. Miss Peepers and Sherlock raced around the room, playing tug-of-war with the capuchin's satchel. Sherlock lunged, grabbing the strap in his teeth. Miss Peepers tugged, bracing her feet against the armchair, flipping head over heels when Sherlock released his grip. Kitty treats and carrot chips spilled out. Sherlock pounced at Miss Peepers with a hiss, skidding through the mess, scattering food everywhere.

Ning woke to animals chasing one another across her lap. By the time she and Bree settled the fight, the living room was in shambles, the warring pets had each slunk into their respective hiding places, and the humans were breathing heavily. But at least Ning's color looked normal and the shadows had retreated from her bruised eyes.

It wasn't enough. But it would do. For now.

CHAPTER 23

"Fancy fee, fancy fee," Ning sang as she sat beside Bree in the car on the way to campus, holding a sleeping Miss Peepers.

"It's fancy free," Bree corrected. "It means not being tied down. Free to do what you choose." Before bed last night, Bree had told Ning about *The Underground* and played some of the videos Grant had isolated of the student performers.

"Free," Ning repeated. "To do what I like. Fee. To pay for something. Right?"

Bree nodded. "That's right. It's probably hard when words sound so similar. Like … pet and vet." She stole a quick glance at Ning, relieved to see the girl smiling.

"I would like to go for underground coffee."

"How about tonight?" Bree pulled into the rear parking lot of the vet clinic. "I can swing by your dorm at six and show you how to get to the coffee house. You'd be welcome anytime," she added, remembering the open invitation Heather and Miriam had given her when she'd last left the coffee house.

After Bree dropped Ning and Miss Peepers off, she headed to her campus office. First order of business was to create an exam for the Concepts in Chemistry class—designed to make sure the football players in the class didn't cheat. As she worked, Bree steeled herself for the inevitable confrontation with Coach when he discovered she wasn't going to give his players a free pass in the class.

I've faced down terrorists and 500-pound tigers. I can handle a middle aged, ex-football player who's gone soft around the middle.

Still, it wouldn't hurt to review some of the self-defense techniques Tugood had taught her. Besides, she needed to stretch and move a bit after an hour hunched over her desk.

Bree closed the door, shrinking the small office even further. She pushed the visitor chairs and desk out of the way to create a clear workout area. After a few stretches, she ran through a series of moves, fighting an imaginary opponent while maintaining her balance and focus.

The moves flowed easily as muscle memory took over. Bree adjusted her position, remembering the warmth of Matthew's hand when he'd guided her through the moves the first time they'd practiced them in the deserted tech-ops center at Sci-Spy headquarters. She'd foolishly allowed herself to think it had been more than routine training.

A few months made a big difference in perception.

Bree broke free of the thoughts of Matthew the same way she'd break out of a choke hold, forcefully, without hesitation and before they could tighten their grip on her and make trouble. She swatted memories away with a block-grab-pull maneuver and kicked them to the curb—which was located somewhere near the groin of her imaginary attacker.

By the time an insistent buzzing from her cell phone interrupted her workout, she'd regained control. And perspective.

"Have you seen the news?" James skipped the usual preambles, his voice terse.

"Which channel?"

"All of them. At least all the local ones. For now."

Bree fumbled with her computer, clicking to a news station in time to see a reporter in front of a SWAP protest. The protest leader held a plastic bag high while speaking in the microphone.

"This is what comes of enslaving animals. We killed them for our pleasure. Now it's payback time. Karma."

The crowd behind him took up the call *Karma, karma, karma,* while he jostled the bag in time to the chant. Bree leaned closer, zooming in on the bag.

"Looks like we've found our missing backscratcher."

The newsreel played all day, looping through footage of the SWAP protesters, interspersed with interviews from Terrance University students and staff. Pundits took turns arguing everything from the legality to the morality of keeping pets, hunting game, having mascots, and a dozen other issues.

One young man wearing a SWAP tee shirt and a T.U. hat told the story of finding the claw in the garbage chute while working a janitorial shift on campus.

It took only minutes before the news teams connected the dots to realize he'd found the claw days after a murder in the same building. Bree held her breath, but no mention of the condition of Quinten Christian's body surfaced.

She let the air from her lungs in a swoosh. When her office phone rang, she picked up out of habit, only to cut the call off when a flurry of questions from a reporter started the instant she'd confirmed her identity. She turned the volume off and ignored repeated attempts at contact.

Thank goodness today wasn't a day when she had classes.

A breaking news banner flashed across the screen. Bree's gut tightened, apprehension turning to dread when a photo of

Quint's mauled body appeared on-screen. She turned up the volume on the computer.

"...source of the video appears to be a Terrance University student reporter who allegedly was asked to keep the footage under wraps in clear violation of her first amendment rights..."

So much for Heather keeping the student reporter quiet during the investigation. Bree chewed her lip as the gristly scene faded, only to be replaced with still photos and choppy video of her with Ning, Lucky, and the police outside of Quint's office. Without warning, the image blurred, as if interrupted by static, then the feed went blank.

"We seem to have lost our video," said a frustrated anchor as the screen returned to an in-studio view. "While our techs try to get it back, let's go to our panel..." Bree lowered the volume again.

Her cell phone buzzed, caller ID indicating the call came from...from The Batcave? Bree picked up.

"W2! Silver surfer here." Grant Mitchelson's voice boomed through the speakers. "No need to thank me."

"Thank you for what?" Bree kept one eye on the news screen but the camera didn't move from the discussion panel.

"What, you aren't watching the news? About the murder at the university where you work?"

"Of course I was watching, I..." Underneath her worry for Ning and her concern for seeing justice served, she'd been freaked out about her own image appearing on the newscast. The larger her public digital footprint, the less useful she'd be as an undercover operative.

"You're welcome," Grant said, as if Bree had voiced her fears aloud.

"You scrubbed my image from the newsfeed? You can do that?"

Silence. And then, "I'm hurt that you doubt my abilities."

"But how? Why?"

"Duuuudette! I may not know what you, Mr. Shoemaker, and Goodie do, but I know that you want to keep it secret. I respect that. You guys not only lead quiet—meaning, *boring*—lives but you have the digital footprint of octogenarians. Heck, even my old granny has more photos online than you do. It's not normal."

Bree held her tongue. Sure, she hadn't gotten into the habit of posting what she ate for breakfast on photo-sharing apps. But octogenarian?

"W2? You there?"

"Yes."

"Was I wrong? Should I restore the files?"

"No." Bree made a snap decision. "But tell me, where are the originals?"

"Without more work, luck, and a virus or two, I can't do anything about images on the original phones or cameras. At least not easily. For now, I just scrambled the information on the news servers. I'll work on a more permanent solution if you like. The only thing I can't work around is an old-fashioned, nondigital camera. One without connectivity." He paused, the clicking of keys in the background indicating he was working on something. "What do you want me to do?"

Her loyalty to Sci-Spy warred with her responsibilities to the Plainville PD. Without warning, an image of her father's face, his lips tight with disappointment, popped into her head. "Keep a single copy of all the footage you find in an encrypted area of our secure servers." She took a breath. "The ones in the Batcave."

"Will do."

"And destroy all other files with the information. Including the original sources if possible."

"If?" Grant laughed, his mirth filling her ears. "There's no if about it. Only a when. And a how. I'll get on it right now.

Meanwhile, you want me to hook you up with some makeup or clothing that can confuse a camera or facial recognition program?"

Bree's jaw dropped. She'd used makeup and clothing before to disappear into a role on stage or during a mission, but this sounded like something out of a sci-fi novel. "That's a thing?"

"Yes, it's a thing. I'll whip up something and leave it in the Batcave. And don't worry, I won't use the stuff that looks like KISS stage makeup. Good?"

"Sure." Bree pulled up a search window on makeup techniques that could fool a surveillance camera.

"Oh, and don't bother searching for it online. You'll only find old references. I'll link you up with the latest and greatest. Silver surfer out."

Throughout the afternoon, Bree alternated between watching local news and scanning the national outlets. No other footage showing her face appeared. Calls to her office phone slowed then stopped altogether.

The next time a breaking news banner appeared, it only announced that the police department had confiscated the tiger claw backscratcher. The story cut to a reporter in the veterinary clinic at T.U.

Bree raised the volume when the camera swung to reveal Dr. Melody Warthan.

"Is it true that the veterinary clinic sponsored the killer tiger?" asked the reporter.

"The veterinary clinic, in conjunction with the Terrance University athletic club, arranged to care for and study the animal," she replied.

"The killer tiger?" the reporter insisted.

A muscle ticked in Melody's jaw and she shook her head. "I don't know what you are talking about."

"I'm talking about this." The reporter shoved a photo at her. "Are these, or are these not, claw marks from your tiger?"

Melody shrugged. "I don't know where those marks came from. But I do know they didn't come from the tiger known as Lucky. She," Melody swallowed, apparently coming to a decision, "she is incapable of inflicting such marks."

And with that, Melody Warthan launched into a discussion of Lucky's soft claw and tooth condition, alerting the general public, and the killer, that the cub was incapable of having committed the crime.

Bree reached for her phone to dial James, just as he called her. "How are you holding up?" he asked as soon as she picked up. "Have you been able to follow the news or were you in class?"

"No classes today. I've been keeping up with all of the news channels I can find. Looks like everything the PD wanted to keep secret is now out in the open."

"Yes. And just like that, any advantages we might have had regarding the investigation are gone. On the other hand, the killer may get careless now that his or her plans to throw suspicion on Lucky have been destroyed."

Bree digested that information. She stared at the crime notebook on the desk where she'd been making notations on the events of the day. "Do you think the crime techs will be able to get anything useful off the backscratcher?"

"They already have." Bree could almost hear James smile through the phone connection. "They couldn't lift any useful prints. It was likely wiped clean before being thrown away. But they did confirm the spacing on the claws exactly matched the spacing on the victim's body. It's almost certainly the weapon used to inflict the wounds."

"But not the murder weapon?"

"Maybe, maybe not. It's all a matter of timing."

"In other words, did the bleeding from his head kill him before the scratches?"

"Exactly. We do know that his head injury wasn't a result of hitting himself on the edge of the desk. Blood spatter and the shape of the wound confirmed that."

"So, we're looking for a tall, strong person with a malicious streak."

James laughed. "Narrows it down a lot, doesn't it?" They chatted for a bit longer before agreeing to meet later to discuss the case over drinks.

At least, Bree thought as she put her phone away, their description of the killer let Heather Beauchamp off the hook. She was strong, but not tall. Unless she'd been standing on the desk, or Quint had been kneeling or ... Possibilities drifted through Bree's mind, but she dismissed each as evidence from her crime book contradicted it.

By late afternoon, when she'd run out of scenarios and hypotheses to test, Bree packed her briefcase and headed to Fiona's office. Thankfully, no news crews or gaggles of photo-obsessed students intercepted her, although she'd taken the pre-caution of turning up her coat collar and wrapping a scarf around her face.

She pulled the suffocating wraps off as soon as she ducked into the administration building, vowing to wear a lightweight hat tomorrow. Or maybe to check out the supposed options Grant promised her.

For now, she focused on Ning and the issues they'd brought to Fiona's attention regarding the harassment by the football players.

When she entered the office, Fiona looked up from a stack of file folders that nearly dwarfed her. "I assume you've seen the news," she demanded when Bree stepped through the door.

"I have."

"This nightmare affects us all. From the Board of Directors to the students. Terrance University's public image will be in shambles if I don't do something about it." Her hands curled into fists, and Bree imagined the manicured fingernails biting into Fiona's skin. "We have to get ahead of this story. Do not," she scowled at Bree, "I repeat, *do not* talk to the press."

"Of course not."

"Good. That's all." Fiona turned back to the papers, dismissing Bree.

"Actually, it isn't. I didn't come here to talk about the news stories. I came to see what you're doing regarding Ning and the harassment complaint against Tanner White and the coach."

Fiona's forehead creased in a frown and her gaze skittered to a desk calendar. She sighed, showing uncharacteristic lack of self-control. "That mess. Fine. We'll deal with it."

She pulled a planner to her and flipped through the pages, running her finger along line after line of apparent chores. "Thursday," she said. "I'll meet with her on Thursday at two in the afternoon."

Bree thanked Fiona. "We'll be here." Bree headed to the door.

"You don't need to accompany her," Fiona said as Bree was about to step into the hall. "I know you feel responsible, but sometimes it is better to let the accuser speak for herself."

"I'll be here," Bree repeated. "I'm her sponsor, after all."

Fiona's eyes were cold as she looked at Bree. She rose from her desk and headed to the door. "Fine. I'll see you both at two on Thursday. Now if you'll excuse me, I have serious damage control to do." With that, Fiona urged Bree out the door, put a Do Not Disturb sign on the window, and—presumably—went back to her work of defusing the public relations nightmares caused by today's media coverage.

⚜   ⚜   ⚜

On the way home from campus, Bree stopped by *The Barkery*. Wendy met her and passed her an envelope containing everything she had on Miss Peepers and Uncle Edward's will. Bree hurried away before either Wendy or Horace could draw her into a discussion of the news stories.

After a quick change of clothes, a few moments with Sherlock, and a sandwich, she headed back to campus to Merveille Hall. Ning met her in the lobby, smiling at Bree while also drawing one corner of her lip between her teeth. Excitement and apprehension radiated from the girl's body.

"Is everything okay?" Bree asked when they set out at a leisurely pace toward the coffee house.

Ning nodded, wrapping her scarf tighter around her and waiting a long moment before speaking. "*Khun* Dr. Bree," she began. Bree leaned close to catch her quiet words. "Do you think I will have to make up poetry tonight?"

"Of course not." Relief flooded Bree at a worry so easily handled. "Unless you want to. The coffee house is all about being free to do whatever you want."

"Fancy free? Like the poem?"

"Exactly. In fact, that's probably why the poem is so popular with everyone at the coffee house."

After they knocked at the door to *The Underground* a student answered and let them in with no announcements. Apparently once you visited the coffee house, you were always welcome. Bree showed Ning around, introducing her to a few people she recognized. They stopped at the bar where an unfamiliar barista offered them coffee or tea.

Bree was grateful when Ning recognized a few students from her freshman class. Others introduced themselves and soon Ning was drawn into a group of dorm mates and others from various countries around the world. Bree gave her a smile and a wave then faded into the background, pleased to see Ning making friends her own age. And her own species, for that matter.

After finishing her tea, Bree slipped from the main room of the coffee house and found a tiny bathroom in an alcove off the landing of the main entry stairs. Instinctively she reached for the faucet to wash grime from the banister off her hands. The sound of voices filtering through the ancient register vent in the ceiling stopped her.

"I hear you've had a spot of trouble," said a voice she recognized as belonging to Nigel.

"Yeah, some class *requirements* my advisor forgot to tell me about." The South American accent didn't soften the sarcasm in his words. "It almost cost me my scholarship."

"Did you take the easy way out? Or the hard way?"

"Let's just say I made arrangements with the university. They're extending my scholarship for an additional semester."

Nigel snorted. "Lucky you."

Bree strained, listening for background noise, but couldn't determine the location of the speakers. No doubt they were in a place they thought secure, unaware that the old building's construction carried their voices.

"I'm sorry my brother can't find a different school to attend," Nigel's friend said. "My mom and sister shouldn't have to put up with the risk of sending their *herbal tea* here. I thought Dr. Christianson's death would have put a stop to the need for bribes."

"Didn't we all." Nigel let out a bitter laugh. "But with Fancy Fee you're never free. *The Underground* will do what it can to help you, but be careful, my friend."

"I doubt even Heather's connections could get me out of jail or prevent deportation."

"She has her ways..." Nigel's voice faded as he and his friend moved away.

Bree finished her business in the bathroom and pulled her crime notebook from her purse. After recording what she'd just heard, she leaned against the sink and closed her eyes, letting her thoughts drift as she tried to make sense of the new revelations. Heather. *The Underground.* Extortion. Murder?

She exited the bathroom and went in search of Ning. Once she found the girl, Bree breathed a sigh of relief when Ning agreed to leave, rather than staying.

The scattered bits of conversation sent Bree's newly-developed spy senses into overdrive for reasons she didn't completely understand. But the warning in her gut was clear. What had Bree gotten herself—and Ning by extension—into at *The Underground*?

The next morning, Bree entered her Concepts in Chemistry class and removed the specialized glasses and scarf Grant had left for her. Her skin itched from application of the makeup concoction embedded with infrared light scattering crystals designed to blur features captured by digital cameras. Her attempt at a selfie this morning indicated the makeup's abilities were worth the discomfort.

When she announced a surprise exam, the class erupted in a chorus of groans. She ignored the protests from the class while directing them to spread out with at least two seats between each student. She handed out the tests, watching as the coded papers passed from student to student down each row of class then sat back to watch their reactions.

Unknown to the students, the exams all had subtle differences. A code on each paper indicated which answer key Bree would use to score it. Two students sitting side by side might be asked to do similar calculations but using different starting numbers. So, the answer for one exam might be (a) while on the neighboring exam (c) would be the correct response. *Take that, would-be cheaters!*

Half an hour into the fifty-minute class, football players began sauntering to the front of the class, slapping completed exams on the desk in front of her. No work showed in the spaces she'd left for calculations. No marks at all, except for a series of circled answers.

Tanner White caught her eye as he added his paper to the growing stack. His blunt fingers rested on the page and he didn't release it when she reached for it. "I'm sure I passed with flying colors," he said, daring her to refute him. "Coach said I would."

"Coach isn't grading your chemistry exam," Bree replied, infusing as much ice into her tone as possible. She held his gaze, waiting until the teen looked away, a snarl twisting his lips.

"We'll see" he tossed over his shoulder as he walked away.

We will, she thought, *but I won't be the one surprised by the outcome.*

One of the last students to leave the class was Josh Gibbons. Scrawled numbers, crossed out sections, looping arrows and question marks covered his exam pages. "I dunno if I got it right," he said, "but I tried."

"I can see that." Bree glanced around the room, taking in the few remaining students. She lowered her voice. "Josh, I know you sent me that sample of Tiger Powder. Why?"

The boy shrugged, his gaze flitting from her desk to the door, not meeting her eyes. "I thought you could help."

"I'm doing my best. Thank you. I know it was a risk."

He met her gaze at last. "It's the right thing to do. Anyway, I'm never going to be a football star, so I don't have that much to lose."

"Josh, believe it or not, there's more to life than football. Success on the field doesn't guarantee success in life. Courage to do the right thing is a much better indicator of how successful your life will be. Your family should be proud."

"Yeah. Um, I guess." A dull flush crept up his neck and he hustled away, but Bree noticed a new confidence to his step that even his slumped shoulders couldn't hide.

CHAPTER 24

The next morning, fresh from her shower, Bree wrapped herself in a robe and headed to the kitchen to make coffee. And promptly stepped in something squishy and warm that oozed between the thin soles of her thin flip flops and her naked foot.

"Ugh. Sherlock." She immediately regretted her tone. Despite bringing the misery upon himself by chugging his food too fast, it wasn't really Sherlock's fault that he threw up. Scanning the mess dotting her pathway, Bree realized at least part of it could be blamed on hairballs. "You poor baby," she cooed, amending her tone.

Sherlock looked up from his position in her favorite chair, blinking sleepily, not an ounce of remorse in his wide green eyes. *Meow.*

"What am I going to do with you?" Bree busied herself cleaning the mess and spritzing the area with odor remover before finally starting the coffee. She hopped back in the shower while it brewed. Once fully dressed, she threw her robe, flip flops, and towels straight into the laundry.

Apparently pleased with her efforts on his behalf, Sherlock sat up, cleaned his whiskers and amused himself by chasing dust motes dancing in the light streaming from the French doors overlooking the balcony. In a flurry of energy, he jumped, twirled and pounced.

"Chasing ghosts again?" Although she didn't believe in ghosts, Bree did know that cats saw wavelengths of light invisible to humans. "Does that mean you can see through my special makeup? Or maybe I should get you to help Nate with his investigations. Which reminds me, he hasn't gotten back to me about the DNA samples yet."

While Sherlock played and Bree munched on some toast, she dialed Nate. He picked up on the second ring.

"How's your vacation going?"

"Ha. Just because I'm not popping into the Sci-PHi corporate offices doesn't mean I'm slacking off."

"Maybe not, but from what I hear tell, your boss Troy is giving everyone an earful about not having you around. I'll let Kiki fill you in on the details. Today is the day she's coming to talk to your chemistry class, isn't it?"

"One of the days. She's addressing the regular freshman chemistry class today. Next week, she'll come back and talk to my Concepts in Chemistry class for non-science majors."

Nate grunted into the phone. "She's happy as a flea on a dog to be gettin' out of here for a bit. Between you and me, I think as much as Troy resents you, he also leans on you. Hell of a situation Tugood put you in by promoting that jackass."

"Don't be too hard on him. He is in over his head. Or at least, he would be if Sci-PHi was a real company."

"Oh, it's real all right. Just because it isn't the only—or main—focus of Mr. Tugood and team, doesn't mean our work isn't real. Take the forensics contracts. Who knows how much having our services speeds up the backlog in our justice system?"

"Speaking of which," Bree interrupted before Nate could get fully warmed up to the subject, "do you have any news for me on our special project?" She crossed her fingers.

"Nope. Hate to break it to you, but the DNA analysis was a bust. Not enough clean sample to run a full panel. But the good news is the gem is sparkly clean after all that trying to get a sample. I gave it to Kiki to pass on to you."

"What did you tell her you were looking for?"

"Blood typing. Just like what you had it logged in for."

"Thanks." Bree chatted for a few more minutes then cut off the call, wishing she'd been able to take the sample directly from Nate. Using Kiki as a delivery service only reminded her that she spent part of every workday lying to her best friend.

With a thud, Sherlock pounced on the floor at her feet, keeping Bree from sinking into depression over Kiki. Instead she laughed at the cat's antics when he batted at an object, tossing it into the air and chasing it. Light glinted off the surface, disappearing when he captured the object between his paws and bent his head toward it.

"Whoa, big boy." Bree grabbed at the whatever-it-was before he could put it in his mouth. "I don't want you to choke on this." She glanced at it, noticing it appeared to be some sort of jewelry before shoving it in her pocket. She'd check her dresser top for missing jewelry later.

For now, she made sure Sherlock's kibble and water bowls were filled and hustled through her morning chores. Between cleaning up after the cat and talking to Nate, she was running late. Applying the photo-confounding makeup took another fifteen minutes.

When she headed to the university, an accident on Main Street and the resulting traffic jam made matters worse. By the time she reached campus, the faculty parking lot was nearly full, and she ended up parking in the very back. She hefted her bag to her shoulder and jogged across the oval.

When Bree reached her office, Kiki lounged outside the door with a bulging briefcase of presentation materials at her feet. Far from looking irritated, she seemed absorbed in playing a game on her phone.

"Have you waited long?" Bree asked.

"Long enough to have a few graduate school flashbacks." Kiki looked up from the screen and sent Bree a mischievous grin. "If I'd had access to a lab, who knows what I might have whipped up? Graduate school labs have so much more interesting stuff than what we work with."

Bree cautiously opened her office door and peeked around the corner after switching on the lights. "Should I be worried that you've planted nitrogen triiodide in my office?" She scanned the floor for telltale dots of purple crystals. Stable when wet, but explosive when dry, they'd been a staple of graduate school pranks.

Behind her, Kiki laughed. "Don't worry. I didn't dot the floor under your chair with contact explosives. But only because I didn't think of it."

"Lucky me," Bree murmured as she ushered Kiki into the office. After getting them both coffee, they discussed the day's events before heading to the class.

While Kiki began her talk, entertaining the students with stories about the history of forensic science, Bree eyed the class, trying to judge their interest. Soon even the most jaded of them were caught up in Kiki's stories of murder, forensics, and crime detection.

When she moved to discussing modern techniques, a dozen hands went up. Students peppered her with questions covering everything from real-life techniques to wondering what popular entertainment got right—and wrong.

"Ms. Bainbridge," one young woman asked, addressing Kiki, "how difficult is it to get into your line of work?"

Kiki outlined a general plan of chemistry study. "It's possible to enter the forensics or other analytical fields with a background in any of the sciences, although I'm partial to chemistry. It's also perfectly acceptable to start out with only a bachelor's degree."

"So, I don't need a PhD?"

"No, but remember, how much education you start with may affect your initial salary and position."

Bree stood, drawing attention away from Kiki for a moment. "Also remember, that what some people learn in graduate school, others learn on-the-job." She flashed Kiki a glance. "It is entirely possible that someone with five to ten years of practical experience is every bit as accomplished—if not more so—than an entry level person with a doctorate."

Kiki nodded in agreement. "On the other hand, the doctorate proves that you can start a course of action and stick with it. So, both ways have their advantages."

A young man raised his hand. "My mom loves to watch those science-based TV shows. You know, the ones where the lab geek always comes up with the analysis that solves the crime. She thinks I'm going to be just like them if I keep studying science." He rolled his eyes.

"We like to call that the *CSI effect*," Kiki began. "Basically, television, movies, and books have trained the public to believe that a brilliant scientist can solve any problem in under an hour. Bree—that is, Dr. Mayfield-Watson—and I have had many discussions with our marketing staff trying to convince them it isn't like that in real life."

A voice from the back of the room called out "that's a relief," and the class laughed.

"Some popular shows do have science consultants," Bree added. "For example, in *Breaking Bad*, a chemist and DEA officials all worked as consultants. The chemistry on the blackboards was always real, but the actual techniques for synthesizing drugs contained deliberate misinformation."

As the bell rang, members of the class clustered around Kiki and Bree, and she ended up moving the discussion to her office in an extra hour of open-door office time.

Kiki declined Bree's invitation to lunch, saying she had a backlog of work to do in the lab. She handed Bree a small envelope as she left. "Nate asked me to bring this to you. It's the sample Detective Hottie asked you to analyze."

Bree ignored Kiki's raised eyebrows and shoved the envelope into her purse. "You know I can't talk about it."

"Sure you can," Kiki gave her a smile, "but you won't, because you promised someone you wouldn't. My curiosity is dying to know more, but your sense of honor is one of the things I love about you, so I won't pry."

"Thanks." Bree's heart kicked painfully at the thought of all the secrets she kept from Kiki and she tightened her lips against speaking. Instead, she gave Kiki a swift hug. "It means more to me than you'll ever know."

"Just promise you'll let me know if you ever need my help. No matter how secret the project or how long you've had to keep me in the dark."

Bree watched Kiki's retreating back, she couldn't help but wonder how much her friend knew—or suspected—about Bree's other life.

The afternoon lasted a lifetime. The stuffy air in the staff conference room lulled Bree into a sleepy state as Heather droned on about the need for harassment training. Bree forced herself to inhale several deep breaths and wondered if the carbon dioxide buildup from the people exhaling in the too-small room accounted for her sleepiness.

When Heather called for a five-minute break, Bree wrestled one of the aging windows open and breathed in a lungful of fresh air.

"Bored already?" Heather propped one hip on the window-sill and sent Bree an assessing look.

"Not at all. Just reacting to the stuffy room. I'm glad we could open the window, at least a little."

Heather's grin reminded Bree of a tiny, sharp-toothed preda-tor. The image of a Tasmanian devil popped into her mind and she shivered.

"Are you sure you want to keep the window open?" Heather asked. "You look chilled."

"It's nothing," Bree suppressed the urge to rub her face to rid it of her irritating camouflage makeup and waved Heather's comment aside. She moved back to her seat, suppressing a sigh of relief when Heather returned to the front of the room.

The class resumed, and Bree focused on what she knew of Heather. A passionate advocate for her students, she'd initially earned Bree's respect. But after her visits to *The Underground,* new information had caused Bree to reassess. Did Heather's unapologetic relief at Quint Christianson's death signal a cold-blooded killer? Or simply a woman who'd had enough and refused to be politically correct in the face of injustices?

And what did Nigel mean about Heather having extensive resources? Was *The Underground* really a refuge for lonely students, or a front for something else? And if it was a front, was it for the purposes of exploiting the students? Or protect-ing them from exploitation—by any means necessary? Her spy senses told her there was more than met the eye at the coffee house, but without further investigation, she couldn't tell what it was.

"Bree?" She looked up to see Fiona staring at her from the front of the room. "What do you think?"

"Sorry, could you repeat the question?"

Fiona frowned at her but repeated a training scenario and asked Bree if she thought it represented harassment. Bree recited the answer she thought Fiona wanted, then returned to scanning the staff in the room. One of the colleagues seated nearby was a killer—or had hired a killer.

And Bree wouldn't give up the investigation until she discovered which one.

CHAPTER 25

B ree had barely washed the makeup from her face when the phone rang. She scooped out a fingerful of moisturizer and applied it liberally while she hurried to the kitchen to answer the call.

"Thank God," Matthew Tugood said in a rush. "Are you all right?"

"I'm fine. What's wrong?" The hairs on the back of Bree's neck stood up and her spy sense went on full alert.

"I've been waiting all day to talk to you. When the security in your condo indicated you were home, I took a quick peek and panicked."

"Matthew, slow down." She hadn't heard that level of fear in his voice since ... well never. She'd never heard him be less than controlled. Even when he was angry, he radiated control. "Tell me everything."

A disgusted noise sounded on the other end of the call. "It's probably nothing. Do me a favor and have the new tech guy come out to check over your security system."

"You mean Grant? Listen, I've been meaning to tell you that he's working out really well so far. The kid is sharp. I don't think Shoe and I will be able to keep our real purpose from him for much longer—at least not without frustrating him to the point where he's ready to quit. He's motivated by making a difference in the world. And he already suspects we aren't just a scientific staffing company."

"Yeah? Well, have him confirm there's nothing wrong with your security system and I'll think about it. All I could see was a blurred mess where your face should have been."

Bree laughed, earning her another snort from Matthew. "If that's what you saw, then I'd say the system is working just fine. Here, take another look." She stepped into the hallway and waved in the general direction of the camera, giving Matthew a smile.

"I'll be damned," he said as she went inside and locked the doors. "You look good. Like yourself."

"It's all Grant's doing. I had a little run-in with some photographers on campus and he whipped up a concoction that scatters light in a way that messes with cameras and facial recognition software. That's what you saw when I came home. What you saw a minute ago was me without the makeup."

Matthew let out a whistle of appreciation. "Believe it or not, that's a new one to me. But do me a favor and don't scare me like that again. I can't afford to lose trained operatives." The forced lightness in his voice didn't fool Bree, but it did warm her heart.

"So, you admit I'm a full operative now?" She tried to match his devil-may-care tone. "Good to know."

"I admit you're the best trained operative I have."

"Hey, I'm the only operative you have."

He chuckled in response, the sound unfamiliar but welcome. "I've missed you, Watson. For the record, I hate being stuck out here, but leaving Sasha on her own wasn't a viable option. And no, don't ask where here is, because I won't answer. Just know that I've missed you."

I miss you, too. The words froze on her tongue. No sense encouraging him. Or deluding herself. He missed her in a professional way, that was all.

"Watson? Still there?"

"Um," she cleared her throat, "yes. I take it you called because the news finally reached you in wherever-you-are. Grant has made sure that my image was scrubbed from all the local news feeds. There wasn't anything for the national outlets or international to pick up about me. I wasn't compromised."

"You weren't … Watson, what aren't you telling me? I don't get the Plainville local news, and you should know that. What are you involved in?"

Bree filled him in on the latest in the murder investigation, including the SWAP protests, news coverage of the crime scene, and everything else she could think of.

"Oh, I bet the Boy Scout is seething over that little leak. Wish I could see it in person."

"Stop salivating over Detective O'Neil and his reaction to the news. For your information, the leak did compromise the investigation. We'd been hoping to keep the tiger claw backscratcher and the tiger's genetic deformity quiet."

"O'Neil will get his perp," Matthew said, a hint of grudging respect in his voice. "He'll have a plan B and a plan C if I know him. He's a good man."

"Why don't you like him?" Bree kicked off her shoes and tucked her legs up on the couch, propping her arm on a pillow. Sherlock staked out a spot behind her knees and curled into a ball.

"I don't … not like him. I just don't see eye-to-eye with sheltered law enforcement types." He cleared his throat. "Enough of that, let's talk about you. How's your Troy-free vacation?"

"If you mean my official suspension from Sci-PHi, I'm doing fine. By the way, I use your office when I need to be on the campus. No one knows I'm there."

"Don't get too used to it. Troy called me, asking me to put in a good word with Charles Angelo about you. Said the events that led to your suspension were all a big misunderstanding."

"I'm not surprised." Bree stroked Sherlock absently. "Both Nate and Kiki told me he's going a little nuts without me there. I think the stress of running the department is wearing on him."

"I'm seriously re-thinking the decision not to put Kiki in that role."

"No, Matthew. Please." *Not cool, Bree. Begging doesn't earn respect.*

"Don't worry. I get it. You hate lying to her. But Bree, don't you think we'd all be better off with Kiki in charge? She won't ride roughshod over the rest of the staff. And she'll let you do special projects without questions. We can make it work."

Kiki's words drifted through Bree's mind. *Let me know if you ever need my help. No matter how secret the project or how long you've had to keep me in the dark.* Bree went out on a limb. "Could we read her in on our real purpose?"

"Not a good idea, Watson. Not a good idea."

Probably not. "What about Grant Mitchelson? Is it time to let him in? Like I said, he knows we're more than a staffing company. By the way, he calls Tech-Ops the Batcave. Which makes you, you know, Batman."

A growl of appreciation escaped Matthew's throat. "Does that make you Bat Girl? 'Cause I remember having a thing for Bat Girl back in the day."

"No. I'm Wonder Woman. And Shoe is Robin."

"I'll bet he loves that."

It was Bree's turn to laugh. "He doesn't know. At least, I don't think so. But Grant is sure—has been from day one—that we're keeping secrets. He knew the moment he had to use a special security code to activate the elevator."

"I thought he might. Have you given him any projects to let him take off the training wheels? Besides formulating camera obscuring makeup for you?"

Bree bit her lip, wondering if she should tell Matthew about the video files from *The Underground.* She still hadn't told James. And she didn't want to look too closely at the reasons why—because they'd show how far outside of the traditional lines she was willing to color to get results.

In the end, she confessed all to Matthew, ending with how Grant had isolated the various files and transformed them into usable pieces of intel.

"Good. I think he's ready for more. Read him in as much—or as little—as you think necessary. I trust your judgement on this. And Watson? Stay safe. Local murder suspects are every bit as dangerous as cornered terrorists. I meant what I said. I care about...what happens to you." With a quick good-bye, he hurried off the line.

Was she foolish for hearing the unspoken words *I care about you?* Or foolish for wishing she did? Why did her flighty little soul insist on chasing adventure and hooking up with the dark-and-dangerous Matthew when accepting the warm, uncomplicated stability she'd find with James would be so much easier?

Why did she always choose to do everything, from her studies in school, to her career, to her love life, the hard way?

Unsettled, she pushed off the couch and headed to her computer. Her evening with Ning at *The Underground*—and the conversations she'd overheard—convinced her that she'd missed something in her prior review of her video surveillance of the coffee house.

An hour of scouring the feeds again, with a focus on her interactions with Heather and Miriam, left her in the same place she'd started—with vague discomfort surrounding both professors but no real answers.

Perhaps instead of looking at the evidence through the lens of trying to find something that was wrong with Miriam's or Heather's actions, she should widen her search.

She cued up the segments Grant had isolated showing the stage and the performers. Bree grabbed a can of caffeine-free soda from the fridge and dumped the loose change from her pockets onto the table before hitting the play icon.

She took down her hair and massaged her scalp, listening to the recitations while scanning the crowd around the stage to try to spot anything out of place.

Nothing. Only a mournful rendition of a student's poem about homesickness. When Nigel stepped to the stage, Bree smiled, remembering how quickly Ning had taken up the "Fancy Free" refrain of his upbeat piece.

She sorted through a pile of loose change as she listened to his melodic voice. "Fancy a coffee? Fancy a tea..."

Her fingers snagged on a chain nestled among the coins. The choke hazard she'd rescued from Sherlock's grip. She pulled the shiny bit of metal from the pile and studied it. A dull stone hung on the end of a bit of chain. Was it a broken bracelet? Necklace? Whatever it was, it didn't belong to her.

Maybe it was Ning's? She'd never seen the girl wear jewelry, much less something this ornate. Her suitemate? Bree racked her brain for other women who may have been in her apartment and came up blank.

In the background, beatnik poets at *The Underground* snapped their fingers, reciting the poem's refrain. "Fancy free ... fee. Fancy fee."

Something wasn't right. Bree's subconscious kept returning to the rhythm and rhyme, which somehow didn't seem to fit. A slight stutter in the rhythm nagged her in the same way a malfunctioning pump on a piece of lab equipment would.

Setting the jewelry aside, she backed up the audio to the beginning. This time, pen in hand, she carefully listened to the words. After several minutes, and lots of rewinding and replaying bits, she'd transcribed the entire poem. She read over the stanzas, searching for the discordant element.

Fancy a coffee? Fancy a tea?
Whatever you fancy, share some with me.
Want cream or sugar? Bring something to barter.
Your life can be easy or very much harder

A shilling, a dollar, an athlete, a scholar,
Fancy free for a fee; fancy free for a fee.

Nigel had spoken with the unseen student about taking the easy or the hard way. Bree searched her purse for her crime notebook, also pulling out the envelope from Wendy Clark and the unhelpful gemstone Kiki had returned to her.

Bree flipped through her notebook to find her observations on her visit to *The Underground* with Ning. There. The student's Bree had overheard had clearly spoken about bribes and how Quint's death hadn't been the end of them. The hairs on Bree's neck stood up.

Could Nigel, the sweet, soft-spoken Brit, be the killer? It was hard to reconcile the idea with the student she thought she knew. But then, his loyalty to Heather ran deep.

The next stanzas took a darker twist, hinting at sinister forces being used to control students.

Fancy a whiskey? Fancy a beer?
Whatever you fancy, come get it here.
Fancy some pills, a needle or coke?
A brownie to nibble or something to smoke?

A shilling, a dollar, an athlete, a scholar,
Fancy free for a fee; fancy free for a fee.

Fancy a flat with one bedroom or two?
If you like it fancy, you know what to do.
Fancy a car, a TV, or advice?
You can have what you fancy, if you pay the price.

A shilling, a dollar, an athlete, a scholar,
Fancy free for a fee; fancy free for a fee.

Can you run like the wind? Throw a great pass?
But your efforts fall short when attending a class?
We've got what you need to help make the grade.
Just bring us your troubles and don't be afraid!

By the time Bree re-read this stanza a prickling awareness sent chills through her body. Coach had gone out of his way to try to bully her into giving his players a passing grade. So much so, that Tanner had baited her, handing in a nearly incomplete paper and stating he was sure he'd pass with flying colors. And where else—outside of the coffee house—had she heard the refrain? She paged through her crime notebook until she'd found the source.

Nigel. Again. At the football game where one of the students had complained of academic issues with the university attorney. The same one who'd admitted to working out a deal with the university to allow him to stay an extra semester.

Had Quint's knowledge of—or involvement in—blackmailing students been what had gotten him killed? All along, Bree had struggled with finding a motive for his death that made sense. Coach—and who knew who else—could have been implicated. Bree stared at her transcript of the final verse.

A shilling, a dollar, an athlete, a scholar,
Fancy free for a fee; fancy free for a fee.

Fancy fee for sale or barter
Fancy fee makes life easy or harder.

Finally, she found the discordant element in the poem. The lines switched from 'fancy free' to 'fancy fee,' the one who could make life easy or harder. Did that refer to a system? A person?

Bree set the clip of the poem so it would play in a loop and began to warm some soup for dinner, hoping to trick her subconscious into noticing something her conscious mind would not. As the soup heated, she cleared the table, dumping her change in a piggy bank, and throwing out trash that had collected in her purse.

Finally, everything but the crime notebook, the gem from Nate, the letter from Wendy and the broken chain remained. She pondered them while eating her soup. To keep her mind from focusing on the crime, she examined the chain Sherlock had been playing with.

It was crusted with dust and other debris. She might as well clean it up before taking it to Tina, Ning's suitemate, to see if it belonged to her.

Bree moistened a soft cloth and ran it along the chain to remove the grime. Ugh. Sherlock must have found it under a cabinet in a nest of dust bunnies and cat hair. As she worked, the stone wiggled and Bree looked closer.

It wasn't a stone lodged in the setting, rather ... a bit of carrot? Orange gummy gunk peeled out of the setting. Where in the world ...

Sherlock distracted her, batting at her knees and demanding treats. Bree set the chain aside and fetched tuna snacks for him. "At least you don't have to fight Miss Peepers for them, this time," she murmured. The image of Miss Peepers flying head over heels and spilling her satchel of treats made Bree giggle. The only thing funnier that the capuchin's somersault had been her reaction to Sherlock launching himself and scattering ...

Scattering the contents of the satchel. Bree left Sherlock to his treats and returned to the table. Could the chain have come from Miss P's satchel? The monkey had been known to pick up shiny objects—including Bree's necklace.

Bree laid the now clean chain on the table. On an impulse, she opened the envelope Nate had sent to her. Nestled inside in a plastic zipper bag was the gem. She spilled it into her palm and examined it. As he'd said, it was now clean. Clean and definitely not a diamond. Or other colorless gem. Without blood obscuring its color, she saw it was clear blue.

Sapphire.

She gently pushed the gem into the empty setting. It fit perfectly, despite a broken prong. And just like the gem clicking into place, the bits that had evaded Bree came together, no longer a puzzle. Instead, a clear picture of a killer.

CHAPTER 26

When James's cell phone went to voicemail, Bree disconnected and dialed again. Finally, he picked up.

"Hey, beautiful, wanna come over?" His sleepy voice poured across the connection.

"Sorry," Bree glanced at the clock, grimacing when she discovered it was after midnight. "I should have waited until morning."

"No worries. Anytime is fine." James cleared his throat, the husky, sleep-roughened edges of his voice smoothing out as he did so. "Are you all right?"

"I'm fine, but we need to talk. I know—or think I know who the killer is." She filled him in on her recent discoveries. She paced the length of her living room, Sherlock at her feet.

"So, let me get this straight. You think you found a blackmail scheme at the university which is related to the murder. And you believe the gem we found at the scene came from a ... what again?"

"An earring jacket. It's a piece of jewelry that women use to transform simple earrings—for example diamond studs—into more ornate ones. This jacket was designed to fit around the post of a stud and add a longer, dangling piece with a second gem in it. Simple diamond studs were transformed into sapphire and diamond drop earrings. That's what was throwing me off. That's why I didn't know she was part of the diamond stud club."

"I'm still half asleep here. Who was part of the diamond stud club? And how does it relate to blackmail? And Quint's murder? Tell me how you figured out the killer's identity. I'm not sure you remembered to tell me who."

"Fiona Fancier. The university attorney. Quint's lover. Don't you see?"

"Tell me more," James said, and Bree heard the rustle of sheets and the slam of dresser drawers. She tried not to imagine him getting dressed.

"I hypothesized," she stressed, using her favorite word, "that Fiona and Quint were part of a blackmail ring. The first day I met Quint, he was irritated about Ning's coming to the university without him having extensive meetings with her.

"And he made a point of showing me his collection of gifts—which I now believe are bribes—from other international students. If I'm correct, the curio cabinet is the key. It's stuffed with evidence of student blackmail. Fiona must have filled out documentation and falsified customs forms for him. She's Fancy Fee—a bastardization of Fiona Fancier—in the poem."

"What poem?" Now James's voice sounded irritated. "Bree, you are normally organized and thoughtful. Tonight, you're rattling on about poetry. What makes you think the earring whatchamacallit belonged to the attorney? And how did it get into your hands?"

Bree struggled for patience. It was late and she'd woken James from sleep. She couldn't expect him to follow all of her rambling. She slowed down. "I think Miss Peepers stole the earring from Fiona's desk when Ning and I filed the harassment claim. It was the only place where she was left unattended. She loves to pick up shiny objects. We were just lucky that she spilled her treasure trove on my dusty floor. Besides, Fiona was the only one to wear sapphire jewelry."

At the kitchen table, Bree arranged the earring jacket and gemstone in separate zipper bags, ready to show to James in the morning.

"You know I'm going to have a devil of a time getting a judge to issue a search warrant based on a capuchin monkey and some beatnik poetry that you illegally recorded, don't you?"

"I'm sure any of the students from *The Underground* would be happy to recite the poem's lyrics for you if that's the issue."

James grunted and continued double checking her thought process, grumbling at the way she'd acted on intuition rather than procedure. She distracted herself by opening the envelope Wendy had given her regarding Miss Peepers.

"James?"

"Yes?"

"Does past criminal activity make a search warrant easier to obtain? Because if it does, I may have what you need."

On bold letterhead, in a curly, stylized font, the words *Fancier Finance and Estates, a Boutique Law Firm* sat above the tag line *Specializing In Caring For All Your Unique Needs.*

At six the next morning, James arrived on her doorstep, coffee in hand. Bree gulped the vanilla-infused brew greedily.

"Whoa, there. Looks like I should have brought you the jumbo carafe rather than a large coffee."

Bree shook her head. "No, I just didn't get much sleep after we talked. Or before."

He took the coffee from her hands and set the cup on the counter. "Neither did I, but who needs sleep?" His lips touched hers and she melted a little into his embrace. The warmth of the contact threatened to undo the energizing effects of caffeine and reluctantly, Bree pulled away, forcing her tired mind to think of the case.

"Do you really think we can get a search warrant for Fiona's office based on all of this?" Bree indicated the earring jacket, gemstone, transcribed poems, and the letterhead from the now defunct law firm.

"If your friends—the ones who own Miss Peepers—are correct about the law firm being dissolved due to malpractice, there should be evidence of it. After we hung up last night, I called in a few favors and set some searches in motion. It'll take a few days, but I should know something—"

"No." Bree grabbed her coffee and downed another slug, wondering if she should have put Grant on the case. "It can't wait that long. Ning is scheduled to meet with Fiona at two today regarding the harassment claim. I don't want her alone with that woman."

"Reschedule."

She shook her head. "It isn't just that. Tuesday—the day the news broke regarding our investigation—I stopped by Fiona's office to set up a time for her to talk with Ning. She was elbow deep in files. My gut tells me they weren't so much about protecting the university as about protecting herself."

"Since when did you start relying on your gut more than on your crime notebook?" James narrowed his eyes and stared as if trying to see inside her brain.

Bree shrugged, refusing to be baited. "The brain is nothing more than a supercomputer taking in gigabytes of information every second. Gut instinct is the brain's way of passing that information to our conscious selves. If we listen.

"Think about it, James. Fiona took charge of Ning almost immediately to keep her from talking to you. She was adamant about putting Lucky down for the crime. She had Quint's confidence, as well as access to his office. For all intents and purposes, she was above suspicion."

"Except until she wasn't." James pushed his untouched coffee toward Bree and removed her empty cup. "If your hypothesis is correct and she is the killer, we still don't know if her motive was related to the alleged blackmail or to a jealous rage."

"Both. Obviously. The claw marks indicate vengeance. Passion."

"It could have been consensual sex play. Maybe Quint forgot the safe word."

"Or," Bree shuddered, remembering the calculating look in Fiona's eyes wherever she toyed with a man's attention, "sexplay designed to disguise murder. And therefore, not spur of the moment. Calculated. And hot blooded, both."

"Do you really think Fiona and Quint would have risked being caught together?"

"Quint had a taste for the exotic, based on his curio cabinet." Bree shrugged as if Quint's tastes didn't cause her skin to crawl. *Liar.* "His office was isolated. No one was expected between the time Ning and Coach left and several hours later when the reporters were scheduled to arrive. What better time for Fiona to confront Quint? Remember, Ning only returned to Quint's office because he *supposedly* texted her."

"In that case," James said, "he and Fiona were both playing with fire. But danger is a turn-on to some people."

Did she imagine he looked at her when he said that? Bree bit the inside of her lip, wondering how much of her fascination with Tugood was the hint of danger he carried.

James framed Bree's face with his hands, scattering her thoughts. "Fine," he said. "I'll push to get the warrant as soon as possible. Before the meeting with Ning. But don't let her go to see Fiona alone. And don't you go without me or the warrant. Understand?"

CHAPTER 27

Later that morning, Bree left her class and headed to the safety of her office, fingering the camera necklace she'd chosen to wear. Before when she'd encountered killers, she'd rushed in, trusting everything would work out.

Yet today, even with preparation and planning on her side, her nerves stretched tight. Should she alert Shoe to watch the video footage in case something went wrong? And even if it did, what could he do from the Tech Ops center across town that James wouldn't be able to do from her side?

She stared at the clock on her office wall. Funny how she hadn't noticed it before. Now each tick of the second hand echoed in the quiet space. Just a little after noon. Less than two hours until they met with Fiona.

Her cell phone rang, caller ID flashing James's mobile number. "Good news," he said after a brief greeting. "We're going to be able to get the warrant. I'll pick it up, gather my team, and meet you at your office by one-thirty. Plenty of time to confront Fiona, take her in for questioning, and search her office."

Bree breathed a sigh of relief. "Thanks. I feel better. I left a message for Ning this morning, telling her not to go to the appointment, but it went to her voice mail. I'm going to double check to make sure she received it. I'll see you soon."

She cut off the call and tried Ning's cell phone, but again, received no answer. She called the dorm and reached Ning's suitemate who said she'd left hours ago for the vet school. Bree decided to check on Ning in person. She'd either assure Ning remained near Dr. Warthan or that she accompanied Bree to her office and remained there while Bree and James met with Fiona.

Bree checked the clock again. With a little over an hour before she met James there was plenty of time to walk instead of taking her car. Bree set off, enjoying the cool autumn air. The walk took some of the edge off her nerves. *You've been in far more dangerous situations,* she chided herself, but the unease wouldn't go away.

Once at the vet school, Bree first checked Lucky's cage. Lucky and Miss Peepers were alone asleep, limbs tangled together like lovers—or best friends. Bree called Ning's number again, but the answering ring came from inside the animal enclosure. Miss P woke and scampered over to the cot, her noisy screech accompanying Ning's ring tone.

Bree hurried to the main lobby and asked the receptionist to page Ning over the intercom. No reply. The desk phone rang and when the receptionist picked it up she passed it to Bree.

"Hello?"

"It's Melody Warthan. I heard you page Ning. She must already be on her way to your meeting."

"No." Bree's mind shifted into high gear. She checked her watch. Nearly twelve-forty. "I told her to cancel her meeting with Fiona about the harassment case."

"I didn't know about that," Melody said. "When I saw her, she was at the front desk talking to the receptionist about a note she'd received."

Bree put her hand over the receiver and turned to the receptionist. "Did you give Ning a note earlier?"

"Not me." The young woman glanced at a notepad by her elbow. "I just started my shift."

Bree grabbed the notepad, ignoring the receptionist's startled gasp, and pulled a pencil from a nearby cup. *Please let this work.* She rubbed the pencil lightly over the pad, praying it picked up indentations from prior notes written on the pad. Relief swamped her as the faint outline of words appeared. *To Ning. Meet Ms. Fancier at one o'clock. Alone.*

Her heart rate kicked up, destroying her momentary sense of relief. She glanced at her cell, surprised to find it still connected to Melody. She cut the call off without saying goodbye and checked the time. Less than fifteen minutes to make it across campus to Fiona's office. Bree jammed her Bluetooth headset into her ear and raced from the vet school.

"Dial James O'Neil," she instructed the voice call feature as she jogged across the campus. At a brisk walk, she'd never make it to the administration building in time. And no matter what risk she took, she didn't dare leave Ning alone with Fiona. Not when the hairs on her neck stood up and every spy sense she developed over the past months warned her against it.

The call went to voice mail, and Bree remembered the Plainville courthouse had a strict no-cell-phones policy. Meaning her only connection to James was stuffed in a tiny locker while he picked up the search warrant. She left a message about the change in meeting time, her voice coming out in labored huffs as she ran across the campus. Nearing the oval, she slowed enough to regain her breath and left a second message at the Plainville police department for James.

She smoothed her hair and tried to catch her breath as she entered the administration building. Whatever happened, it would be better to appear calm in Fiona's office and hope that she didn't suspect Bree had identified her as the killer. On the way to the third floor, Bree switched the necklace camera on and called Shoe.

"Monitor my camera and audio. Starting immediately," she said when he picked up. "I'll explain later." She cut off the call and stuffed the earpiece in her pocket as she exited the stairwell. She checked the time. One-ten. She hurried down the empty hallway.

The door to Fiona's inner office was nearly closed, but light from the office escaped through the sliver of open space. Voices drifted toward her.

"I know it looks daunting," Fiona's voice sounded soothing, relaxed. "We call it legalese. But all you really need to know is that by signing this paperwork, we can assure that your tiger cub doesn't have to be put to sleep."

"But Lucky did nothing. Dr. Warthan said—"

"Dr. Warthan isn't responsible for the cub. You are. And no matter what anyone has told you, you and the cub were found— alone—beside Dr. Christianson's body. By allowing the tiger to roam outside of its cage, you've placed yourself, the cub, and the university in grave danger. I've done my best to take steps to be sure you won't be deported and the cub won't be put down. But you have to understand, it's difficult."

"I will read the papers first," Ning insisted. Bree thanked every deity she knew for the girl's stubbornness. At the moment, Ning seemed to be holding her own. Bree crept close to the door, careful her shadow didn't show through the frosted window, and listened at the crack between the door and the frame, ready to enter at a second's notice. Lifting her cell phone, she pressed the video icon then carefully slid the top of the phone in the opening and angled the camera lens so she could see part of what was going on in the room.

Fiona's sigh was heavy. "If you insist."

Ning's chair scraped against the wooden floor of the office. "I take to Dr. Bree and read it with her."

"Don't you trust me?"

"I read the papers with Dr. Bree."

"There's no need to bring Dr. Mayfield-Watson into this. She could not only lose her job, but she could go to jail for a very long time if we don't settle this matter immediately."

"Dr. Bree did nothing—"

"Unfortunately, she did. I'm sorry." Fiona's voice dripped fake sincerity. "I didn't want to have to tell you about the illegal maneuvers she took to get you and the cub into the university. I know how much you looked up to her."

The chair scraped across the floor again and through the camera screen, Bree saw Ning sit heavily in it. The girl's lips quivered.

"Trust me. If there was any other way, I'd have found it. But there isn't. You need to sign these papers." Fiona moved from her position behind the desk, extending a pen to Ning.

Bree didn't wait any longer. She stashed the phone and pulled the door open. Fiona heard her coming and stepped between Ning and Bree, gripping the girl's arm tight enough to leave a fresh set of bruises.

"You need to leave before security arrives," Fiona said, dragging Ning with her behind the desk.

"We both know security isn't coming. And nothing you've told Ning is true. What's really in those papers, Fiona?"

With one hand, Fiona stuffed papers into her briefcase, keeping a grip on Ning with the other. She grabbed the unsigned pages from the girl and added them to the bulging leather bag.

"It's something I guarantee you won't like." Fiona draped the strap of the briefcase over Ning's neck. While Ning struggled with the unexpected weight and bulk, Fiona reached into the desk drawer and palmed something.

A weapon.

She jammed the barrel into Ning's ribs as she forced the girl in front of her. Ning, who'd faced down tigers and bitten an unwelcome attacker, stood wooden, frozen, as if she'd finally broken. Tears dripped from her eyes. "I am sorry Dr.—"

"Shut up," Fiona commanded. "Come with me. If Bree stays quietly here while we leave, nothing will happen to you. If not …" She shrugged.

Keeping Ning between herself and Bree, Fiona walked to the door, moving to back through it. A flash of movement behind Fiona caught Bree's eye.

"Wait." Bree lunged toward Fiona, drawing her attention and forcing her to move the gun from Ning's side to aim it at Bree.

"Don't make me shoot—"

Ning shouted something in Thai and stomped on Fiona's instep at the same time Bree lunged again, knocking the gun arm sideways. Fiona's snarled threat ended in a scream as James grabbed her arm from behind, wrenching it up and taking the gun from her grip.

Seconds later, a uniformed officer had Fiona in cuffs, reading the Miranda rights to her while a Detective Shana Westerman took the briefcase from Ning.

While the others led Fiona away, James secured the office, directing Bree and Ning to wait on the couch in the receptionist's office outside of Fiona's door. An hour later, they walked away from the scene, leaving the office in the hands of a search team. A uniformed sentry stood posted at the door.

They'd caught the killer. And everyone knew it.

Hours later, Bree slid into a booth across from James at *Mama Marinara's*. "The atmosphere here is much nicer than the interrogation room," she said.

"I don't know." James studied the warm honey-gold walls painted with scenes from a vineyard. His gaze lingered on straw-wrapped wine bottles and olive oil flasks clustered on the decorative shelving. "It has its charm, but nothing beats the privacy of our interrogation room."

"You're such a romantic," she teased.

"I could be. If you'd give me the chance." His eyes lit with a question, and Bree was grateful when a server slid a basket of warm garlic knots on the table, interrupting the flow of conversation. They quickly ordered their food and drinks.

"So," James continued, ignoring the tension that stretched across the table, "how is Ning?"

"Hard to tell." Bree reached for a roll and broke it into buttery, garlicky bits. "Facing Fiona rattled her more than she's letting on. But after I reassured her—over and over again—that Lucky and she would be fine, she started to calm down. Before you arrived on the scene, Fiona threatened to have Ning deported, Lucky euthanized, and me imprisoned."

"That's a lot to take in. It's a wonder she didn't crumble under that kind of pressure."

"Ning's tough. Resilient. She seemed more concerned for me and Lucky than for herself. I have you to thank for her confidence in the police. The time you spent gaining her trust paid off.

"The mention of deportation would have frightened most of the international students into doing whatever Fiona wanted." Bree wiped her greasy fingers on a napkin, leaving the roll on her plate, untasted.

James reached across the table and captured her hand, his grip warm and gentle. "She's a good kid with lots of courage. For the record, I understand why you rushed to Fiona's office to protect her. But please. Never do something like that again."

His grip tightened, and his gaze sharpened, making it difficult for Bree to look away. "I couldn't live with myself if something happened to you and I wasn't there to protect you."

"I know." She gave his fingers a squeeze then tugged her hand free as the server returned with steaming plates of linguini in vodka cream sauce.

"Did you discover anything in the papers you confiscated?" she asked, turning the conversation back to him.

James twirled a strand of pasta and popped it into his mouth before answering. "Fiona was a great help to us—she'd filled her briefcase with incriminating evidence. Of course, we're still searching the rest of the office and now have a warrant for her home as well. But what we have so far is more than enough to incriminate her on a number of charges."

"I suppose your warrant includes phone and computer records?"

"Of course." He nodded at her untouched plate, and Bree picked up her fork. "By the way, the paper she tried to get Ning to sign was essentially a confession, incriminating you. In it, she said you killed Dr. Christianson and threatened Ning if she didn't go along with your version of the events."

Bree paused, her forkful of linguini halfway to her mouth. "That bitc-, er, woman, tried to blame me?"

"Anything to throw suspicion off her long enough for her to cash out and get far enough away to avoid arrest. The information you found on her prior law firm will likely establish a pattern of unethical—or criminal—behavior followed by an attempt to rebrand and reinvent herself." He shrugged. "If she'd done a better job of it the first time, we may not have caught her this time."

Bree dug into her pasta, listening as James filled her in on what they'd learned so far. Fiona had confessed to taunting Quint, expressing her anger against the way he looked at the young, exotic students. She told him she could be as rough and exotic as he'd like. They'd fought, breaking a crystal decanter and turning from angry to amorous—or so Quint thought—in the process.

A shiver of disgust raced down Bree's spine as James described Fiona raking the claw across Quint's torso in a twisted, passionate rage.

"She says she doesn't remember anything more until she saw him dead at her feet." James shrugged. "I think she's laying grounds for an insanity plea of some sort. But my guess is we'll find a club or umbrella or some other heavy item in her home with Quint's blood and DNA on it."

He went on to describe the evidence piling up to indicate that Quint and Fiona were indeed running an extortion scheme on the international students.

"You've learned quite a lot in the few hours since you took the files from her office. Were others involved? Or was it only Fiona and Quint?"

"You tell me. You're a budding investigator." He leaned back and raised his eyebrows, encouraging her to fill in … something.

Bree took a swallow of wine and thought for a moment. "You found evidence that they were also dealing in the performance enhancement drugs for the football team."

"Got it in one. But then, you were the one to find and identify the Tiger Powder. So far, we don't have firm evidence that points to Coach Fleek being involved, but my guess is it's only a matter of time. I'm sure his quarterback, Tanner, will be implicated as well. It won't punish him for his abuse of Ning, but it's a step in the right direction."

Bree pushed her plate of pasta away and took another sip of wine. "When I was at *The Underground* with Ning, I heard the British student Nigel with another student—I think from South America—discussing *herbal remedies* he'd supplied to the university in exchange for keeping his scholarship."

"As in code for illegal drugs." James sighed. "That's a tough one, but I'll work with everyone I can to protect the students. They've already been abused by Quint and Fiona's blackmail setup. They shouldn't have to be abused by a cold legal system as well." He scrubbed a hand across his face, suddenly appearing tired.

Bree reached across the table and took his free hand. "I know you'll do the best you can. You'll fight for them. I have faith in you."

"It might not be enough."

"It is for me."

She squeezed his fingers, offering friendship. When his eyes lit with anticipation, another part of her resistance crumbled. *Not every hero is wounded,* she reminded herself. Ten minutes later, when they left the restaurant, for better or worse, her hand was still tucked in his as they strolled into the deepening twilight…

Author's Notes

In *The Tiger's Tale,* I introduce several new animals. Lucky the tiger was inspired by my real-life adventures in Thailand where I was able to feed, bathe, and interact with tigers, from small babies to large, lazy cats!

For the purposes of the plot, I invented a disease that makes Lucky's claws soft and nearly nonexistent. The disease is entirely fictional but was inspired by two real-life human diseases: hypophosphatasia and osteomalacia.

I also took the liberty of inventing makeup that helps the wearer hide from cameras. While such technologies exist, at this point, they are not as advanced as described in the book. For the safety of us all, let us hope the idea remains fictional.

I hope you have enjoyed reading *The Tiger's Tale.* Honest reviews are always welcome—authors rely on reviews to help them gain new readers, and our publishers use reviews to decide if a series will live or die. Posting reviews on Amazon, Barnes & Noble, or Goodreads is a great way to support authors. My only request is that you warn review readers if you decide to post "spoilers" which give away plot points!

For more information about the books in the Undercover Cat series, please visit my website at www.kellezriley.net.

As always, thank you for taking the time to live in my story world. I hope I have entertained you.

EXPERIMENTS FROM BREE'S
RECIPE BOOK

Basic White Cake Recipe   (~2 dozen)

Raw Materials List:
- 1 ½ C (360 mL) granulated sugar
- 1 C (240 mL) oil
- 2 tsp (10 mL) vanilla
- 6 large eggs, whites only
- 3½ C (840 mL) cake flour
- 4 tsp (20 mL) baking powder
- ¼ tsp (1.2 mL) salt
- 1 ½ C (360 mL) milk

Synthesis:
1. Mix together oil and sugars.
2. Add vanilla.
3. Add egg whites, a little at a time. Beat until fluffy.
4. In another bowl, stir together flour, baking powder, and salt.
5. Alternately add dry ingredients and milk into the sugar mixture until well mixed.
6. Preheat oven to 350°F (180°C).
7. Line a muffin tin with paper cupcake liners. Spray the inside of the liner with nonstick cooking spray.
8. Fill the wells 1/3 to 1/2 full with the cupcake mix.
9. Bake for 15-20 minutes or until a toothpick inserted in the cupcakes comes out clean. Cool.

Happy Experimenting!

Coconut Cupcakes
(Co, periodic element)   (~2 dozen)

Raw Materials List:
- Basic white cake (or boxed mix)
- 1 C (240 mL) sweetened, flaked coconut
- 2 tsp (10 mL) coconut extract

Synthesis:
1. Prepare cake as directed with these modifications:
   a. Use coconut extract instead of vanilla.
   b. Mix in coconut with the dry ingredients.

Frosting
Raw Materials List:
- 1 C (240 mL) shortening
- ~4 tbsp water, milk, or coconut milk
- 1 tsp flavoring (vanilla extract)
- ~4 C (960 mL) powdered sugar
- Coconut flakes for garnish

Synthesis:
1. Beat shortening and liquids until smooth.
2. Mix in powdered sugar slowly, until desired consistency. Adjust with more sugar and/or liquids if necessary.
3. Add frosting to a pastry bag or a zip-close bag with a tiny corner snipped off. Pipe in a swirl pattern on top of cooled cupcakes.
4. Sprinkle of coconut flakes for garnish.

<u>NOTES</u>

1. For a flavor variation, add both vanilla and coconut extracts.

Happy Experimenting!

Curry Spice (or coconut curry) Cupcakes (~2 dozen) (Cu, periodic element)

Raw Materials List (Curry Spice Mix):
- 2 parts ginger
- 2 parts turmeric
- 2 parts allspice (may substitute pumpkin pie spice for a sweeter mix)
- 1 part ground red chili

Mix spices and store in airtight container.

Synthesis:
1. Prepare basic white cake OR Coconut cake (see above)
2. Add 1-3 tsp (5-15 mL) curry spice mix to dry ingredients

NOTES
1. The curry spice adds a warm complexity, much like a spice cake. When used with sweet batters it can calm the sweetness.
2. Try adding a bit of curry spice to the frosting as well. Dissolve spice in liquids before creaming with the shortening. Remember, a little goes a long way!

Happy Experimenting!

Basic Chocolate Cake Mix

Raw Materials List:
- 3 C (720 mL) sugar
- 1 C (240 mL) oil
- 2 tsp (10 mL) vanilla
- 4 large eggs
- 3 C (720 mL) cake flour
- 1 tbsp (15 mL) baking soda
- 1 ½ tsp (7.5 mL) baking powder
- 1 ½ C unsweetened cocoa powder
- 1 ½ tsp (7.5 mL) salt
- 1 ½ C (360 mL) milk
- 1 ½ C (360 mL) water

Synthesis:
1. Mix together oil and sugar.
2. Add vanilla.
3. Add eggs, one at a time. Beat until fluffy.
4. In another bowl, stir together flour, baking soda, baking powder, cocoa powder, and salt.
5. Combine milk and water.
6. Alternately add dry and wet ingredients to the sugar mixture, until well mixed.
7. Preheat oven to 350°F (180°C).
8. Line a muffin tin with paper cupcake liners. Spray the inside of the liner with nonstick cooking spray.
9. Fill the wells 1/3 to 1/2 full with the cupcake mix.
10. Bake for 15-20 minutes or until a toothpick inserted in the cupcakes comes out clean. Cool.

<u>Peanut Butter Cupcakes</u>
<u>(Pb, periodic element)</u>   (~2 dozen)

Raw Materials List:
- Basic chocolate cake (or boxed mix)
- ½ C (120 mL) oil
- ½ C (120 mL) smooth peanut butter

Synthesis:
1. Prepare as directed in the chocolate cake recipe with these modifications:
   a. Cut the oil to ½ C.
   b. Add ½ C smooth peanut butter (to replace missing oil).

<u>NOTES</u>
1. Notice peanut butter is substituted for part of the oil. As a fat-based food, peanut butter can easily substitute for part of the fats in recipes. Because peanut butter is 25 percent protein, it can't be used to substitute all of the fat. A quick trick is to mix equal parts peanut butter and oil (or shortening) and then substitute the mixture for all of the fat (e.g. oil or shortening) in a recipe.
2. *A note on butter*: butter is about 20 percent water and 80 percent fat. (Exact ratio will vary based on the processing.) When substituting fat for butter or vice versa, take this into account. For example, if a recipe calls for 1 C of butter, substitute ¾ C of oil or shortening *plus* ¼ C water. (Sharp eyes will see this is a 25 percent ratio—but that is within a reasonable margin of error for recipes!) Conversely, if a recipe calls for 1 C of oil, substitute 1 ¼ C of butter, and reduce the water or other

liquids in the recipe by ¼ C. Once you know the science behind baking, all kinds of possibilities open up!

Frosting

Raw Materials List:

- 1 C (240 mL) shortening
- ½ C (120 mL) smooth peanut butter
- ~3 tbsp (45 mL) milk
- ~4 C (960 mL) powdered sugar
- 1 tsp (5 mL) vanilla
- Peanut butter chips for garnish

Synthesis:

1. Beat shortening, peanut butter, and liquids until smooth.
2. Mix in powdered sugar slowly, until desired consistency. Adjust with more sugar and/or liquids if necessary.
3. Add frosting to a pastry bag or a zip-close bag with a tiny corner snipped off. Pipe in a swirl pattern on top of cooled cupcakes.
4. Sprinkle with peanut butter chips for garnish.

NOTES AND SCIENCE-OF-BAKING TIPS

1. You may need to add small additional amounts of liquid and/or powdered sugar to reach the right consistency. It should hold soft peaks but spread easily for best frosting results.

Happy Experimenting!

Pad Thai

Raw Materials List:
- 8 oz (227 g) pad Thai noodles
- 2 tbsp (30 mL) lime juice
- 2 tbsp (30 mL) brown sugar
- 1 tbsp (15 mL) fish sauce
- 1 tbsp (15 mL) soy sauce
- ¼ tsp (1 mL) cayenne pepper
- 2 tbsp (30 mL) vegetable oil
- 1 sliced bell pepper
- 2 cloves garlic, minced
- 2 eggs, lightly whisked
- 1 lb. (~0.5 kg) shrimp
- Ground black pepper
- Kosher salt
- 2 green onions, thinly sliced on a bias
- ½ C (120 mL) roasted peanuts, chopped

Synthesis:
1. Cook noodles in salted water 7 to 10 minutes or until tender. Drain and set aside.
2. Whisk together lime juice, brown sugar, fish sauce, soy sauce, and cayenne pepper. Set aside.
3. In a large nonstick pan over medium-high heat, heat oil. Add bell pepper and cook until tender, about 4 minutes. Stir in garlic and cook until fragrant, about 1 minute more.
4. Add the shrimp and season with salt and pepper. Cook until pink, about 2 minutes per side.
5. Push the shrimp and vegetables to one side of the pan and pour in the egg. Scramble until just set then mix with the shrimp mixture.

6. Add the cooked noodles and toss until combined. Pour in the lime juice mixture and toss until the noodles are coated.

7. Top with green onions and roasted peanuts.

Happy Experimenting!

Panang Curry

Raw Materials List:

- 5 tbsp (75 mL) curry paste
- cooking oil
- 4 C (~1 L) coconut milk
- ⅔ lb. (0.3 kg) skinless, boneless chicken, sliced
- ½ C (120 mL) each: thinly sliced carrots, bell peppers, mushrooms
- 2 tbsp (30 mL) palm sugar
- 2 tbsp (30 mL) fish sauce, or to taste
- 6 kaffir lime leaves, torn
- 2 fresh red chili peppers, sliced
- ¼ C (60 mL) fresh Thai basil leaves

Synthesis:

1. Fry curry paste in oil over medium heat until fragrant.
2. Stir in coconut milk; bring to a boil.
3. Add chicken and vegetables. Cook 10-15 minutes until the chicken is done and the vegetables are tender.
4. Stir in palm sugar, fish sauce, and lime leaves. Simmer for 5 minutes.
5. Garnish with sliced red chili peppers and Thai basil leaves.

Happy Experimenting!

Autumn Apple Nachos

Raw Materials List:
- 4 Granny Smith apples, cored and thinly sliced
- 1 C (240 mL) white chocolate chips, melted
- 3/4 C (180 mL) caramel, warmed in microwave
- 1 C (240 mL) chopped pretzels
- 2 Heath candy bars, broken into pieces

Synthesis:
1. Arrange apple slices on top of one another.
2. Drizzle half the white chocolate and caramel.
3. Top with pretzels and Heath bars.
4. Drizzle with remaining white chocolate and caramel.
5. Serve immediately.

Happy Experimenting!

SEE WHERE IT ALL BEGAN:

The Cupcake Caper: Excerpt

What would you do if you found your boss dead?
Bree knows exactly what she has to do: find the killer.

Bree's grandmother often said she remembered every detail of the day President Kennedy died. Her mother remembered every detail of the day man first walked on the moon. Bree remembered every detail of the day she found Buckster Davis dead under his desk.

She could still smell the coffee with its bitter burned tang, see the wild mess of papers on his desk, hear the barely audible beep-beep-beep of his computer monitor reminding him of their appointment. She remembered the way his fingers curled, as if clawing at life itself. The mottled, unnatural purple-red of his skin, normally a warm olive tint, swam before her eyes whenever she closed them ...

Click Here to Buy the E-Book
Click Here to Buy the Print Book
Click Here for Multiple Copy Discounts